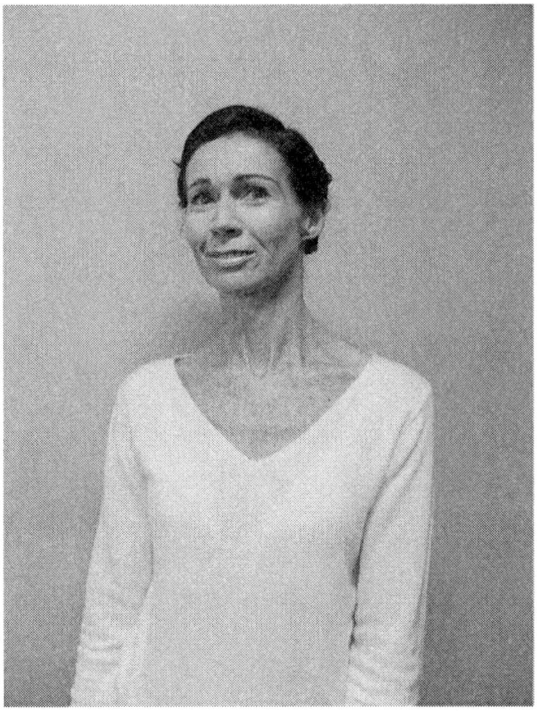

Photograph: *Kathy Tierney*

By: *Kate Thomas, Kate Thomas Media.*

Kathy Tierney is a writer who has won six literary awards, her most recent international award in the 2021 Bridport Prize UK, and published in various literary journals and anthologies. She has an Associate Degree of Creative Writing from Southern Cross University and, in February 2021, graduated with a Bachelor's degree in Creative Writing with distinction from Deakin University, Australia. *The Social Prophet* is her second novel.

To Ashley Albanese, Hani Soliman, and Izabel Soliman, social prophets of Armidale. With thanks for your friendship. And to Sydney social prophet Christopher Hewitt ("Toff"), with thanks for inspiring this novel with your social prophecy.

Kathy Tierney

The Social Prophet

Austin Macauley Publishers™
London • Cambridge • New York • Sharjah

Ordering Information
Quantity sales: Special discounts are available on quantity purchases by corporations, associations, and others. For details, contact the publisher at the address below.

Publisher's Cataloging-in-Publication data
Tierney, Kathy
The Social Prophet

ISBN 9781643780832 (Paperback)
ISBN 9781643780849 (Hardback)
ISBN 9781647508784 (ePub e-book)

Library of Congress Control Number: 2020909460

www.austinmacauley.com/us

First Published 2021
Austin Macauley Publishers LLC
40 Wall Street, 33rd Floor, Suite 3302
New York, NY 10005
USA

mail-usa@austinmacauley.com
+1 (646) 5125767

Thanks to my family for their love. Thanks to Jess and Alise. Thanks to Arts Law Centre of Australia for their assistance. Thanks to friends: Ashley Albanese, Alan Hughes, Angelo Rimpici, Ken Scott, Hani Soliman and Izabel Soliman for their encouragement and support. Thanks to Beth Coop, Smith House, Armidale, NSW, Australia, for her kindness.

‘Men make their own history,
but not in circumstances of their own choosing.’
Karl Marx

1

Black Crag

Sydney, NSW, Australia

March 2000

The town regarded him, Hamish McColl, as a social tsunami, a disaster cracking over their heads, about to ground zero them all. The black parish priest of the Church of Saint Thomas, Father Matthias, had been called on many times in the past to do an exorcism on Hamish's mind, as he refused to accept the Word of God. Father Matthias, weary of picking among the wreckage for ideological survivors, had quietly spoken to Hamish after each Sunday Mass, but never asked him to leave. He, Hamish, had most fortunately been saved by the Church of Saint Thomas's Lost Sheep parable policy, where he was cautiously welcomed back each Sunday, as possibly returning to God.

This hope had been held close to his parents' hearts for a long time, as they lit a candle for him each week, praying his mind would sleep in the arms of Jesus. One time, he found his mother, Josephine, kneeling in front of the statue of the Virgin, begging her to put a blackout in his mind, so he would stop questioning the parables.

His father, Wallace, had taken him off to Father Matthias soon afterwards, for urgent exorcism. Hamish was first fed peanuts, a recommended Catholic method for ridding the body of evil substances, and then inoculated with The Word again by Father Matthias, who reminded him *not* to question the Word of God. People questioning the Word of God were why, Father Matthias told him, there was a social plague of evil out there. Hamish must refer continually to his parables, to avoid growing into one of the Devil's bubonic sores.

Pointing out to Father Matthias that parables were full of incorrect facts had earnt him, Hamish, more time in the confessional box, confessing to the sin of pride.

'But Father,' Hamish argued through the confessional box, 'the parable of the mustard seed *is* wrong. It says that the mustard seed is the *smallest* of all seeds on Earth. But it's not. *And* it doesn't become the largest of all garden plants either, with huge branches which shade birds. Father. The mustard seed only grows a tree of five feet tall. They would have to be very skinny birds, Father, to find shade in that.'

Hamish thought he heard a choke of laughter behind the confessional grille, but he couldn't be sure.

The priest cleared his throat. 'I assure you, Hamish, with Jesus around to produce loaves and fishes, the birds wouldn't have been skinny at all,' he reprimanded. 'And the height of the tree is irrelevant. To interpret a parable correctly, Son, you must ask yourself, *what does God mean by this word?* Not, *are these words scientifically accurate?* And for all you know, Hamish, the mustard seed *may* have been the smallest seed on Earth *at* the time of Jesus. The other thing to consider is the mustard tree *may* have grown a lot taller in Jesus' time, because Jesus had the power of miracles.' The priest was quiet for a minute. 'And maybe, Hamish, if you want to talk in scientific language, the possibility is, the mustard tree, at the time of Jesus, *wasn*'t stunted by global warming. They may be only five feet high now, *because* of the global warming. But these ways of thinking are not encouraged in the Church, Hamish. You have to think in the ways God teaches you, not the ways man teaches you, or the way science teaches you. God is outside measurements. He is outside the measurement of a mustard seed, outside the measurement of a mustard tree, outside the measurement of the bird's body that you have taken it on yourself, to determine as skinny. Remember, God is above all that. He exists in transcendence. That is, transcendence above the ways of man.'

'Transcendence…' Hamish said doubtfully.

'Read up on that, Little Mr Science. And say three *Hail Mary's* after you do. You need to repent, to realise there are things bigger than your mind sitting above you, which know better than you. Pray to that. Because it won't be something called science, coming to collect your soul on your passing away.'

Father Matthias fell silent. Hamish muttered some reluctant *Hail Mary's* and felt the words stoning the soap bubbles in his mind, cementing the fragile, transparent gleams of his thoughts with religious repetition. Hamish waited for the pronouncement of his religious sentence, given to all who refused mind traps: those thou shalt nots, parables, and psalms snapping shut the mind. *Just a big lockdown on thinking*, Hamish thought sullenly.

Minute after minute passed, and still Father Matthias had not pronounced the sentence.

'Father Matthias? Are you still there?' Hamish whispered nervously, remembering to keep his voice quiet in the Church coffin box. 'I can't hear you.'

Had the priest been raptured, and he, Hamish, been left behind? Stamped with 666? For thinking outside locks?

Hamish sagged in relief against the back wall of the confessional box, as the priest spoke again. 'Well I'm barely a whisper to you anyway, Son. So, what does it matter if I'm here or not? You are more interested in listening to the Devil's tempters, interested in acquiring you, as the son of pride.' Father Matthias's voice lowered, snapped into sternness. 'You remember this, Son. The sin of pride makes you forget what is divine in you, what is dignified and right. You forget your own humanity, by inflating yourself so much, you end up the helium of Satan. Do you want to be that balloon, Hamish? Do you?'

Hamish thought about it. Church dignity or Hell's balloon. Helium or candlestick. Neither fit him. Hamish stared at the floor in dismay, at his possible future as nude. Father Matthias just wasn't offering anything outside those two choices.

He was outside lost sheep range. In the abyss, no one was going to find him.

'See? You're not talking back to me about that question, Hamish, and that is a concern to me, as you may be considering Hell's vacancy as a residential satanic balloon. Puffed up and sinful with pride.' Father Matthias's voice rumbled through the confessional box. 'So, before you joust with Jesus' academia, Son, you remember that the sin of pride comes from evil thought. If you don't get the evil thought out of your head, it will always speak through your mouth and make you look like a social idiot.'

'Yes, Father,' Hamish forced himself to say. Hamish was more of the opinion that social idiots were people who didn't read enough, and just parroted everyone else. Hamish decided to keep this quiet, as he had learnt that saying *Yes, Father* was the only way out of the confessional box. He had once been made to stay in there for six hours, until he learnt to agree with his penance and the sentence given to him by Father Matthias, declared one of God's Jury members. And further to that he, Hamish, was to understand that the penance and punishment, handed down to Father Matthias by mysterious forces, were given a lot more gently to him, than by those on judge and jury duty in society.

Hamish left the confessional box, before he kicked it in.

'Hamish! Come back here,' Father Matthias's voice boomed after him.

He pretended not to hear and hurried out of the Church.

When he got home, Hamish got out his father's Oxford dictionary, which, he'd been told by his father, had strict usage terms around it. It was only meant to explain the English language to him, his father said, and not to design or construct poems and songs. His father told him he did not want him learning pagan arts, which would turn the ears of Pan his way.

Hamish stuck the dictionary under his armpit and walked to the table, to do The Word of Father Matthias, and this week the word was "transcendence". He tossed the dictionary on the brown table. A dark-blue vase of pink flowers was sitting on it. Some dead leaves were floating near the top of the vase; the water was murky looking. There was an odd damp smell he didn't like. Hamish thought he saw worms in there. He peered closer. The worms were suddenly gone. He looked away uneasily, sat down, and turned to the blue cover of the dictionary, finding a strange and unusual comfort in its dry, factual language. *It makes a change from appearing and disappearing worms*, he thought miserably. He ran his fingers over the cover. It was torn around the edges, just like him; torn as if it had been read many, many times and carried many, many places.

Hamish smudged the dust on the dictionary cover, panicked about what he saw appear in the dust. A skull, and some bones littered around it, assembling and climbing out of the book cover. Hamish frantically smudged the dirt again, breathing hard, trying to stop the skeleton leaping out; was his father hiding something? Had a skeleton appeared to show him there was a nasty secret in the cupboard? If so, *where?* He didn't want to think about it, in case more skeletons started climbing the walls and hanging out of the windows: *What if there was a murder in the family?*

Hamish hastily opened the dictionary, not wanting to think about it. He hesitated to turn the page, fearful there was another skeleton hiding there, ready to unleash *Fright Night* on him. He forced himself to turn to the *T* section, frantically turning pages over, before he glimpsed bone or blood.

Hamish knew he would be asked all about the priestly prescribed word, "transcendence", by Father Matthias after the next Mass, in a confessional follow-up to see if he had done his penance; and he also knew that skeletons living in his father's dictionary would not be considered an excuse by Father Matthias. Hamish had been caught out before not doing his religious penance, and had earnt even more penance. Penance was religious therapy, Father Matthias informed him, and he must do it as required, to stop his head from going mad.

'Son,' Father Matthias had reminded him, in yet another confession, 'the way you know an evil thought, is by the repeated urge to do the evil thing. It makes you want, want, want, and it does that until you give in to it and do the evil thing. Like, when you ate all of the jam and cream scones after Mass that day. You remember that day, Hamish? You had the urge over and over, until you committed the gluttony and stuffed the scones all in your mouth, one after the other, at great speed. Like you had not eaten in weeks. Do not be a horned puppet on the marionette of the Devil, Son. You cut that puppet string; you hear me, Son? Do not do the evil thought!'

Hamish thought about committing more gluttony, so he would be too fat to fit in the confessional box, which he seemed to find himself in week after week. But he hated the idea of being a puppet more than he hated confessing. He couldn't stand the thought of someone else in control of his mind, other than himself. Hamish did not want anyone telling him what to do, human or devil.

He decided not to be on the Devil's marionette, being lowered into scones and jam and cream each week, and yanked out again, only to be lowered into some other sin. Father Matthias had alerted Hamish that his long-dreadlocked hair would get him an interview with Sloth as well.

'Get out of the social slobber, Hamish,' Father Matthias had warned him, 'before it's too late.'

2

'Father. There are some unnatural things happening in this Church.'

'I think there are some unnatural things happening with you, Hamish,' Father Matthias said.

Hamish looked away, his eyes falling on the large wooden crucifix on the back wall of the church. It loomed out, growing larger and larger. He stumbled back from the sight, wondering if he should say any more. *Church objects are not what they seem*, he thought, panicking. They were the secret weapons of God, secret stashes of altar TNT. He looked around, panicking again, his eyes falling on the statue of the Christ Child, clutched in the Virgin Mary's arms. Any minute, the Christ Child, lurking in his statue, may hurl a grenade out at him. One year old and already killing the strange.

Hamish hesitated. The cross snapped back on the wall. Hamish sank down against the wall of the church, looking anxiously at the cross.

'Hamish?' the priest asked, coming towards him, his face concerned.

'I've only committed three of the seven sins, Father. Only three. And God is throwing weapons at me.'

'Well, three counts and you're out, usually applies,' Father Matthias said. 'So if you've committed three sins, and you're not telling me about them, you better let me know.'

'You already know about pride and gluttony…'

'And what is the other sin, hiding in the cupboard?' the priest asked.

Hamish looked away. 'Wrath,' he mumbled.

'What? I can't hear you,' Father Matthias said, leaning down, his hand cupping around his ear.

'Wrath,' Hamish said irritably, rubbing his forehead, feeling pain run through his head.

'And what sins have you committed under the spirit of wrath?' Father Matthias asked.

'I just feel angry a lot of the time,' Hamish said.

'About what?' Father Matthias asked, sitting down in a pew, clasping his hands together and leaning forward.

'Slow people. They piss me off, they don't understand quickly enough, and I see snails coming out of their mouths because they are so slow.'

'You see snails, coming out of people's mouths… Son?' the Priest asked, scrutinising him closely.

'Well, yeah. Because I can see the truth about them. About how slow they are in the head.'

'You see snails coming out of people's mouths and believe this is something showing you that the person is stupid and slow.'

'Father, I'm telling you: I can see the truth about people.'

'What are you talking about?' the priest scolded.

Hamish kept a wary eye on the cross. 'I can read the truth as well, Father. And I read that the seven sins aren't real. The real sins are in Solomon's writings. And I read that Solomon wrote *six things the Lord doth hate…* It's *six* sins; six, not seven.'

'I know Solomon's writings and I know what comes after the sixth sin he mentions. It's called "abomination", and I found it in you,' the priest said sternly. 'You stop reading those books, thinking you know it all, and stay with the guidance system provided for you.' The priest stared hard at him. 'You stay with the A to Z of parables, OK?'

'Father, I'm telling you—'

The cross blew out again in front of him, this time with his own self hanging off it. On it was written *Hamish, King of the Seven Sins.* Blood dripped off the nails, from his hands, splashing to the floor.

'Father,' he said panicking, clutching the priest's arm, looking at the cross.

The priest stared hard at the cross, and then at him. 'What? Are you seeing the Christ bleeding, Son?'

'No…it's…can't you see it?'

'See what?' The priest looked closely at him, 'Are you seeing things again… Son?'

Hamish bit his lip.

'I think you have pagan eyes and are seeing things,' Father Matthias said firmly. 'See what paganism does to you? Makes you see birds as demons. People as trolls. I can't record anything miraculous, Son; with what you say, you see. I think you've got the pagan sight. You go home tonight, Son, and you pray that God makes your eyes normal.'

'What happened to "those who have eyes to see"?' Hamish asked irritably, rubbing his forehead again. The pain in his head was getting worse, pulsing in waves he couldn't get away from. They kept repeating over and over. It was poison to his head.

'You have *strange* eyes to see with. The eyes of a pagan. Not the eyes of Christ, who sees the truth. And it's because you're reading *outside* what is recommended by the Church. You'd be best off reading the work of Alexander Pope, who got the phone call from God in the sixteenth century and God said to him, *a little learning is a dangerous thing*. You, Hamish, got the phone call of the Devil, who seduces you with knowing things, not of Christian sources. You remember what happened to Eve, Son, when she bit of the pagan apple. She was cast out from what is safe. You will end up an outcast from the things that keep you safe. I warn you now, in my duty as a priest, do not talk or listen to the pagan talk or read the pagan works. I don't want to see a little demon called Hamish, with horns, next time I see you in Mass.'

'I don't know what you mean, Father. I find things in books. I find the truth.'

'Stay out of the Devil's apple tree,' the priest said warningly.

'It was in the pages of a book. As writing. I didn't go down to hell to get it,' Hamish protested.

'Son. There are forces operating in this world, you know nothing about,' the priest said, giving him another long warning look.

Hamish stopped thinking about Father Matthias's mini-sermons at him and opened up the *T* section of the dictionary. It said: "Transcendence: (mass noun) Existence or experience beyond the normal or physical levels."

Hamish thought about this for a while, thinking his mind must have been in that experience since his womb days. His school teacher had sarcastically said it to him once, that in the womb, his mind grew first and it was too big for his head. The lightbulb flickered above him and he looked up hesitantly, wary of what he might see, but not able to resist what truth it might show him.

Hamish watched uneasily as the lightbulb on the ceiling grew larger and larger.

Fuck! he thought, *it's going to explode*. He scrambled off the chair, fell to the floor and hid under the chair.

'Hamish…?' he heard his mother ask from the kitchen. 'Hamish? What are you doing down there?'

Hamish heard the lightbulb explode and ran into his room, shutting the door and leaning against it, his breathing hard and fast.

There was no way he was turning on his light.

After Sunday Mass the next week, Hamish was dutifully asked by Father Matthias about his understanding of transcendence.

'Father,' he said, his thoughts rapid as pistol fire, 'I get it. The mustard seed and the mustard tree were beyond the normal and physical levels when looked at with Jesus' eyes. Because he had transcendent eyes. Everything looked bigger. And I sat there, Father, after reading the definition of transcendence, and I thought, that's what Jesus really meant. He was talking about the mustard seed and tree in a transcendent way, like out of their measurements? And not in an actual way, or the way of science.'

A laugh flew out of the Priest's mouth. 'Oh, I've almost cancelled your next inevitable confession, just for thinking of that, Son. But you have to tame your mind to the recommended ways of thinking. You push your mind too far out of its recommended shape, and it can become strange.' He paused, considering Hamish's flushed cheeks and confidence. 'Your mind has become like a cliff, Hamish: too tall, and steep, and rugged, and broken away from its homeland. Your mind, Son, you need to make it like the church rock of St Peter. And, this St Peter's rock mind, it stops you falling into the lower ways of thinking, of the social bubonic, which people get when their mind's like a cliff.' Father Matthias put his hand on Hamish's shoulder, and walked with him to the morning-tea table neatly draped with a clean, white cloth, with steaming silver urns of coffee and small glass milk jars sitting on it. 'You know, Son, all I asked you to do, was look up the definition of the word "transcendence", so you knew in what sense God operated. Instead, you decided to be clever, pulling the word right out of shape, into Hamish meaning. Were you being deliberately clever, Hamish? Were you?'

'It's just something I thought of,' Hamish said, shrugging.

'I will put it down as unintentional ego, then. Because being deliberately clever like that is ego, Hamish. It's your mind assuming its own greatness. You must take precautions against that Hamish. Think in the ways Jesus has taught. Those parables he made. They are behaviour parables. They teach you how to respond and act. You read those parables 1 to 46, Hamish, and you will see it's an A to Z roadmap on how to live your life,' Father Matthias said, giving Hamish's shoulder a rub.

'I don't know if I want a roadmap like that, Father,' Hamish said doubtfully. 'I would be cutting out half my mind following it.'

'Then your mind was born too big, Hamish, and just like a big, wild tree, it has to have some branches cut off. That doesn't hurt you know, Son. You won't have to carry so much weight, with some of those branches cut off. Do you really want a heavy mind, full of thoughts which are here, there and everywhere? No. It's best just to have one branch on that tree, full of healthy leaves.'

'Why are the other branches there, then?' Hamish pondered.

'Those branches are just different paths you can take in life. An unfortunate product of free will. Now. Did you say the three *Hail Mary's* before you read the dictionary? Did you put yourself in a reverent space first? Because I don't think you did. Otherwise, you would not have come up with all those strange explanations and sights…' He turned Hamish around by his shoulders, to face the church. 'Look at that. What do you see?'

Hamish studied the bleached sandstones of the church. People walked quietly through the dark brown arch, their heads bowed. He wasn't sure whether their heads were bowed in reverence or penitence; or they were trying to avoid the suspicious eyes of Father Matthew, who was recruiting for the confessional box that day. Hamish looked up at the stone steeple and the big brass bell swinging gently in the breeze.

Hamish backed away, as he saw a small black-winged thing, clawing at the sun-bleached red tiles of the church.

'What is *that* doing on the House of God?' Hamish asked suspiciously, pointing at the small black-winged thing.

He saw Father Matthias squint at the church roof, 'What d'you mean, Son?'

'Is that what I am supposed to be seeing, Father? That thing?' Hamish asked, looking hard at the roof.

'*What* thing, Hamish?' Father Matthias asked, exasperated, staring hard at the roof. 'I can't see what you mean, Son.'

'The thing that looks like a small, skinny bat, trying to eat the roof.'

'You are seeing things again, Son,' Father Matthias said, looking hard at him.

'I'm telling you. It's there,' Hamish said angrily.

'I think you may have schizophrenia,' Father Matthias said firmly. 'It comes from asking too many questions. You get a devil-split mind. From wanting to know things outside what is recommended for you to know. For today, I will pass that bat thing you saw off as a tree shadow. But the next day I won't. You don't go around talking about things like that. You understand?'

'Yes Father,' he mumbled, looking down at the ground. 'Yes, I understand.'

Father Matthias patted him on the shoulder. 'Good lad.'

Hamish looked up at Father Matthias. 'What is it you *did* want me to see, Father? When you asked me to look at the church?'

'Your ticket out of free will, Hamish. And all the suffering it brings with it, because you do your will, not God's. Now. Off you go…' He turned his head, looking around at the parishioners congregating at the front of the church. 'Where's that mother of yours? Ah. There she is. Have some scones,' he said, waving at the table. 'But remember not to commit the sin of gluttony on them, please.'

Hamish fought the urge to eat all the steaming hot scones, with their deep-red slathers of strawberry jam and thick cream melting down the sides. He looked away desperately, as the urge to grab all the scones at once and stuff them in his mouth smashed through his mind.

That's when he saw her.

Justine.

3

She looked like a doll. Big blue eyes, porcelain-white skin, and lightly flushed pink cheeks. Her hair was straight and blonde, cut sharply just above the breast area. *Not that she has much of that at thirteen*, he thought, hastily looking away from the small swells underneath her light pink dress.

But it was enough to stir his fourteen-year-old interest. He looked quickly again at her soft, curvaceous body, how the pink dress draped over her full hips; his eyes dropping to the ruffled pink hem fluttering in the wind around her legs. His gaze skittered away from her soft, inviting body, falling onto the hot steaming scones, dripping with jam and cream.

He was sure of a lot of things, because his mind was deft and quick, and he could work most things out very quickly. But girls? There had never been a beginning point he could work from, so he could work Justine out. No precedent to refer to, as he'd always, until now, regarded girls biologically, not with personal interest. He looked at Justine again, his cheeks flushing. His mind could not work out the shape of what it had been presented with and what angles to explain her with.

As he looked at her, the deftness and the quickness of his mind slowed, the way a day slows to purple before sunset. She sent him into a state of dusk. A state of falling and fading, out of the hot sun of his mind and the heat of his thoughts, spitting like a wildfire through him, igniting his senses, making him rapid, fast, and agitated. He blinked rapidly, not used to the deep dusk cooling his mind, and the quiet tides of blue in her eyes, washing into him. He could not pass through her as he passed through most things.

Her solidness made her a mystery; paused his mind.

'Who are you?' Hamish asked with interest, coming closer to her.

She looked steadily at him. 'Justine Wright.'

'Hamish McColl,' he said.

'Yes. I know,' she said seriously.

Hamish did not know what to say next. Her cerulean-blue eyes were disturbing the quick movements of his mind, and he couldn't think of any words that were native to his mind, to say to her. She belonged to things around her; to things that were solid, defined, and unquestionable.

Justine smiled politely at him. Her politeness and silence told him she was a person of social rhythm: *You speak, I speak, you speak, I speak.* He knew she was politely waiting for him to say the next line. She kept looking at him with the patience of a church, her eyes like quiet spaces.

He didn't know how to talk to her. There was no drifting in her. Nothing he could recognise as something of his own.

She was made of too many solid things.

School closed around him for the day, forcing him into stone. Another day like a vaccination, inoculating his mind with the curriculum of Saint Francis' High School, Sydney. He stood at the entrance of the high school, the sandstone bricks of the school buildings thickening through his mind, slowing the comet-like ability of his thoughts. Hamish closed his eyes, trying to stop the effect of the bricks on him. He could never name this strange thing that happened to him, where he stared at something and its texture would enter his mind, affecting him with its composition.

He didn't want to tell anyone about it either. Once, he had started to try and tell his sister, and saw a cuckoo on a clock arm flying out of her head.

She would think he was mental.

So, he didn't tell her. Just kept quiet about it; quiet about the secret ways he saw the truth, and the way buildings and people just seemed to pass through his head.

He had learnt to glance quickly at things, so they didn't affect him so badly.

Hamish looked away from the thick sandstone of the two-storey building, his eyes hitting the dark wood of the arched entry students were disappearing into. He looked quickly away from its shape, so it didn't produce a dark arrow to hit his thoughts.

Hamish lowered his head so as not to see the shape of the arch as he followed the stream of students, vanishing one by one, out of the natural territory of the dark husks of tree trunks, sun-buttered grass and drifts of wind, surrounding the school.

Hamish sat down on his assigned school seat, staring wearily out the window, avoiding the eyes of his teacher Mr Sorokin; slimy, impatient, like grey stingrays. His mind had trouble hardening or sharpening under his strange, grey, jelly-like stare.

Hamish could not accept the boxes Mr Sorokin made for his thoughts. They put fences around his thinking, made cows of his thoughts. He saw those cows on assignment papers handed back to students after marking; cows which stepped out of the marked papers, shuffled off, and sat behind the teacher's desk. He couldn't stand looking at those cows with their dumb stares, chewing slowly on cuds, excreting out the same shit every day; just like he had to learn the same stupid shit every day.

He was sick of it and couldn't understand why no one could understand his non-acceptance of things. As far as he could see, everything and everyone was just a copy of other people's beliefs. He wanted to be who he was, not some dust-bible or classroom lesson. Sorokin once said to the class that maths taught a certain way of thinking: this plus that equals this; to prepare you for later social thinking, like woman plus man equals child.

Hamish had thought desperately about this for days, his mind sinking into holes. *A plus Hamish equals C. Hamish plus B equals C. A plus B equals Hamish.* He'd spent days desperately wondering what A, B and C would be, and if, in fact, he could escape from them.

'Hamish,' Sorokin called out sharply.

Hamish looked away from the window which, he decided, held back all natural things. He wished he could make the window pane between the classroom and nature disappear, as he felt too glassed into measurement, into exactness; yet, he felt like an inexactness in the classroom, sitting in the layout of five exact rows of twenty-five small brown desks, and twenty-five mustard-yellow chairs.

All exactly placed on lightly pebbled brown carpet.

It gave him vertigo.

He looked at Sorokin, thinking how much like a vicious hawk he looked with his narrowed, grey eyes, and his sharp nose narrowing in and hooking over like a beak, almost reaching his thin, tight lips. His blonde tuft of hair, cut sharply to one side, sticking up like a stiff, predatory wing.

A vicious hawk, stuffed into a white shirt. Sorokin's dark grey tie loomed out like a slipknot.

Fuck! Hamish almost yelled, as the slipknot came close to his own neck and snapped back again, into its disguise as a tie.

‘Yes?’ Hamish replied belatedly to Sorokin, his voice uneven, as the slipknot snapped out and snapped back in again. At least, it didn’t come close to him this time. Which meant Sorokin had pulled back from completely killing him. He felt Sorokin in his head, hovering like a predator over his mind.

‘Yes, what?’

Hamish’s mind rebelled against the expected social politeness he was expected to show Sorokin, but which Sorokin was not expected to show him. Why was it that Sorokin could call him, Hamish, by his first name, but he, Hamish, could not call Sorokin by *his* first name?

Hamish decided against social politeness. It was too much like glass; a window pane separating what was natural between people.

‘Yes, Peter,’ he said, raising his chin, staring defiantly at Sorokin.

‘Excuse me?’ his teacher asked, his face deadly, his eyes flickering with toxins. Hamish scrambled back in his seat, as he saw shadowy predator-wings come out of Sorokin’s face, beating slowly, together and apart.

Hamish found it hard to keep talking with those predatory wings flapping out of Sorokin’s face, but he managed to say something. ‘Yes, Peter,’ he repeated.

The veins across Sorokin’s face mottled purple. Hamish looked away, deeply disturbed by the sight of Sorokin’s purple-veined face between the flapping wings. He grew even more alarmed seeing Sorokin’s hands turning into talons, curling into fists.

‘That is *not* how you address a teacher, Hamish.’

‘It’s how you should address a teacher,’ Hamish said, his anger now stronger than his fear. His voice rose. ‘You may be an adult, which means you get called Mr Sorokin; and I may be a teenager, which means I get called Hamish; but you are not mentally taller than me. *You are not mentally taller than me!*’ he yelled.

‘And how have you measured that, Hamish?’ Sorokin asked, staring at him coldly. ‘How have you measured that I am not mentally taller than you?’

‘It’s not something you do with a ruler, Peter,’ Hamish sneered.

Sorokin’s breath sounded slowly through the classroom. Sorokin had done that before, that slow breath which made Hamish feel on edge. Not only because it was slow and he hated anything slow, but it made him feel tense and agitated, waiting for the next minute to take place; to him it was always like a question he had to solve. Waiting for Sorokin’s breath to end almost sent him mental, waiting to know if Sorokin was going to finish him off or concede defeat to him.

Hamish stared at the ceiling, waiting for the drongo to speak.

'God will not be helping you this time, Hamish, no matter how much you raise your eyes to the ceiling. The cloud will not come down with his best wishes for your future. As far as your somewhat strange and odd intelligence goes, Hamish, I have measured it on many, many occasions. *With* proper educational assessment tools. And I *know* I have more intelligence than you, Hamish, because I *know* the answer to the questions already. You are still working the answers out. Your scores show that.'

Hamish felt his face heating the same way it did when he was forced to run round and around in a circle in athletic carnivals; something he found irritating and pointless. And that's what he felt like he was doing with Sorokin. Just arguing around and around in circles. Hamish had read once that circles had no entrance or exit, so he knew there would be no way he could go into Sorokin's point of view, and no way he could get out of it either.

Hamish clenched his fists. Rage was like a clumsy walker in his mind; it kept banging against the walls in his head, knocking his intelligence out. He couldn't reach for the words he wanted to say, because all he could feel was rage. The words just stumbled out of his mouth, without thought, without question, and without answer. 'You know the answers, *Peter*,' Hamish fumed, 'because you read them in the teacher's part of the book. The answers were already written there, and *not* worked out by you.'

'*Wrong*,' Sorokin corrected, 'I already *learnt* those answers when I was a student at high school.'

'Then you are just more educated than me, *not* mentally taller,' Hamish said hotly.

Sorokin's eyes narrowed, predatory as the hawk suddenly swooping down on its prey struggling way beneath it. 'My completion of my education *makes* me mentally taller than you, because I have *learnt* more things than you,' Sorokin told him. 'That makes my mind bigger than yours.'

'No,' Hamish spat out, 'it makes your mind smaller. Because all you have learnt, and all I am learning now, is *useless*.' He held his maths book up. 'All these maths equations I'm never even going to use. When am I going to use trigonometry? Or algebra? I'm not going to go into the bank, and ask for 90 degrees of my savings, am I?' Hamish told him belligerently, throwing his maths book on the floor.

Sorokin put both hands on his desk, leaning forward, staring hard at Hamish, his voice low and quiet. 'Let me tell you something, Hamish. That sort of thinking is called vigilante. It's part of a personality disorder, Hamish, where your thinking is off and not on. Where, instead of just being Hamish McColl, you are the secret Batman of Sydney. Something mythological and bigger than what you actually are.' Sorokin locked eyes with Hamish, as if he was trying to padlock him into his seat; stop him flying out as the St Francis High School Batman. 'Being the secret Batman, up here,' he tapped his forehead, 'doesn't get you anywhere, Hamish, except a place in mental hospital.' Sorokin walked around the front of the desk, folding his arms, studying him. 'We are trying to get you into correct thinking habits, Hamish, so you can function as a good citizen. Now and as an adult. Lose your Batman, Hamish,' he said warningly. 'We have things in place in our society, that stop little nuclear weapons like you going off and causing social blasts. Do you understand?'

'No,' Hamish said stubbornly, kicking the floor underneath the desk, 'and I don't want to.'

Sorokin looked at him, his face tight and severe, each word screwing up like a piece of paper into a tight ball. 'What is it you don't understand?'

'Why asking questions about what other people say is called vigilante,' Hamish answered impatiently, his feet shuffling under the desk.

'It's called vigilante because you are thinking outside the systems in society which exist to protect the people, Hamish. Social systems, Hamish, social systems. Religion, law, education, family, tradition. Even the way we all greet one another is part of a social system. A greeting, said the correct way, as taught by tradition or family, makes you part of a social pattern that helps you stay inside a social place. Social systems stop you skidding outside the lines, Hamish. When we all skate together within the lines of a social system, Hamish, life works out. So, you must understand, Hamish, that within the lines of a social system, you are Hamish, the student; and I am the teacher, Mr Sorokin. Student is your social place and teacher is my social place in the social system.'

'I don't want to do a puppet skate with a whole lot of people, all saying and doing the same thing,' Hamish said hotly. 'I have a mouth of my own.'

‘Yes. And it’s too big,’ Sorokin said sarcastically, ‘like most Batman thinkers.’

‘No. Your mouth is too small,’ Hamish snapped.

Sorokin smiled thinly. ‘Your mouth is too big because it is stuffed full of things outside the social system. You have a type of mental obesity, Hamish.’

‘I have Maccas thoughts,’ Hamish said sarcastically.

‘Another strange statement, from Hamish, the resident class Batman. McDonalds has nothing to do with it. Your Batman thinking does. You have the sort of thoughts, Hamish, that lead to social riots. The reason prescribed thought exists, such as what you learn in school or church, is so you know how to live in peace with others, in an ordered society. We don’t live in the Stone Age anymore, Hamish, where we club each other over the head because our thinking urge is instinctual, instead of ordered. Society is designed in systems, not caves, so people do things in a reasonable, civilised manner.’

The lunchtime bell echoed in the school grounds.

‘And why do we have a bell to announce it’s lunchtime?’ Hamish demanded. ‘It’s stupid. You should just look at the clock and say *lunchtime*.’

‘The bell ringing is part of a school system,’ his teacher answered dismissively, turning away and gathering the papers together on his desk. ‘The sound of the bell ringing tells you what to do, and when. You hear it, you get up, you walk out of the classroom and you have lunch. Then you hear another one, which tells you to pack up, and return to the classroom.’

‘Why do you need your larynx then?’ Hamish asked sarcastically.

‘My larynx is part of my biological system. The bell is part of a school system,’ Mr Sorokin said coolly, ‘which is part of a larger social system called education.’

‘You have to use your larynx to teach us,’ Hamish pointed out. ‘So your larynx is part of the school system.’

Mr Sorokin grew quiet, staring at Hamish; his eyes like grey, wet stones at the bottom of a creek. Eyes that drowned things, so they lay quiet and still. And did not speak.

‘Hamish. Don’t question the system,’ Sorokin said quietly.

‘It sucks,’ Hamish said, and went out the classroom door, slamming it behind him.

4

Father Matthias smiled tolerantly at Hamish, as he walked through the open church doors with his mother, Josephine, and his father, Wallace. Hamish looked at Father Matthias's crisp, green robe flowing in the wind, and the symbolic items of the body and blood of Christ stitched on his robe in white cloth. His black face was shining with sweat and grace, his shaved head gleaming like a black dome in the sunlight.

His father impatiently pushed Hamish towards Father Matthias.

'You need a new commandment, Father, just for Hamish. *Thou shalt not speak.*'

'The eleventh commandment is for God to decide, Mr McColl, as much as we want to write more to help us with our earthly problems. Now, what exactly is the issue with the Last Supper?'

'Hamish here—' His father drew a deep breath, exhaling loudly and began again. 'Hamish here is speaking rubbish again. He's half leprechaun, I tell you. A changeling,' his father said, looking suspiciously at Josephine. She clutched her handbag, raising it to her chest, her eyes pleading with him. She shook her head *no*.

'Hamish?' Father Matthias asked, not taking his eyes off his face.

'I read some stuff in Dad's books,' Hamish said reluctantly, 'after I received the penance for stuffing myself on host wafers. I just couldn't stop eating them, Father, I couldn't stop...' Hamish looked down at the ground again, shuffling from foot to foot. 'Dad says what I'm reading is different to what's there.'

'Ah yes.' Father Matthias ruminated a moment, before continuing, his voice rumbling. 'The host wafer penance, for committing gluttony on the host form. Your interesting reading ability, I will not comment on.'

'We are very embarrassed about his gluttony, Father, very embarrassed,' his mother said, her voice low, her eyes downcast, her head bowed.

'I'm hungry a lot,' Hamish complained. 'My stomach, it doesn't feel like it has any walls in it and the hunger is big as space itself. I just can't stop eating.'

'I will not house a fat leprechaun in my home,' his father said. 'Fat Catholic leprechauns are not approved of.'

Father Matthias looked away from his father, narrowing his eyes suspiciously at Hamish. 'You have the Devil's hunger. People who eat like that, scoffing down host wafers and scones…it's the Devil's hunger.'

'And he eats all the leftovers at home,' his mother added.

'Eating off our plates. Like a little leprechaun pig,' his father said, his eyes hostile.

Father Matthias held up his hand. 'Please. Let me continue.'

His mother looked down at the ground again, her head bowed. 'Yes, Father.'

Father Matthias looked at Hamish, his eyes troubled. 'People who scoff food down like that, Hamish, and then go to the cupboard for more, have a Devil's runt growing in them.' He walked forward, looking at Hamish intently, and clasped his shoulders firmly. 'And we will not welcome Hamish-with-horns into our church Masses, Son. Oh no, we won't.'

'I will do my best, my absolute best, Father, to make sure that doesn't happen,' his mother said, her hands twisting together, as she looked worriedly at Hamish.

'I know you will, Josephine. You are a good woman. But Hamish's mind, it keeps wanting to do the bungee jump into matters of the abyss.' The priest turned, looking meaningfully at Hamish's father. 'Please. He has too much thought already; and those books of yours are making his imagination planet-sized, instead of the very small seed it should be, if at all.'

'Ask what the little leprechaun read in planet-sized chapter eight,' his father told the priest, folding his arms and rocking back and forth on his heels.

Hamish shrugged, trying to act casual, saying, 'It was a chapter about how when we eat of the body of Christ and drink of his blood, it changes our inner reality.'

'Son, all that meant was that the ingestion of the sacraments changes our sinning natures.' The Priest looked at Hamish's father warningly. 'Please, put those books away, Mr McColl. He's reading things too big for him.'

'I don't remember any of that being in my books, Father,' Hamish's father said, scratching his head. 'He's making magic out of them, turning ordinary pumpkin words into fraudulent Cinderella's strange dressed-up words. You best check him for leprechaun blood, Father, with the Church. I have no way of knowing if he's of my flesh or not.'

Father Matthias looked at him sharply, then at Hamish. 'How long have you been reading words that aren't there, Hamish?' he asked carefully.

'I don't know,' Hamish said, rubbing his face irritably. 'Words which tell the truth about things have always been there in the books I read.'

'Put a lock on your bookshelf,' Father Matthias said quietly to Hamish's father, then turned to Hamish. 'You don't need to concern yourself with complex theological business, like transubstantiation and meiosis.'

'Transub…and mes…what?' asked Hamish.

'Theological terms, for what changes the inner reality in parishioners who drink of the blood of Christ and eat of the body of Christ to purify themselves,' the priest answered.

'What should I do? About his imagination?' his mother asked anxiously.

The priest looked troubled. 'It is indeed peculiar. Please. Keep a strong and steady eye on him. If you notice anything more…please, let me know.' He leant forward and whispered in his father's ear, '*…medication…and…stop it now…and…'*

The priest finished whispering. Hamish's father nodded, his eyes bristling with hostility. Hamish was not sure if his eyes were hostile because he didn't like anyone, even a priest, telling him what to do; or if the hostility was more to do with himself, as his father believed he was the love-child of a leprechaun, who had it off with his mother.

'I will do as you ask,' Hamish's father said abruptly.

Hamish looked from Father Matthias to his father, and back at the priest again. The priest looked at him carefully, as if examining him for soul disease.

Hamish tried to smile, but couldn't.

The priest's hand landed on his shoulder. 'Is everything alright, Hamish?' His voice rumbled deeply like he had thunder in his larynx.

Hamish looked up at the priest.

'Yes,' Hamish lied, feeling as if he was regarded as the syphilis of the Church.

'You're not smiling, Hamish,' Father Matthias said, looking at him closely.

'I'm thinking about something,' Hamish said.

'What exactly are you thinking about? And, is it confessional material?' Father Matthias asked.

'No, Father. Unless wondering what sort of smile I should give you is a sin of free choice.'

The priest threw back his head and roared with laughter.

'Hamish,' his mother said, embarrassed, 'you should really stop thinking about such things.'

'I have to think about the multiple choice of smiles,' Hamish said seriously. 'I could give someone the wrong type of smile, and they could get the wrong idea. I could give a piranha person a sacrificial lamb smile, and that would be the end of me.'

'Oh dear!' his mother said, mortified.

'I apologise for Hamish, Father Matthias,' Hamish's father said. 'He has a tendency to complicate what is really very simple. I think it may be a leprechaun trait.'

'Ah. He was born with a few extra brain cells than most,' the priest said.

'Extra brain cells are not what is needed, Father; common sense is,' Hamish's father said determinedly. 'But he doesn't seem to have been born with a whole lot of that. Too much leprechaun wandering in his head.'

'You seem to be a little obsessed with leprechauns, Mr McColl,' Father Matthias said. 'And I don't feel heritage, whether it's leprechaun or goat or chicken or human, is the problem. The problem is in his brain design, and that's what you need to take note of; not assign his mental phenomena to leprechaun DNA.'

'You think it's mental phenomena? No, Father, I think not. There is no doubt in my mind that he is a leprechaun; a changeling here from the other world, wearing a skeleton and flesh.'

'I see,' Father Matthias said, his face solemn; although Hamish could see what looked like the *Joker* out of *Batman* springing out of both of his eyes, and he knew that Father Matthias thought that *Hamish's leprechaun-self* was just a big joke.

Hamish thought he should keep quiet about that one. Or Father Matthias might quietly pick up the phone, and call the whitecoats to come and remove him, the Pan-possessed Hamish, from the sanctified Church grounds.

Father Matthias looked from Hamish's father to his mother. 'I don't think you will ever teach Hamish how to be common or sensible. He's just not made that way. And in a practical and systematic society, he is going to find things somewhat difficult, because of his make.'

It was like he wasn't even standing there, Hamish thought, his cheeks heating, his breath ripping through his nose and mouth. Anger flared in his eyes as he stared at the three of them, the sight making him feel like a rabid bull looking at a red flag.

'Please pray for him, Father,' Hamish's mother said earnestly, dropping her head again, shame burning her cheeks. 'He knows not what he does.'

'I don't think the rosary can work a miracle that big,' the priest said drily. 'And let me tell you, Mrs McColl, it will take a lot of praying to bring that mind down.'

'Hail Hamish, full of mental tallness, we are against thee,' Hamish said furiously, elbowing his way out of the small crowd gathered around the priest. Like he was some sort of Sydney Jesus leaving the temple.

'Hamish!' his mother called out, her beseeching voice buzzing like a dying bee. He turned quickly, feverishly wishing he hadn't, as the rosary beads came flying out of his mother's mouth, strangling him around the neck.

Fuck! He gripped his neck, trying to get them off, but felt they weren't there anymore, just a projection of the truth. Dismayed, he wondered if his mother thought about coming into his room at night and strangling him with her rosary beads, because she was so ashamed of him.

Hamish ignored his mother, given her possible homicidal intent with her rosary beads, and went to find a pew. He looked around, noticing for the first time how the people in the stained-glass windows were all in suffering or condemning positions. Christ in twisted agony on the cross. The Angels and Saints and Prophets, glassed-in by stained windows, looking at him accusingly: *I know what you did, I know what you did, I know what you did.* His eyes fell on the Virgin holding her bleeding heart, her eyes raised in anguish.

He sat down at a pew near the front, wondering why things in the church were presented in ideas of suffering and condemnation. *Why isn't Christ pictured as resurrected, but instead torn and bloody? Why isn't the Virgin pictured ascended, with her heart whole and healed? It was like their stories got paused halfway*, Hamish thought.

Kept always in that suffering state.

Hamish had heard Father Matthias speak one Sunday, after the second reading, about how all Catholics must suffer in the spirit of Christ. Father Matthias had reverently held up a hammer, like it was the holy smash-instrument of God, looking intently from member to member of the congregation. 'This hammer, it's like God's tool, to bring the suffering to you. But he waits a bit, before he drives in the nail. To say to you, you will get the suffering, oh yes you will; because you are spiritually lazy! As it says in his good book,' his voice played across the congregation like a deep, dark, and husky cello, 'in the Hebrews, 12.6: *For those whom the Lord loves, he disciplines and he scourges every son he receives!*'

Hamish shrank back in the pew, looking at Father Matthias in terror as the hammer went Hulk, growing larger and larger. *Fuck!* he thought, *Fuck!* pressing hard against the back of the seat; as the Hulk hammer went from head to head, and skulls started cracking.

He looked frantically behind him for an escape route as God's holy instrument demolished the people in front of him. All the doorways were blocked off by Roman soldiers gripping hammers in their hands, tapping them lightly against their palms.

Fuck, he thought panicking, *no escape from being smashed.* He closed his eyes, not wanting to see God's holy instrument coming for him.

Nothing happened.

Slowly, he opened his eyes.

The hammer snapped back to normal, and Father Matthias's calm, black face graced him, with the serenity of a man who had escaped God's hammer. Hamish's heart slowed down, as mental panic about being hit over the head with a holy tool stopped. Hamish looked hesitantly at his father, now sitting in his pew. Should he ask his leprechaun-averse father the question sliding out of the ten minutes of panic he'd just been through?

He knew the question would just keep repeating in his mind until he had an answer for it.

Hamish quickly and nervously tapped his father on the arm.

'Dad,' he whispered urgently.

Hamish's father looked at him, annoyed.

Hamish decided to ask anyway. He had to have that question answered. He didn't want it sounding in his head, like a loud drill for the rest of the day. And the next. And the next. And the next.

'Dad,' he said loudly, 'why doesn't God receive daughters for scourging? Father Matthias only mentioned sons in that Bible verse he quoted.'

'As it says quite clearly in the Bible passage, Hamish, which the good Father quoted and quite rightly so, *those whom God loves*...and then the passage says *sons*. Not daughters. Sons.' Hamish's father ground his teeth together, his hands clenching into fists. 'It is clear, Hamish, why God does not love the women of the Earth. It was *Eve* who ate of the apple offered to her by the daughter of Satan, *not* Adam. So, he loves the sons. God makes *sons* suffer so they grow spiritually wise and don't eat an apple from the tree of the daughter of Satan again.'

'I get it now,' Hamish said. 'God keeps hammer-beating sons up, until they wise up to evil skank-women handing out poisoned apples.'

'That is the story, Hamish,' his father said, satisfaction crossing his face. 'That is the story. So, don't you be going putting your leprechaun-self in the story, going into penile drool at the things offered to you, by a daughter of Satan, or one of his she-tempters.'

'Right,' Hamish said, 'don't date an evil skank.'

'Or become gay,' Hamish's father said, 'because I will give you a family sentence of eunuch if you do.'

'Dad. I'm not gay.'

'If you make the un-Christian choice to be a gay, or partake of apple slop from a daughter of Satan, I don't hold out much hope for you, Hamish. You still have the wee brain of a leprechaun, wearing big boots. You will just suffer and suffer and suffer because of that.'

Hamish looked unhappily at Father Matthias solemnly moving the hammer in an arc, his eyes weighty on each congregation member. The priest continued, 'It is said: *The greatest souls are awakened out of suffering!*' His words roared through the church, making some parishioners flatten themselves against their pew seats, and others drop to their knees, their mouths moving in prayer. Hamish leant forward, clutching his head, fearfully thinking about the religious fate of his soul opening its red-rimmed eye, as people hammer-smashed him into greatness. *Why awake broken?* he thought, not able to work out the logic.

Hamish decided, right then and there, he was going native. He was zipping his soul up in a sleeping bag and leaving it out in the wild somewhere—somewhere where stars weren't hammers; and the gently-waving leaves weren't hammers; and the soft rush of the river wasn't a hammer.

When it came to being a great soul like Jesus, or a native under the non-hammering stars, he would be the native, Hamish decided. Be with what was natural. Because he didn't think smashing each other with hammers was.

People rose from the pews, murmuring, crossing themselves. Father Matthias swept up the aisle, his crisp, green robe flowing behind him, like some scurrying angel behind him was holding it out in the wind. Hamish tried to ignore the hammer coming out of Father Matthias's mouth, but it was too large for him to dismiss.

Hamish quickly turned his head away, and turned to see Justine standing at the end of his pew. Like a Saint. Like the Virgin. Like one of the Angels, with her golden hair, blue eyes and faintly flushed skin; the soft drifts of her rose-pink dress; her soft white arms and her small cherubic hands, held together.

She looks like she has just stepped out of one of the stained-glass windows in the church, Hamish thought, *the arch around her keeping everything out and keeping her in a consistency of glass, where the picture was already drawn and coloured.*

'Hi,' Hamish said, his voice plunging down and shooting suddenly up; still not certain of how he should greet her, or anyone else for that matter. His sister Niamh, who had etiquette lessons each Friday, had tried to teach him British social customs to cure him of his social disregard for people. The formal phrases snapped his mind like a rat trap. He came to dread the soft knock at his door; Niamh standing there. A black coffin, with a British flag wrapped around it, sliding out of her mouth as she said, 'How do you do?' Hamish could barely bring himself to talk to Niamh after each soft knock, fearful his mind would be murdered by the next instalment of her language pesticide.

Aside from his fear of Niamh's language pesticide, regularly sprayed on him, his thoughts were so rapid, firing off at least every three seconds. He could not remember or retain or even take notice of such careful and consistent formality of language. Hamish could never quite remember to say *How do you do?* to anyone when meeting them; *Hi* or *Hello* or *Yo* or *Fuck off* shot out of his mouth instead. The lighter handshake for girls, gently taught to him by Niamh, was never remembered when he was bouncing up and down in a thought, taking it up, taking it down, rebounding it off the walls of his mind for its multi-possibilities. One of Niamh's friends he'd practised *la feminine* handshake on, had never returned to the house, whingeing on and on to Niamh about having her arm half-ripped out of her socket by him, Hamish.

He didn't want to be associated with her friend, known as a sook, anyway. She irritated him every time she spoke, sounding both like a high-pitched cat and a thin whistle blowing off, 'Niiiiaaaammmmhhhh' yowling down the hallway. She'd actually asked Niamh, right in front of him, when he was going to the pound, comparing him to an enthusiastic and untrained bulldog. Cat bitch.

Hamish had closed the door on yet another human face, finding something strange in its place, and using the only words he knew to deal with strange things. 'Fuck off,' he scowled, walking past the strange thin cat, coming out of the wall into his room.

'Hamish?' Justine asked, jolting him back to the present moment.

'I was just thinking about something,' Hamish mumbled.

'You do that at home, Hamish,' she said, her voice reprimanding, 'not when you are talking to people.'

'I'm one big room,' Hamish said.

'Hamish. That doesn't make any sense to me,' she said unyieldingly.

Hamish looked away from her, not wanting to even speak about the house with cement walls and rooms like boxes he saw coming out the top of her head. Each room had a neatly typed and labelled name. He looked at the room on top of her head called 'Thinking' and the next room called 'Talking'. His eyes rested on the next room, called 'Category'. On the impeccably vacuumed carpet was a brown cardboard box, with the word 'Hamish' written in thick, red letters on it, and a big blue question mark underneath it.

She hadn't decided what he was yet. He wondered if he was going to be stored in the garage he could see, or taken out of the box and housed comfortably in one of her rooms. In any case, the sight of such categorical order left him unable to speak.

'Can I sit here?' Justine asked politely.

He nodded quickly, looking away until the tight little house on top of her head snapped back into her skull. That tight little house had everything to do with why she suffered so badly with social politeness. He, Hamish, would never have asked if he could sit next to her. He just would have done it. Like many others, she weirdly believed everyone had to do things the same way. Like, everybody was just one big face and one big mouth. His mind gripped this idea and threw it around, wondering how he could rip the social house off its arse; so he didn't have to sit in it anymore.

Hamish looked cautiously at Justine, paused at the end of the pew, her hand lightly resting on top of it, looking patiently at him.

He realised she was waiting for him to speak the social butter.

'You don't have to ask if you can sit here,' Hamish said, unwilling to be part of the one big mouth of everyone. *You say this, and then I say this, and then you say this, and then I say this...piss off to the puppets*, he thought. He would say what he wanted to say.

'I'm being polite, Hamish.'

He looked away, appalled.

'Politeness is a disease,' he muttered, 'everyone seems to have.'

Justine's blue eyes became reserved, bored almost. 'Why don't you have it, Hamish?'

'I'm different,' he said confidently. 'I can see that everyone is squashed into one big car together. And I can see it because I'm standing outside the car, looking at everyone in church here squashed together. Faces flat against the window.'

'You're not different, Hamish. You're mental,' she answered firmly. 'The whole church is not in one car. They just wouldn't all fit.'

He didn't like how she called him mental.

And, he didn't like how she sprayed her lemon-starched collar of logic on his ideas.

It took him three days to do a Jesus job on the idea, and bring it back from the dead.

Despite this, he was strangely drawn to her.

Sorokin held Hamish's assignment in his hand, as if it was something he wanted to quarantine. An infectious piece of material, which failed his mental hygiene standards. Sorokin dropped the assignment into Hamish's hands, like it was a wipe of dirty toilet paper from the arse of an unclean mind.

'That,' Sorokin said scathingly, 'I have absolutely no words for.'

Hamish looked at his assignment and saw *0/20* written on it. Humiliation violated his mind, wrecking his certainty and confidence about his intelligence.

His face burned with anger at this insult of a grade from Sorokin. He did it on purpose, Hamish knew he did, denying Hamish's 'superiority' to him.

Hamish looked at him furiously. 'This is not fair,' he yelled at Sorokin, 'this is not fair!'

His teacher regarded him coolly. 'Yes, it is fair, Hamish. You didn't give me an answer. You gave me a mental dump.'

'I did not,' Hamish said hotly, throwing the assignment back at him. 'Give me my real mark. That's a pretend mark.'

'Now, who's a little paranoid boy,' Sorokin taunted. 'That mark means you didn't answer the question, you just did what you wanted to do, in your strange little Batman way.'

'My thoughts aren't a mental dump!' Hamish said angrily. 'They mean something.'

'They mean you *didn't* answer the question,' Sorokin said firmly. 'You answered it the way *you* wanted to answer it. Now pick that assignment up. Batman spats won't be tolerated here, boy.'

'How about a Hamish spit,' Hamish said, spitting at him.

Sorokin's face flamed, his grey eyes like hot flint. He rapidly walked over to Hamish, grabbing him by the hair.

'Get you and your nit hair off this chair, and pick that assignment up. Now.'

Hamish stumbled off the chair, falling in front of the assignment. Sorokin pushed Hamish's face down onto it.

'Pick the rubbish up,' Sorokin said, his foot kicking the assignment. Hamish's hands fumbled over it, until he grasped a corner.

Sorokin released his hair, his face becoming calm. 'Now give it to me.'

Hamish handed the assignment up, and clasped his hands around his head, shielding his hair from Sorokin's pulling hands.

'Stay in your place in this classroom, Hamish,' Sorokin threatened.

Hamish scrambled back into his chair.

'Sit straight, Hamish; not like something vomiting,' Sorokin said.

'I don't feel too good,' Hamish said. 'I want to go home, I—'

'*Sit* straight in your chair and I will calmly and logically explain to you why your mark was zero. We do live in a civil society, after all. Now. Let me show you an example…' Hamish watched bleakly, as Sorokin turned the pages of Hamish's assignment over. 'Ah, here,' Sorokin said determinedly, his eyes narrowing. 'Now listen to this:

I don't think much of Jane Trainer's novel "The Knowing of the Fifth Day". It's the most boring thing I've ever read. I mean, she writes lines like

"The sky looked grey today". How fucking unimaginative. The boring bitch should use words like "charcoal" instead of grey. There is enough of the boring in people lives. We shouldn't have to find it in fiction as well.'

Sorokin lowered the paper, looking at him, and said sarcastically, 'Hamish, really?'

'The words in that novel, they weren't words, they were bones,' Hamish said hotly. 'Dead, dry, words. Why should I have had to read it? None of us should have. It's an insult.'

'And *you* are insulting your own intelligence, by writing that piece of rubbish. You were asked to write a factual review of the novel, not an opinion piece on it. You have taken something very simple, and turned it into something complex. All you had to do, Hamish, was answer the question; not *think* about the question,' Sorokin told him as if he was some school runt, whose mind was smaller than everyone else's.

'I thought school *was* about learning to think,' Hamish said.

His teacher gave him a disbelieving look. 'School is designed to teach you certain things. So you think in certain ways. Get used to it, Hamish.'

'I don't belong here. I *don't* belong here,' Hamish said angrily, flipping up his desk lid, getting his books out and tossing them on the floor. 'You won't even let me think the way I want to; you want me to think spastic.'

'Try and think of school as a street full of *Give way* signs,' Sorokin said. 'There's no *Give way* on what is being taught to you. It's part of an existing system you have to learn how to exist in.'

'You should cross out *Give way* and write *Run away* over it,' Hamish said bitterly, throwing his books in his bag.

'There is no running away from it, Hamish. School is an indoctrination into how to be part of society, as it is designed. And *your* ideas, Hamish, are unacceptable and outside the design.' Sorokin cuffed his hand down, as if giving Hamish the axe. 'You need some fences around the wild paddock your mind is, Hamish, to keep your mind in your head, not sprawling out on the streets.'

Hamish stared at him in disbelief. 'I don't see why I have to think like everybody else and not myself.'

'It's an agreed way of thinking, Hamish,' his teacher said quietly and coldly. '*Agreed*, meaning the way we think about that tree out there, in the *agreed* way. At school, in your science class, we think about the tree as a species type. We all agree to call it *Melaleuca quinquenervia;* not a gnome or guinea pig. Someone, before us, has already decided what to call that tree. And we have all agreed to think about the tree that way.'

'Did *the someone* have more IQ points than the rest of us?' Hamish demanded. 'That, what he calls the tree, matters more than what I call the tree?'

'What you decide to call the tree is irrelevant, Hamish,' Sorokin said. 'There is an educational and societal agreement to call that tree by its species name. And it's the same with thinking, Hamish. You agree to think in the ways authorities have decided. It's how we all commonly understand each other. If a nurse trained in medical thinking decided to talk like a poet to her colleague or patient…well…it is not what they want to hear, is it? They want to know about the treatment of a urinary infection, not a poetic description of their urine sample looking like saffron sunlight. Do you understand this, Hamish? The vigilante type thinking you clearly are developing, only gets you kicked out of society and into new accommodation called a mental hospital.' Sorokin placed both hands on the desk, staring hard at Hamish. 'Learn to belong.'

Hamish felt his mind go into revolt again. And couldn't stop it. 'I *don't* belong to ways of thinking thought up by other people,' he yelled, wondering why Sorokin could not understand the logic of what he, Hamish, was saying. 'It's stupid. Why have a mind at all, if you are going to think everyone else's thoughts?'

Sorokin folded his arms, lowering his chin, staring at him like a bull, ready to charge. 'Your mind is just a container, Hamish. The Establishment—being law, religion, philosophy, politics, and education—decide what thoughts go into that container.'

'I don't care,' Hamish said. 'I don't give a fuck. I want to be out of this classroom; somewhere where trees are called elephants; and teachers like you are rotting on the shores of the strange and weird; and where I don't have to see you; and where I don't have to listen to you, *or* anyone else, about how to think and I don't want to be here anymore. I don't belong in places where trees are called melaleuca and you are called a teacher.'

Hamish stopped; his lungs felt like they were ballooning from lack of air, from talking too fast and not breathing between his words. His eyes skittered away from Sorokin, as he saw a melaleuca tree cracking out of his ribcage, its roots rapidly growing, coming straight for him.

‘Fuck!’ Hamish yelled, scuttling out of his chair and stumbling back, ‘Fuck!’

‘Oh, what now?’ Sorokin said, his voice caught somewhere between pity and irritation.

‘Your fucking tree roots. They’re coming for me. They’re going to strangle me, in your teacher thinking, and I’ll be stuck here, grown over by your tree roots.’

‘You are right,’ the teacher said, grabbing him by the arm, and dragging him to the door. ‘You don’t belong here. In fact, you don’t belong anywhere. Go to the principal’s office now, Hamish. Go explain your unextraordinary mind to him.’

Hamish stared stubbornly at him.

‘*Now.*’

5

Hamish's school principal, M. George Funnell, stared intently at him, his fingers tapping on the desk.

'This is what you *don't* get, Hamish. Society. It is already finalised. Decided on and designed a long time ago; a social apparatus of religion, law, education, politics, and philosophy.'

'The social...what?' Hamish asked, looking at him suspiciously. 'Is it something you hang school students on?'

'Hamish. That is paranoid, uneducated thinking. The social apparatus is a social design. And it works in much the same way as the engine of a car. Society is the car, you understand? It doesn't run without the engines of religion, law, education, politics, and philosophy.'

'Fuck that,' Hamish said belligerently, folding his arms across his chest. 'When I get out of here, I'm going to blow all the car engines up.'

'With what, Hamish?' Funnell asked, mildly tolerant. 'With what?'

'A Hamish bomb,' Hamish said confidently, tossing his head.

'A Hamish bomb.' Funnell leant back in his chair, linking his fingers together over his fat belly barely covered by his shirt buttons straining in their holes. 'And what is that made of?'

'The Hamish,' he blurted out, feeling his mind sloshing around in liquid with bits of garbage in it; bits of lava; bits of Sorokin's piss. He didn't know what was worse: mind slosh like he was feeling now, or mind comets, where his thoughts shot through his head so fast and so hard, he felt like his mind was being carried inside a meteorite, hurling through space.

'The Hamish,' Funnell said interestedly. 'Are you a biological body, made of grenades, Hamish? Things that explode?'

Hamish felt the saliva in his mouth grow hot and moist, as his mind sweltered with irritation at Funnel's inane comment.

'Should I list you as a terrorist, Hamish?' Funnell asked indifferently, as if nothing of what Hamish said, or who he was, really mattered. Hamish knew, just knew, that people would only take him seriously when he became a part of one of the stupid social engines Funnell was talking about. Part of religion; part of law; part of politics; part of family; part of school.

His mind did not start with any of those stupid social engines. It seemed to start on something not even listed, not even known, not even defined.

'Well, Hamish?' Funnell asked.

'I'm just someone who doesn't want to come off the photocopier; Hamish, off the same page as everyone else.'

'That's interesting, Hamish. Interesting wording. Yes, it is. You feel like you might shoot out of the photocopier; another copy of the blueprint citizen; just another part of the pile.'

'Well, who wants to live like that?' Hamish demanded, looking at him.

'Can you see that we have all shot out of the same photocopier, Hamish? That we all have skin, bones, blood, veins, body organs? Are you going to take off your skin, empty your blood, and remove your body organs, because you don't like being the same design as everyone else?'

Hamish decided to scoff, as he was still wrestling with Funnell's logic and looking for a combat response. 'That's a stupid question.'

'It's not so stupid,' Funnell remarked, leaning back in his big black leather chair, placing both hands on the arm rests. 'People like you, Hamish? Free thinkers, who challenge the agreed way of thinking, cause chaos and riots in society.' Funnell folded his arms behind his head. 'Look at those people who chain themselves to trees, Hamish, because they disagree with the way the economy makes money and just want the trees to sit there as supposedly sacred objects, worshipped by the indigenous people, contributing oxygen and nothing else.' He picked up his glossy and fat black pen, with the school insignia shining in gold on it. 'This is what you don't understand, Hamish. There is *no* other way of thinking about things, outside what society agrees on. You better get used to that now.'

'It sucks!' Hamish said vehemently, walking out and slamming the door behind him.

6

Black Crag
Sydney NSW Australia,
April 2003

'Hamish?' Justine asked calmly.

Hamish didn't answer, just looked at her. Expected responses like 'Yes', after someone called his name, still annoyed him. He had once spent the entire week just watching how many people said 'Yes?' after someone called their name. 139 people out of 140. The 140th had said, 'What the fuck do you want?'; a fringe rat, too pissed off with people to respond the polite way of the insider.

'Are you hearing me, Hamish?' Justine asked reprovingly, her hand touching his arm. 'Or are you thinking about things you shouldn't?'

Hamish looked away from her, at the church; shadows loomed over where they sat on the grass, waiting for all the parishioners to come out after the Ash Wednesday Mass. His eyes narrowed at some dark shapes gliding through the shadows the church cast.

Fuck! Hamish thought, panicking, scrambling back from where he sat, as he saw saints emerging from the shadows, covered in ash, loose robes floating behind them, their ash-dusted halos magnifying, as if they had lost the tightness and lightness of their holy positions.

'Hamish? Did something bite you?' Justine asked, looking at him sitting back away from her.

He looked silently at Justine, the one certain and stable presence in his life, not knowing how to explain to her what he saw; the things changed depending on where he was, who he was looking at and what situation he was in, but she, Justine, never changed. He looked at her, barely able to restrain the gratitude in his eyes, just for being who she was. She was like his paracetamol, easing the pains in his head, which were lately getting worse and more frequent.

'Hamish? Have you sat on a bull ant nest?' Justine asked, concerned, looking carefully at the grassy place he had sat on and moved away from, then looking closely at him.

'I'm just thinking about things, in the *me* sort of way,' Hamish said, as casually as he could.

'Uh-oh,' Justine said, looking at him in dismay. 'Hamish. You've worn out three teachers, two priests, one nun, and given your mother a nervous breakdown because of thinking in the *you* sort of way.' She caught his gaze, holding him in the cerulean certainty of her eyes, drawing the tension of thinking in too many different ways out of his head. He thought like multiple storms, cracking in venous light across his mind. He thought like the North, sweating painful blood-red citrus thoughts out of the steaming tropics, sweltering in his mental ecology.

It's fucked, but interesting, he thought, rubbing his forehead.

'And thinking about things *your* way is not how you answer questions, Hamish.' Justine continued, 'The answers are already there. Like they are in the back of the schoolbook, when you check if your maths answers are right. You just have to pick the right answer for the question asked. Like when a man marries a woman, Hamish. The priest asks the question already there, on the page. The woman or man answers the question, already learnt from the page. You don't go making up your own answers.'

'I find new questions and new answers,' Hamish explained, 'because it stops me from becoming automatic or thinking like everyone else.'

'You're not making sense, Hamish,' Justine said, looking away.

Hamish picked unhappily at the grass. 'It's like this. You have to stand guard on your own mind. Because it's trained to follow. And it will follow automatically,' he warned her. 'It's like this. You've got everyone in cars, at a stop sign, waiting in a queue. Waiting those three seconds, to check the road is clear, before they cross to the other side of the road. But unexpectedly, a car doesn't stop for those three seconds. It goes straight through. And if your mind is on automatic, the driver behind him just goes through as well; because he's not watching if the road is clear, he's watching the lead car in front of him, or the leader. So, he goes straight through, following the leader, and ends up killing the driver of an oncoming car, and he himself ends up in a wheelchair. All because he followed the leader and didn't look for himself.'

'That's a very long, complicated explanation, Hamish,' Justine said, frowning, then standing up and brushing the grass off her long, pale pink skirt. Hamish quickly lowered his eyes, as he felt excitement shoot through his cock, when he caught a glimpse of her pale, smooth legs. He hurriedly pulled his jumper off the grass and bunched it over his erection. He didn't want her noticing it and she noticed most things. To his relief, she was looking over at her parents, standing by the church gate talking to Father Matthias. He tried to calm his cock down, by thinking of his very fat aunty who had thick moustache hair over her upper lip and smelt like urine.

Hamish decided to talk as well, move his mind away from her pale, smooth legs, into something mathematical, which didn't promise luscious, ripe, mango females, but dry equations.

'It's not really a complicated explanation,' Hamish explained to Justine. 'Automatic behaviour is an example of how two-dimensional thinking operates in humans.'

'What?' Justine asked, staring down at him in disbelief. 'What do you mean? Speak in English, Hamish.'

'I am,' he said.

'I mean *our* version of English. Here in Australia.'

'Would you like that with church, school, court or tomato sauce?' Hamish asked bitterly.

'Oh, Hamish!' she scolded, 'It's not a menu I was asking for.'

'OK, Justine,' Hamish sighed, 'no menu. I'll do straight speak, just for you.'

'You should just do it for yourself, Hamish. So you are understood by others, most of whom speak in plain language.'

'You are an exemption to my own law, Justine. For you, I will speak in photocopies.'

'Hamish. That was another unintelligible sentence I have no dictionary for.'

'It means I am being considerate of you, Justine, and ignoring myself. I will pull out the chair, only for you, Justine; be the gentleman, and not the strange thin thing.'

‘Let’s…not go there, Hamish…pulling out the chair for me, like we’re on some date…’ she said.

Hamish’s face fell at her easy dismissal of him. She did it so casually, like he, Hamish, didn’t matter and, even worse, did not even consider the possibility of him as a boyfriend. His thoughts fell rapidly into the ghoul in his mind, the ghoul which held all his darkling six o’ clock hours, of disappointment and hopelessness.

Hamish looked away from her, pained.

‘So, what were you saying, about two-dimensional thinking, Hamish?’

With a painful effort, he pulled his thoughts back from the ghoul in his mind and looked at her dully. ‘Two-dimensional thinking is found in collectives like politics or the Church. It’s the sort of thinking characteristic of the person who says *this is right, this is wrong*, or *this activity is good and this activity is bad*.’ He looked up at her, shading his eyes with his hand, wondering if he should say anything more, knowing she was as solid and definite as skin. He didn’t have solid mental skin like her, he was made of citrus-red fire, leaping high into native winds. And, he did not want to tell her how he symbolically saw her spirit: honest and straight, white feathers drifting around her, falling through strands of her blonde hair, pink roses blooming out of her cheeks, infusing the cells of his body with her fresh, clean scent, reassuring and quietening his fire spirit.

Finally he spoke. ‘I just see things differently than most people, Justine.’

Justine’s blue eyes softened. ‘What do you mean, Hamish?’ she asked.

Hamish hastily stumbled around in his mind, looking for words which wouldn’t scare her, or make her think he was some mental Frankenstein. He couldn’t stand to lose her from his life, even if she didn’t want him as a boyfriend. To his hot and tense senses, Justine felt like that drifting moment just before falling asleep.

Hamish looked away, deciding not to tell her about her angel-feathered hair or the roses growing out of her skin, and quickly chose a general, non-scary response. ‘I’m a free thinker, not a reactive thinker, characteristic of a Catholic or an atheist. You know, the us and them thing, which either makes you friend or enemy. I don’t see people that way, Justine. Most people just come over as strange to me because they think oddly and because of this they are the enemy to me.’ Hamish looked at her quietening, calming whiteness, and said, ‘You aren’t, though. You are an angel to me, Justine.’

Justine looked solemnly at him. 'What are you doing here, Hamish? In a place you don't belong?'

'My parents are extremely hopeful of a white sheep outcome.'

'Oh Hamish!' Justine scolded. 'You are not a black sheep. Just a confused one.'

'And the other point to make is, I found you here,' he said, 'an angel in a place of thorns.'

Hamish looked down, unable to meet her eyes. He didn't want her to see how he was clumsily reaching for her, trying to tell her what she meant to him, in his own awkward way.

Justine stood up and reached out her hand. He grasped it, feeling her soft white skin, palms which held Bibles between them, palms which had never been hit by a hammer. Palms which feathers drifted out of, floating around her, keeping her under the wing of God, not under the hammer of humans.

She pulled him up so he was standing, feathers drifting around them. Justine looked at him, her blue eyes steady, calm, reassuring. 'I'm Catholic, Hamish, but I'm not your enemy.'

'Are you trying to save me?' he asked.

'That's for God,' she said.

7

Black Crag.
Sydney, NSW Australia
March 2004

You don't belong anywhere.

Peter Sorokin's words still echoed through Hamish's mind, at AC/DC volume. Every time he felt lost and separate from people around him, he would hear Sorokin in his head: *you don't belong anywhere, you don't belong anywhere, you don't belong anywhere.*

He just had trouble feeling part of a sum total, whether it was family, church or school. He was like this separate, strange-looking number, which didn't fit the equation. He had noticed recently how much society was aggregated and presented in sum totals: twenty-two church members, seven family members, fifteen scouts, twenty-eight classmates, three pets, merging together to form one large water, called the community ocean.

Sometimes, he found it hard to breathe when he looked at the ocean. It was a type of threat to him, an expanse where his existence was caught in established rhythms and tides, no matter what his own individual rhythm was. Which, at the moment, was a little riptide, going off on its own. He, Hamish, was the isolated B minor, sounding outside the repetitive notes of A.

Hamish looked away from the ocean, unable to look at the way it washed over everything, swamping like loss.

Hamish turned away from the cliff edge, looking at the town beneath him divided into straight, even, intersections of churches, halls, houses and schools. *Crucifix intersections*, he thought, preventing random angles like him. Those systems. He couldn't stand them. They suffocated him like a tight cloth over his mouth and he knew there was something outside of social suffocation, knew it by the motion of the wind.

Those ideologies he grew up in were like artificial lungs around his thoughts. Squeezing metal through his mind, fracturing and hardening his natural flow. It was only when he watched things which flew, he remembered his mental wings. Dragonflies, butterflies, fireflies, words containing yellow and fire.

He knew his mind was flying too high, as Icarus had flown too close to the sun; he was burning himself on the height of his thoughts. He could feel a strange heat in his cheeks, pains pulsing through the front of his brain, his mind wide open like an eye, keeping him awake night after night.

He longed for Justine. She was soil, and tree roots, solid rocks; substance which grounded his thoughts, clenched the wings in his mind and fettered them. When he looked in her eyes, he lost the quickening in his mind, his thoughts fell out of their question marks, and he stopped going into a mental pandemic, where one idea infected the next.

Hamish squatted down on the grassy cliff, looking at the silvery-blue water rippling in tides towards the shore, thinking about how people would politely tolerate him at first. And then, after nine or ten sentences, came their cautiousness, their wariness, their avoidance, and then the silence. His ideas and his conversations just didn't fit in with the ideas and conversations of other people he met. He was just losing people, week after week, making him more and more silent, and more and more closed into rooms; as his life lessened and thinned around him, making him feel unwanted, lonely and confused about why his thoughts were so offensive to people. He pondered whether it was because his high intelligence didn't fit into the set beliefs prescribed by The Establishment; and because of this, he was pushed out of society.

Hamish remembered Father Matthias's words: *You have a bright mind, Hamish. Use it to help people up, not tear them down.*

Hamish thought a lot about what he could do after Father Matthias's remark. Something where he was not continually examining the deficiencies in other people's minds. Something where he could solve the deficiencies in society, like the isolation of social vigilantes such as himself, who did not have a preference for social exactness or social reverence for ideologies worshipped by the people at the social altar.

Hamish thought of Mozart, whose name was on the sick list in one of his father's black-leather notebooks. Mozart, who wrote rude letters for hours and hours, yet made some of the most beautiful music ever heard. Hamish feared he would kill his own Mozart, by becoming part of a social system which had no octaves; just a flatline of beliefs, like a dead heart preserved.

Would he make his own Requiem by taking up Father Matthias's suggestion? Would that mean bowing and kneeling down to social systems? Hamish rubbed his forehead, tired of thinking all the time. Too many questions, causing riptides in his mind. He was feeling weary and down, suffering as part of the 15 percent of the Mozart-type population which were called innovative. Yet, he felt he was putting himself in danger of mental catatonia, by stepping into the 85 percent of the population called conformist, a social stiff. Corpses hit his mind, as he saw himself white-faced, in that fading moment just before death. His eyes sightless.

He struggled with the riptide thoughts fracturing his mind and tried to calm himself with Justine's face. It usually worked, but today it did not bring him the peace he craved; only unbearable sexual excitement, as his mind lingered hotly on the cat-like curve of her eye, her soft pink lips, her silky blonde hair; making him so hard, he felt like he had a volcano cock.

His mind splintered and cracked as he looked at the ocean, like something was ripping his entire cellular structure apart. Something he couldn't explain or name. Something which made his mind haemorrhage. His body burn and radiate with heat. Hamish rubbed hard at his eyes, as the ocean appeared to dip and fold into vulvar folds. *The ocean*, he thought, his eyes widening with sudden realisation, *it's one big watery cunt over the land. And it always has been, it always has been, I just never knew it. It's doing things to my head, with those seductive vulvar folds, I am going to explode out of my volcano cock; I, the Hamish, am going to ocean come…*

Hamish tore his clothes off, throwing them in a heap beside him.

He was unable to come, even though he was standing as she, the ocean, had asked him to; naked with his cock ready to stick in her giant vulviform folds. She continued to tease him with her vaginal dilations, making him throb painfully, but unable to come.

'Bitch!' Hamish screamed at the ocean, taking his shoes off and hurling them at the ocean. 'Bitch! Fucking driving me mental! You're a cock tease, just like her!'

The ocean crashed loudly in his ears and he clapped his hands over them, as a roaring went down his ear canals.

He felt arms and hands dragging him back, and he stumbled, almost fell. 'Bitch!' he screamed again, 'Tempting me like that! And I can never get into you, I can never get into you…I can never fuck you…'

The ocean roared around him and within him, mixing with the yelling of the crowd around him and in him. Hamish roared as well, as he felt his flesh gripped by other people's hands, his body dragging backwards, backwards, backwards, backwards…

8

It was too white. The walls, the bedsheets, the uniforms. White, white, white. Hamish had seen, after he arrived here, a lot of mental blood running down the hallways; patients stumbling out of the blood flow, and collapsing face down again. His mind could not equate the whiteness and cleanness girdling the patients, with all the blood howling in their minds.

'Now, Hamish,' his mother said, giving him a quick kiss on the cheek and stepping hastily back, as if he was in the infectious diseases ward, and not a mental health ward, 'you're not to come out of here, until your mind is all fixed up. Your father and I can't have you standing nude on top of a cliff, screaming to no one about the ocean being a tormenting…' she trailed off, lowering her eyes, 'well, you know what.' She looked up at him, her face tight with anxiety, her eyes without hope. 'I don't know how you thought of such things, given your Catholic upbringing. We do not encourage those sorts of thoughts or behaviour.' His mother looked away, lowering her eyes again. 'Your father also suspects you may be a homosexual, as you've reached eighteen and have never had a girlfriend. In fact, you don't even speak about girls and he's worried that you will only have intercourse with an ocean.'

Hamish's father looked at him grimly. 'I've said it to you, since you were a little one, Son. God made Adam and Eve, not Adam and Steve.'

'I'm not interested in the Fundamentalist Word, Dad,' Hamish said irritably, looking away from him.

'That you don't listen to the Word of God, is why you are in here,' his father said firmly, 'and the Word of God is very clear, about those gay feelings I suspect you have. In the book of Leviticus, Chapter 20:13, Son, it says "*If a man has sexual relations with a man as one does with a woman, both of them have done what is detestable. They are to be put to death; their blood will be on their own heads.*"' His father leant forward, both hands on the table. 'Son…if you become a pagan gay…'

'What? Are you going to do a Leviticus job on me? Cut my head off? Feed my cock to the sharks?' Hamish demanded. 'And I've already told you, I'm *not* gay.'

'But you may…go that way,' his father said darkly, 'if you are not treated.' He slid his hands off the table and straightened up, looking at Hamish with condemnation. 'The Church is very clear on this, Son. Homosexual orientation is considered an "objective disorder" by the Church, something which will make you commit an inherent moral evil. Do you understand that, Son? That homosexuality is a *disorder.* The great pontificate Pope Paul VI, worship his name, in the document he sanctioned called *Persona Humana*, agreed that homosexuality is pathological and depraved. Son, it's a *disease.*'

'So, I am here, in this mental hospital, to stop me from becoming gay,' Hamish said sarcastically.

'Homosexuality is a mental sickness, Son,' his father informed him, his face grave. 'And in the Church, there is specific pastoral care for such a condition. Cardinal Joseph Ratzinger in a document he signed called *Homosexualitatis Problema,* says the clergy needs to treat people with those disordered sexual orientations, with pastoral care. He says so in 1986, in a letter called *On the Pastoral Care of Homosexual Persons.*'

'So, I'm here, in this mental hospital, as part of pastoral care,' Hamish said in disbelief, 'as a precaution against becoming gay.'

'With all due respect, Mr McColl,' interrupted the psychiatry registrar nearby, 'Hamish is not in here for any gay-related issue. In fact, witnesses say he was screaming about the ocean, which he perceived as a *vagina* tormenting him.'

'To be against the vagina is the sign of a male homosexual,' Hamish's father said, raising his chin, his eyes hostile.

'I feel you are taking this out of context, Mr McColl,' the registrar said calmly.

'The anomaly of homosexuality is a strong possibility with my son,' Hamish's father insisted. 'He has no girlfriend. And I have presented many suitable dates for him from the ages of fifteen to eighteen. He is not interested in any of them. Not one bonny church lass.'

'So, it's the possibility of me, being homosexually sick in the head, is what concerns you most about this whole thing,' Hamish said belligerently.

'We just can't have it, Son. A homosexual in the family. It is the sexuality of pagans. It would be too much for your mother. We would face exclusion, possibly ex-communication, from the Church if we don't take precautions against this terrible event,' his father said.

'Yes,' his mother said sadly, 'we would have to take you to Egypt and sadly leave you there, where such practices were accepted.'

'Or, have the Canaanites accept you as their new pagan son,' his father added, nodding, as if he were seriously considering the idea, 'a new leprechaun for their culture.'

'So, you going to drop me off in Egypt, a thousand years ago, and have me petted by gay Canaanites,' Hamish said in disbelief, 'or leave me here to get treatment for gay thoughts and leprechaun infection?'

His father looked at him with dislike. 'Can you put Hamish in the locked ward please,' his father said to the psychiatry registrar, 'until he gets over his thoughts of homosexuality?'

The registrar looked at him and said stiffly, 'Homosexuality is not a mental illness, Mr McColl.'

'Catholicism is against this unnaturalness, *Sir*. Please don't let him out, until he is cured of it. There will be no gay pagan in the family, to shame me,' his father said vehemently, 'so you are to cure him of his darkling thoughts, *Sir*.'

'We are not a sexuality rehabilitation centre, Mr McColl,' the psychiatry registrar said, his eyes frosty.

'You are to treat him for penis inclination to the pagan anus,' his father insisted.

'Mr McColl,' the psychiatry registrar began.

'*Just* get him treatment for the possibility,' his father demanded. 'I don't want my son turning into the Son of Pan, because he acted on a gay feeling and sinned with a man.'

'I need to arrange an interview with your son to confirm a diagnosis,' the psychiatry registrar said, his eyes now at zero degrees Celsius, 'but I can assure you now. Nowhere in the Diagnostic and Statistical Manual, the DSM-IV, does it list homosexuality as a mental health condition or a thought disorder.'

'You forget, *Sir*. Judeo-Christianity rules in this country. It has since the first fleet. If the Church says homosexuality is a disorder, then it is.' His father gave the registrar a threatening look. 'You best remember that.'

‘Right,’ said the registrar flatly, looking away and regarding Hamish a little kindlier. ‘Go into the interview room there, Hamish. The psychiatry team here will be in shortly to speak with you.’

Hamish sat down in the interview room, looking around at the thickly painted cream walls, cream carpet and cream lounges. There was a small, square, wooden table in the centre of the room, with a glass top. On top of this table was placed a glass cube on a wooden base, the cube propped up at an angle, so a cube corner edge was pointing to the ceiling. Hamish tried not to look at the design, as its geometry made him feel strangely infected, almost feverish. The glass flattening his spirit; and the sharp cube corners piercing and popping the soft balloon of his mind.

Hamish looked wearily at the creaminess of the walls around him, washing through his mind like a tide of cleanliness; making him feel every worm thought there. The square table, the square cube, the square walls…he had trouble not punching it all, too many squares tormenting him, boxing his mind, keeping it coffin contained.

Hamish looked down, refusing to look at the secret square persecutors posing as objects and walls, unleashing weapons on unsuspecting patients. He suspected mental health staff put those weapons there, deliberately, on government orders. To destroy people like him.

People who refused to obey The Establishment.

Hamish put his head in his hands, tired of the effect of colour and shape on his mind. Other people seemed to be able to just see a square and have it register as such in their minds, as a simple thought like, *I see a square.* He, on the other hand, felt the square imprint on his mind, constructing vertical and horizontal lines, locking up the rivers, the breezes, the dragonfly motions in his mind.

He had asked Justine, once, what happened when she looked at a colour. ‘Nothing,’ she had told him, ‘it’s just a colour.’ He didn’t tell her that her sister’s red dress made him feel mental: the red flaming his thoughts, and making his cheeks heat, to the point where he felt cranky as an Alzheimer’s patient. He had spent all day looking for something yellow to look at and hold, as it was the only colour he didn’t have some strange sensory reaction to; yellow made him feel like he was in a soothing hot bath, pores of the sun opening up in his skin. The yellow made all the strange prickling he felt on his scalp like a thousand pins were inserting in and out, ease and stop.

Yellow was his Valium.

Three psychiatrists walked in, faces solemn as a funeral, gripping their wooden brown clipboards, their white shirts throwing silence into his mind. Hamish stared hard at the clipboards, seeing brown coffins form and magnify, floating towards him, with their lids slightly raised. Ready for him.

His mental funeral was here.

He knew it.

Hamish looked down at his navy blue and white pajama pants, checking his cock was not hanging out, and tried to wipe a milk stain off his green sloppy-joe. It wouldn't come off. He looked up, as the psychiatrists sat down, and he smoothed down his dark brown, fuzzy dreadlocks.

One of the psychiatrists slid his large framed glasses up his nose, looking at him compassionately. 'I'm Dr Bruce Beyer, a psychiatrist based here, in the hospital.'

Hamish considered this new piece of antiseptic in his life. The psychiatrist's gleaming silver hair was cut short, and parted with military precision to the left. His skin was olive and sagging, as if he'd seen too many disappointments in life.

'All hail Bruce!' Hamish said, throwing his hands up and making worshipping motions. 'The God of Psychiatry is here!'

Hamish watched in satisfaction, as Bruce's face creased in dismay. He liked upsetting those who belonged to The Establishment, those who determined what was normal in society and what was not. Mental health doctors, he thought, were as much as a social institution as the church or the courts, deciding what was appropriate behaviour in public and what was not. He did not cut it as Catholic Hamish; he did not cut it as School Hamish; and he didn't qualify for the family; and now here were the latest social stiffs in his life.

He, the Hamish, would not lie helpless in their anally retentive arms. No, he would not.

'And you are…?' Bruce prompted, like he, Hamish, was some intellectually disabled child, who did not know how to introduce himself.

He simply didn't see the need for shrinks.

Hamish fixed Bruce with a bubonic stare. 'I'm not introducing myself,' Hamish said belligerently, tightly folding his arms around himself, 'as I don't believe in the social disease called politeness and I can predict, without a doubt, that my name is already written on those anal clipboards of yours. *Yet* another thing snapped over my name.'

'Right, right,' Bruce said, his eyes already distant, as if preparing to survive another session of client insanity. 'Sitting next to me,' he glanced at the clipboard, 'Mr McColl, are my colleagues: psychiatrist Dr Johanna Rigby and psychiatrist Dr Golu Gupta. We're here to review your case...er...Mr McColl.'

Hamish stared aggressively at him. 'Case? *Case?* Like I'm an object? Just a file?'

'He does not mean to insult you,' Golu explained to Hamish. 'It's part of the language used in mental health. Not a personal statement about you.'

'And Mr McColl, objectivity is a better way to view you,' Bruce added, 'because it gives a more accurate picture of you, than someone who is viewing you subjectively and may decide you are something you are not, because of a biased impression.'

'How comforting,' Hamish said sarcastically.

'No one here will put dummies in your mouth, Hamish. Comfort is not applicable here,' Johanna said.

'I don't know about that,' Golu said mildly. 'There's a lovely knitting group of grandmothers, who make rugs with those colourful knitted squares. They drop them off for the patients here, to bring some colour and comfort to their raining and storming minds.'

'Hey,' Hamish said, 'you're lower on the mental corpse factor than these other two here.'

Johanna stared at Hamish, as if he was a dangerous specimen that needed containment.

'Right, right,' Bruce said, as if he was pretending none of this conflict was occurring and generalisations were best. 'Now, Mr McColl,' Bruce continued, 'we need to do an interview with you, to ascertain the current state of your mind and how it is functioning at the moment.'

Hamish looked silently from one to the other. He could almost hear the knives sharpening in their minds, preparing for psychiatric dissection. Johanna actually scared him with her narrow, vicious-looking face and dark brown hair, cut sharply and bluntly at chin length. The short, dark, bluntness of her hair made him think of knife edges and things which killed and maimed. Her brown eyes were dismissive and uninterested, as if bored by cracking minds, like he was just a spore of ugliness in the world, infecting it with disorder.

Hamish looked away from Johanna, irritated by her. Just another person who existed as a procedure, as far as he could see; no rivers in her, nothing that curved like a moon. People like Johanna were flat and straight and measured as a ruler, her thoughts straight out of the policy and procedure manual. Hamish's eyes slid to Golu, who was looking at him interestedly, as if he was a novel specimen which had arrived for examination and he had yet to name. Golu's shrewd brown eyes held none of the dismissiveness of Johanna, or the distance of Bruce. More an exploratory openness, which told Hamish he was a man who at least didn't want to cage the wildlife.

Hamish studied Golu for a minute, trusting him more because of his loosely combed black hair curling around his neck and the gold stud in his ear, which suggested an inch away from social conformity. Golu's collar was undone as well, telling Hamish he did not always take notice of the precise way things should be done; like completely buttoning up the shirt, because the number of buttons dictated so. Golu was not a methods man, Hamish concluded, looking at Golu's brown face regarding him contentedly. Golu's hand gestured towards him, as if waiting for Hamish to speak.

'Can you just call me Hamish, all of you,' Hamish said annoyed, 'and not Mr McColl? I'm not into formalities.'

'Clearly,' Johanna said, looking contemptuously at his pajama pants and his green sloppy-joe, still wearing some of his lunch.

'You are a condescending bitch,' Hamish said to her, his voice erupting with anger. He clenched his fists hard, trying to stop himself from saying anything further. He knew it could earn him more time in this morgue. His mouth tightened, as he saw Golu lean over to Bruce, making one of those hurriedly whispered side comments, which made him feel small and just not relevant. Hamish decided such an exclusionary practice was intolerable, and decided to include himself. He leant forward, listening closely to the side comments Golu was making to Bruce.

'…he has no filter there, see? No processing happening, before he speaks. He just speaks…'

'Right, right, yes,' Bruce agreed, looking at Hamish with consideration, 'I see what you mean.'

'Hamish. I find your comment inappropriate,' Johanna said, talking as if a peg was pinching her nose. Nasal and tight. Hamish looked away from her, appalled.

'It was completely appropriate,' Hamish said in disbelief. 'Your eyes, your voice, your attitude, all say *bitch*.'

Johanna nodded at Bruce, her face dogged and determined.

'Paranoia,' she proclaimed.

'Oh, it is not,' Hamish said sarcastically, shifting back in his chair. 'It was an opinion. You have some sort of condition, cat snapper, where you can't perceive reality correctly. I was not making a paranoid statement. I was just giving my opinion on you.'

Johanna's pale face mottled red, as she stared at him. 'People who act appropriately don't just blurt out their personal opinions. They consider the other person's well-being first.'

Hamish looked at her in disbelief. 'You didn't consider mine.'

Bruce hastily held his hand up, saying, 'Now, Johanna.'

Hamish watched in satisfaction, as the red mottled stains of anger on her cheeks deepened. The bitch was going to lose it. He knew she would. Women like her couldn't stand being called out by anything with a cock. *Whether it was The Hamish cock or The Bruce cock or The Golu cock.* He'd seen her type before, screaming and gripping placards outside a church, protesting against the Patriarchal Penis; *What pisses you off more, you fucking Catholic bastard,* a woman had screamed at a startled priest coming out of the church, *my intelligence or my vagina?* The priest had considered the Vagina Activist briefly, told her she was infected with Eve syndrome, and was last heard on his mobile phone, calling an exorcist.

Hamish brought himself back, to the argument between Bruce and Johanna.

'Bruce,' Johanna snapped, 'I have the right to say no to coercive and threatening behaviour.'

'This is a mental health patient, Johanna,' Bruce reminded her quietly, holding up Hamish's file for her to see, 'not a person who operates within normative social parameters.'

Johanna looked at Bruce, humiliation washing across her face, her neck pushing out. *Like a diseased turtle*, Hamish thought, tightening his folded arms around his ribcage, nodding to himself.

'Bruce,' Johanna hissed, 'you've just called me out in front of a patient, and a colleague.'

'See me about it later, Johanna. Not now, while we are assessing the patient,' Bruce said, waving one hand at her, while he wrote some notes.

'Would you not call me *The Patient,* like I'm a psychiatry title on one of your mental bibles,' Hamish complained. 'I am not *The Patient.* I am a sad sea of depressing waves, washing up on the unwanted shore.'

Golu looked at him interestedly, clicking on the end of his pen, ready to write. 'And how does this sea imagery of sadness and waves and washed up, relate to your—'

'Delusion,' Johanna said vehemently.

'Please,' Golu said with courtesy, holding up his hand, 'let me finish.' He checked his notes again. 'Hamish, it says here in these notes, that you believed the ocean was in fact, a vagina, whose purpose was to torment and tease you. How is this so?'

'The vagina ocean,' Hamish said sighing, unhappily picking at his pajama pants with his hand. 'I don't know how you could miss it, really. There is nothing phallic about its appearance at all. It looks like one big flat cunt,' he leant forward in his chair, putting his forehead in his hands, 'but on *that* day, the ocean was dilating her watery folds, and tempting me, and tempting me, and tempting me, just like *her.*'

'Ah. We've got somewhere,' Bruce said in satisfaction, writing some notes. '*Her.* We have a psychological link.'

Golu leant back in his chair, crossing one leg over the other. His foot swung back and forth, giving Hamish vertigo. Hamish rubbed his eyes, trying to keep his vision from keeling over as the offensive foot swung through his senses.

'Hamish,' Golu asked, 'do you actually *think* the ocean *is* a vagina, or it just looks *like* a vagina, in the…ah…poetic sense?'

'You mean cunt water?' Hamish asked bluntly.

'Ah…' Golu trailed off uncertainly.

'Are you referring to vaginal secretions?' Johanna asked, her brown eyes flickering with distaste, 'because if you are, that's disgusting.'

Hamish shifted restlessly in his chair, 'I think you are *all* reading too much into it. I just looked at the ocean, and *thought* that thought.'

Golu leant towards Bruce. 'Thought disorder,' he said, in a low voice.

'Right, right, possibly,' Bruce said absently, writing quickly on his notepad. He looked up at Hamish with clinical interest. 'Hamish. You have told us that the ocean is a vagina, teasing and tormenting you. And you have just mentioned a female, who you think has similar characteristics of a…er…tease. Is it possible, Hamish, do you think that your frustrated sexual feelings about this woman, are, in fact, related to your perception of the ocean?'

Hamish leant forward, putting his forehead in his hands. 'There is just too much Justine in my head. Just like there is too much cunt water in the ocean. It's causing a volcano in my cock and a volcano in my head. I've never *had* such sexual agony.'

'Right, right,' Bruce said. 'That sort of sexual intensity can be a sign of Bipolar 1 Disorder, Hamish.'

'Well it's just with her,' Hamish said, folding one hand over the erection straining in his pants.

Bruce eyed Hamish's hand over his dick uneasily.

'I'm not going to sit here and wank off, if that's why you're looking at me like that.'

'Right, right, yes,' Bruce said, looking discreetly away and checking his notes, 'let's move on. Now. You have stated to us the word *her* and you've also referred to a female named Justine. I take it that *her* and Justine are the one and same?'

'Yes. Her. Justine,' Hamish answered irritably. He shifted restlessly in his chair, scratching his ribcage. 'I mean, I look at other women, and they don't really do it for me, but lately, the thought of her crucifies my cock. The fuck-urge is so *bad* and is causing me *so* much wank suffering.'

'Right, right,' Bruce said, looking at him alarmed and writing more hurried notes.

'Do you believe you have the crown of thorns…on your cock…' Johanna said disbelievingly.

'Is that what I said? Is that what I said?' Hamish said irritably, leaning forward and slamming his hands against his forehead. 'You are pissing me off.'

'You didn't say those *exact* words, Hamish, but *that* is what you are implying,' Johanna insisted.

'Perhaps it's *you* having delusions, cat snapper,' Hamish spat, looking up, his eyes glowering. 'You're hearing my words different to what they are actually are.'

'It's called paraphrasing,' Johanna snarled.

'OK,' Golu said, looking at Johanna warningly, 'OK. No more interplay, *please*. This is a mental health assessment. Please continue, Bruce.'

'Right, right, yes,' Bruce said thoughtfully, slowly tapping his pen on his clipboard.

Hamish looked irritably at the tapping pen. 'Would you get on with it?'

'Listen, Hamish,' Bruce said carefully, 'it sounds like you are experiencing hallucinations, delusions, thought disorder and uncontrollable sexual urges. You also talk very rapidly, and get angry very easily if someone disagrees with you. All these symptoms are indicative of Bipolar 1 Disorder, but we would like you to stay in here for a couple of more weeks, so we can fully assess you.'

'I talk fast? You think I talk fast?' Hamish demanded.

'Yes,' Bruce said mildly.

'You talk *slow* is the problem,' Hamish came back at him with. 'Anything outside of that, sounds fast to you.'

'I'm a moderate talker,' Johanna said, 'and you sound fast to me as well.'

'You are not moderate anything, sweetheart,' he said sarcastically, 'you are all one angle.'

'I'm not sure what that means, Hamish,' she said, her nasal voice irritating him, and making him tense. The *whining*. He didn't know how any of her mental health patients survived it.

'No. You wouldn't,' he said, bored. 'You are not a 90-degree, or 180-degree or 360-degree person, so you don't understand the different angles of people's minds. You are a straight-line sort of a person. Your mind doesn't go around a corner. Your mind doesn't go up a hill. Your mind doesn't go down a hill either. Which is why you don't understand a fucking word I am saying.'

Johanna's cheeks mottled red. 'Going up a hill or down a hill, is obviously for Bipolar people, like you,' she said.

'Johanna!' Bruce exclaimed, horrified.

Golu dropped his pen. It clanged loudly on the floor. Hamish looked at the pen irritably, then at Johanna.

'You're not very professional, Johanna,' Hamish said, folding his arms across his chest, glowering at her. 'I don't know how you can call yourself a moderate person, really. Moderation takes mental discipline. And you don't have it. You just speak your anger. Speak your sarcasm. Speak your scorn. *That* makes you just as mentally messed up as me, cat snapper.'

'I don't think so,' Johanna said, that nasal twang in her voice like a rubber band in action, stretching and snapping. Hamish rubbed his forehead, trying to ease the small snaps of pain he felt in his head.

'Johanna,' Bruce said quietly, putting a finger to his lips, 'please remember you are talking to someone with a mental illness.'

'You just did it again,' Johanna said furiously, slamming her foot down on the floor, and her clipboard down on the table. 'Called me out in front of a patient!'

'Hello! I am here,' Hamish yelled, hurtling out of his chair and waving his arms up above his head, trying to get their attention, 'in the room. You are talking about me in the third person. Like I'm not *here*.'

'Well, the point is, you shouldn't be here,' Bruce said soothingly, turning the page of his file. 'You should be out there. Working. Going home to a wife. Doing things people normally do.'

'How horrific,' Hamish said, looking around for an escape from the room. The door looked firmly locked. They could have at least left it a bit ajar, as a bit of reassurance for him, that he wasn't going to be trapped in the room like an animal about to be caged.

But, alas, no, he thought, staring morosely at the door. It was as firmly closed as their minds, and he could feel himself being shut in their analytic little rooms, more and more compressed into a diagnosis. His hand went to his throat, as it started to tighten. Panic shot through him at the thought of being trapped in their heads.

And he couldn't get *out* of their heads, because *they* were the authority, not him.

Bruce gave him a mild look of pity, his hands coming to rest firmly on Hamish's file. 'Now, Hamish, that you think normal things are horrific is why you are here. Aside from what appear to be symptoms of bipolar disorder, you also have a type of vigilante thinking…gone wrong. It's called—'

'Intellectual Normality Order,' Hamish said sarcastically.

'What?' Johanna asked, staring at him in disbelief.

Hamish sighed impatiently, shifting restlessly in his seat. He was tired of her intellectual catatonia. 'What you call vigilante thinking…and it's not the first time, I've heard that, cat snapper—'

'Hardly surprising,' Johanna said sarcastically, folding her arms tightly around her breasts, her fingers gripping her ribs. He was sure there was no heart beating in there. Not with the way she spoke to him, like a mental health corpse without compassion or understanding of him.

Anger flared through him, the same way red flared in the sky, just before night shut it down.

Just like she, cat snapper, shut people down.

As his anger towards Johanna pulsed through him, he felt his mind surge degrees above the Celsius barometer in his head. 'Oh, fuck off and let me finish,' he snapped.

'Do you like having enemies…Hamish?' Bruce asked, concerned, pushing his glasses back up his nose. 'See, you seem to have a persistent grudge against Dr Rigby here. Persistent grudges are a sign of vigilante thinking gone wrong. When vigilante thinking goes wrong, Hamish, it's called Paranoid Personality Disorder. You, Hamish, actually seem to *like* having grudges. You become animated, you have purpose, you have a goal. And I hasten to add that, ordinarily, amination, purpose and goals are healthy things. But *not* when they are orientated towards vengeance and paranoid vigilantism. You see, the problem is, Hamish, none of that is mentally healthy. It is making you ill.'

Golu leant forward, clasping his fingers together around his knees. He looked at Hamish unaffectedly, with the same casual interest he would as if seeing a moth in the room. Just something flitting through, there for a day.

Hamish stared at him suspiciously.

Was Golu's easy, casual interest a psychiatric trick, designed to gain his trust? He, the Hamish, was on to him, he was onto the Golu.

Golu looked at him mildly. 'And we are here, Hamish, to try and help you get better. Not to lock you further into your own mind.'

Hamish looked at him even more suspiciously. He suspected the sneaky Hindu had peered into his head, saw what he had been thinking about mental lock-up. Yes. Golu had Hindu x-ray eyes in his mind, bloody bastard.

He looked away from Golu, trying to struggle out of the pulsing lights, bones and locks he could see coming out of Golu's eyes. Finally, he managed to say something. 'It seems I'm locked up in *your* minds. You have already decided what I am.'

'And what are you, Hamish, in your own mind?' Golu asked benignly. Hamish looked at him, warily. That balmy face and mild tone was *extremely* deceptive, given his Hindu specialty to burgle his mind.

'An escape,' Hamish told Golu, 'I'm an *escape.* I'm an escape from what's *out* there.'

'And *what* is out there, Hamish?' Bruce asked, bemused, tapping his pen again. Hamish ground his teeth, looking at the pen slowly tapping.

Bruce stopped tapping his pen, giving Hamish an encouraging look. 'What are you escaping from out there?' he asked.

Hamish leant forward, rubbing his eyes. 'People sick with history,' he mumbled.

'Meaning?' Bruce asked interestedly.

'People doing things the Moses way, the Plato way, the Hitler way,' Hamish said rapidly, counting the names off his fingers. 'All those mothball ways that preserve the thoughts of passed-away brains.'

'Those thoughts or ways you've just talked about, are preserved and practised, Hamish, because they have ordered society in some way,' Bruce said sagaciously, 'and it's our job here to help create some order for you.'

'Get the corkscrews out of your mind, Hamish,' Golu said comfortingly to him.

'Oh, purge me of vigilante sickness!' Hamish yelled to the startled psychiatrists; he stood up, flinging back his head and throwing his arms out, like he was on a crucifix. 'Save me, mental health, from the sickness of self-thinking.'

'Now, Hamish,' Bruce said, alarmed, 'that's not what this is about.'

Hamish lowered his head, and saw Johanna looking at him pityingly.

'You are very sick, Hamish. Very sick,' she said, shaking her head and clicking on the end of her biro to write some notes.

Hamish looked at her darkly. 'You have a sickness too,' he said. 'It's called Gestapo thinking.'

'Are you accusing me of being a Nazi?' Johanna asked, her cheeks mottling red again.

'Well, I wouldn't stop at one disease with you, cat snapper. You have another disease called literality. And you may have others, yet undiscovered,' Hamish said speculatively, nodding his head. 'You, mental health's most ungracious pussy, literally thought I was calling you a Nazi. It was just a metaphoric reference to your obsession with model citizens.'

'Excuse me,' Johanna said abruptly, pushing back her chair.

'Where are you going, Johanna?' Golu asked, looking at her with concern.

Johanna tapped her watch. Hamish narrowed his eyes suspiciously, as Golu and Bruce looked knowingly at each other.

'Is that some secret mental health signal? A code between psychiatrists?' Hamish demanded to know.

'It simply means time out, Hamish,' Golu said lightly, leaning one arm, crooked at the elbow, over the back of his chair, 'something we could all do with, I think.'

'You should never have given *her* time *in* this place,' Hamish said, rubbing at his temples. 'She's the sort who does people's heads in. She's a threat to the mentally ill.'

Golu clapped his hand to his mouth, as if trying not to laugh.

'Well she is,' Hamish insisted, tossing his dreadlocks over his shoulders.

Bruce looked at him carefully. 'That sort of thinking is typical of thought disorder, Hamish.'

'It seems anything outside careful and noted facts is thought disorder,' Hamish said sarcastically, shifting in his chair. 'Only the quantified mind is accepted. I have more of a qualitative mind, Mr Sheen. I think in stories.'

'I'm not clear on what you mean, Hamish,' Bruce said, bewildered, 'calling me Mr Sheen like that.'

'You know. The cleaning product, Mr Sheen polish. You have a very polished mind, Bruce, all glossy and smooth with The Establishment thinking. I'm sure they can all see their own faces mirrored in your mind, it's that shiny with their thoughts.'

'Er...Hamish,' Bruce said, lowering his clipboard, 'the problem with thinking in...er...stories and metaphors, is that there are no mental parameters in place. To you, it is an interesting description, but to a psychiatrist such as myself, calling me Mr Sheen could end up in the mental health assessment tool; as a delusion, you think I am a cleaning product.'

'What?' Hamish said in disbelief. 'It was just a description.'

Golu spoke patiently, 'And I would add that fiction is a very large place to be in, Hamish. Anything can happen. There are no established maps there, so to speak. No road to follow, no traffic lights *already* in place. The writer makes it all up. You have to get out of that place, Hamish. Put some traffic lights in your life that tell you when to go, when to be ready and when to stop.'

Hamish linked his fingers on top of his dreadlocks, staring at the ceiling, as he said, 'We are living in fiction already, Golu. None of it's real. It's design thinking by other people. Something they have made up; we are expected to be characters in. The Priest. The Student. The Teacher. The Father. The Mother. As written by them.' Hamish lowered his eyes to stare straight at Bruce. 'No one would even know their real thoughts, because of design thinking.'

'Can you give us an example of what you mean by design thinking, Hamish?' Bruce asked, twiddling his pen between his fingers.

Hamish linked his fingers together under his chin, staring broodingly at the psychiatrist. 'My father, his thoughts go straight to a parable or a proverb or something the Pope fucking wrote, he doesn't express just himself. And I don't think he even knows what he himself is. Dad's first word, at one year old, wasn't *dad* or *mum*. It was Jesus.'

Golu smothered a laugh. Bruce gave him a warning look, then looked more kindly at Hamish.

'Now, Hamish. You can't think in those anti-systematic terms and expect to mentally survive in established society. If we go back to the theme of traffic lights in your life, which Golu used to illustrate his point, you might want to examine what traffic lights do.'

'Fuck. I hate literals,' Hamish mumbled, rubbing at his forehead with his hands.

'A function of traffic lights, Hamish, is to stop people having crashes,' Bruce said pointedly. 'You, my boy, will keep having mental crashes, if you don't have traffic lights at the right places in your life.'

'We have a similar function to traffic lights here, Hamish,' Golu said in a helpful tone. 'We're stopping you from crashing. Stopping you from becoming a complete write-off.'

'One of your traffic lights seems to be cracked,' Hamish said, sliding his eyes meaningfully towards Johanna.

Golu's mouth twitched and he looked away, covering it with his hand as if trying not to laugh.

'Now, Hamish,' Bruce said sternly, 'talk like that is not necessary.'

'Talk like yours is hard for me to understand, Bruce. The Golu, at least, has a little imagination to his speech,' Hamish said generously. 'You think more in tin-can thoughts Bruce, produced straight from the psychiatry factory. And your cat snapper, Bruce, she just doesn't think at all. She speaks like a disease, no condom over her tongue, to stop what's spilling out and infecting us all and—'

'Right, right,' Bruce interrupted hastily. 'I think we have to be careful about what we say here…er…Hamish. Thinking differences…and so on.'

'Golu, you Indian bastard, your sari land knows about thinking differences, and you should remember this when ticking off Vote 1 for Hamish, the Fucked Up,' he said, his fingers grasping and twisting the skin on his chin. 'I saw a TV show about perspectives in India; and your mad people are regarded as sacred.'

'Yes, it's true. In Hinduism, there is such a thing as divine madness, which is behaviour related to mystical or religious activities. It can be mistaken as psychosis by conservative society,' Golu confirmed, nodding his head.

Hamish looked pointedly at Bruce and Johanna. 'Hear that you two textbook stiffs? Who are you to disturb a sacred state?'

'We don't really have that cultural belief, here…er…Hamish,' Bruce carefully explained. 'Here, mental illness is regarded as a psychiatric issue, not a sacred state.'

'We are a country of tin-can people,' Hamish said despairingly, throwing his head back, rocking backward and forward on his seat. 'Nothing is held sacred here.'

'There are many different religions in place in our country, Hamish,' Bruce said with consideration, his fingers bending and resting on the clipboard, 'which people hold sacred, but your bipolar disorder belongs in psychiatry. It doesn't belong to a church, or to India.'

'Don't throw that subject–object crap at me,' Hamish said belligerently, 'of who belongs to what. I'm on a higher intelligence level than A-B-C.'

'Right, right,' Bruce said abstractedly, turning pages of his file. Hamish could see the front of the file now, labelled with a sticker on which was written: ***Hamish McColl***. There was a red, round sticker on his label.

'What the fuck is that?' Hamish said, pointing at the red round dot. Bruce closed the file, looking at the label.

'What in particular are you referring to?' Bruce asked. 'Or…are you seeing something there, Hamish?'

'The red dot on the file.'

'Now, Hamish. There is no red dot on the file.'

'Yes, there is. Am I a coded patient, Bruce? Am I a coded patient? I am, aren't I? You better not be putting cyanide in my food here, Bruce, I have ways of knowing things, I—'

Bruce held up his hand. 'Any more talk like that, Hamish, and we will have to get out the straitjacket. The only code on you is a bipolar diagnostic code of 296. After that, there is another number which refers to the severity of your diagnosis. There is no red dot on your file.'

'Yes, there is,' Hamish insisted.

Bruce was silent for a minute, considering him; his face looked disturbed. 'You are a highly intelligent man, Hamish,' he acknowledged, 'but—' He stopped, searching for words.

'But you're like a wild river out of control,' Golu said, his hands lifting and widening out. 'Your mind, you know, it splashes everywhere.'

Bruce looked at Golu warily. 'Let's get back to calling this as it is. Bipolar Disorder,' he turned another page of Hamish's file, reading for a moment, 'untreated for some time. Years, in fact.' He looked up resolutely. 'We have to medicate you, Hamish.'

'What? *Medicate* me? I don't want no mental poison, killing my mind, Bruce.'

'Now, Hamish, try to think of medication in a different terminology than poison. Medication is for sedating the disturbances in your mind. Medication will help adjust your neurotransmitters, because they are not firing properly. This means that one neuron in your mind is not conducting the message to the next neuron. Because of that, other parts of your brain and your nervous system are not receiving the messages needed to function properly, and mental illness results,' Bruce explained, methodically rubbing his glasses with a tissue.

'So, I've got a dysfunctional postman in my head,' Hamish said in disbelief.

'Now, Hamish,' Bruce said reprovingly, 'that's exactly what I mean. That is not entirely accurate, is it? Your untreated mental illnesses, and it appears you have more than one, means you have a dysfunctional perception of people, conversations and the environment you are in. This dysfunctional perception means your thoughts are not forming properly, Hamish. This is why you are producing strange language, like mental poison, to describe medication. Or calling neurological anomalies, a dysfunctional postman.'

'No,' Hamish said angrily, 'what you call dysfunctional perception, I call a metaphor.'

'You are having delusions, Hamish,' Bruce said firmly, putting the tissue down and carefully placing his glasses on. 'There is no other word for it.'

'I think you are getting a little anal about all of this,' Hamish told him, upset. 'You'd tell all the writers in the world they are suffering from mental illnesses because they don't always write about things in realist terms.'

'Right, right,' Bruce said absently, 'and when you use the word "anal" about my professional opinion, Hamish…what do you mean?'

'Oh, for fuck's sake, I'm not referring to your arsehole, I'm talking about your thinking type,' Hamish said, restlessly shifting in his seat.

'Which is?' Bruce asked, his pen poised above his notes.

'I just said it. Anal.'

'And if you could describe it another way, what would you call it?' Golu asked.

'You have small thoughts. Anus size. You cut out the bigger paths in your mind, meandering through the forest, where lush thoughts grow, wet, deep and green.'

'That was rather poetic,' Golu mused.

Bruce looked hard at Hamish. 'Do you really believe…thoughts grow in forests?'

Hamish looked contemptuously at him. 'Your training doesn't include analysing literary metaphors, does it?'

'Right, right,' Bruce said absently, turning another page of the file. 'No. No it doesn't. This is a psychiatric profession, not a literary one.'

'And that's why you have immediately contextualised my metaphor to some sort of delusional belief about thoughts growing in forests, instead of contextualising it to a metaphor,' Hamish said defensively.

'What I'm looking at, Hamish, is how your mind is functioning. That is what I am psychiatrically trained to do. At present, your mind is highly dysfunctional. This is something observed from the quality and content of your thoughts, your behaviour and somewhat…er…defensive responses and vigilante arguments with us.' He paused, turning another page on the file and looking thoughtfully at Hamish. 'The other thing to point out, Hamish, is that you are not a poet by trade, or a writer. Otherwise, your claim that your language is metaphoric would indeed be considered. The fact is, Hamish, you are unemployed and have no particular…well,' he paused again, 'social title, that your mind could be considered contextually with. Therefore, your mind cannot be assessed relationally to creativity, or any other occupation, in fact. You are simply suffering from mental illness.'

'So, you have to consider my mind in relation to a social title or occupation for it to pass your standards,' Hamish said, scowling, leaning back and folding his arms.

'A social title, like receptionist, hairdresser, manager, psychiatrist or poet, gives context to your mind and what's coming out of it,' Bruce explained, 'and the issue here is, Hamish, you have no social context in your mind, it's just reactivity and dysfunction. It is, as Golu said, without those social maps which people follow so there is no mental crashing.' He leant forward, putting both hands under his chin like a steeple. 'So, given these facts, Hamish, we need to keep you here longer, to further assess your mental state. The results of these mental health assessments will give me a full psychiatric map of your mind.'

'It's just one big, black, burning field,' Hamish said, folding his arms across his chest and rubbing at his biceps.

'Right, right,' Bruce said looking at him concernedly, clicking on the end of his biro.

Hamish winced, looking away. 'Ready to record more of my postal delivery failure thoughts?'

'Now, Hamish, I've already explained to you, why you should not talk like that and what it is indicative of.'

'Is your mind really like that, Hamish?' Golu asked. 'One big, black, burning field?'

'Sometimes,' Hamish said abruptly, 'but you, being Indian, should understand that.'

'And that means what, exactly?' Bruce asked, his pen poised above his clipboard.

Hamish looked at Bruce impatiently. 'Indians believe that the divine is present as burning grounds in impure places.'

'Hamish,' Bruce said, 'the connection between your mind existing as one big, black, burning field and Indian religious belief is not really clear to me.'

'No. You are thinking from your arsehole again,' Hamish said.

'Now, Hamish…' Bruce said disapprovingly, pointing his pen at him and waving it a little.

‘What Hamish is referring to,’ Golu said placatingly, ‘is a belief of the Bhakti, a Hindu sect, which says that the divine manifests in contaminated places and things as burning grounds, in sexuality and…’ He paused, as if searching his memory.

‘Blood as well,’ Hamish said helpfully.

‘Right, right,’ Bruce said pensively, linking his fingers together and pausing a moment. ‘So just to get this clear, Hamish, you believe that the burning black field you describe your mind is, in fact, divine presence?’

‘Well, that should be obvious to you, Bruce,’ Hamish said. ‘My mind is a burning black field because of the impure social shit, which you call social systems, being dumped into it.’

Bruce looked worriedly at him. ‘So, you believe there is a divine presence burning social impurities in your mind.’

‘As I said, that should be obvious to you, Bruce,’ Hamish said impatiently.

‘The other words for what you are describing, Hamish, is thought disorder, which is a common symptom of bipolar disorder,’ Bruce said firmly.

‘Don’t pull out one of your lingo words out of your psychiatry post-box and stick it on me as a mental address. Hamish McColl,’ he yelled, standing up and raising an arm, ‘lives at 200 Thought Disorders Street, in the suburb of Bipolar!’

‘Now, Hamish,’ Bruce said, the worried expression on his face intensifying, ‘that’s thought disorder happening in your head again.’

‘You are not hearing the metaphors in that statement, are you?’ Hamish demanded.

‘Right, right,’ Bruce said distractedly, ‘you think I’m not hearing what you are saying, and just categorising your speech to a disorder.’

‘Exactly,’ Hamish said, regarding this man’s stupidity with disbelief.

‘Please. Tell me about your burning black field,’ Golu said quietly, gesturing at Hamish to sit down.

Hamish sat down, leaning back in his chair, flinging his dreadlocks back over his shoulders. ‘I have already stated my divine case,’ he said insistently.

‘You think you have divine madness,’ Golu mused, scratching his head.

‘I am being divinely burned. A Joan of Arc job by God on the impurities in my mind. Impurities put in by social corpses such as yourselves; dumbly reciting exclusionary passages of textbooks at me, so I become the theory of us all, not the theory of I.’ Hamish turned as Johanna opened the door, emerging from whatever mental health hellhole she had flown out of, gripping a new textbook evil to torment him with. He looked quickly at the title of the textbook in her hand, so it didn't claw at his mind and dump itself there.

'*Peculiar Disorders of Non-Conformists*,' Hamish said, repeating the title out loud. With ridicule, he said, 'Johanna, really?'

'Hamish. It doesn't say that,' she said, staring at him incredulously.

'Yes, it does,' Hamish argued, 'it very clearly says that.'

'Now, Hamish,' Bruce said, 'that is your Bipolar perception hallucinating a different title on the book. The title actually says *The Statistical and Diagnostic Manual of Mental Disorders*, and not *Peculiar Disorders of Non-Conformists*.'

'No, Bruce,' Hamish said, eyeballing him, 'I can see the truth about that so-called mental health manual.'

'Right, right,' Bruce said, looking at him in dismay. 'You believe the truth about the mental health manual is manifesting to you *as* a title.'

'Truth is not a mental illness, Bruce,' Hamish said, 'it's a gift.'

'So, you think you have gifted sight, Hamish? Where you see the truth about things?' Bruce asked, quickly writing some notes and looking up at him with a disturbed expression.

Hamish was silent for a minute. 'Bruce, my brain is about 200 years ahead of yours and—'

'Hamish,' Johanna interrupted, 'when—'

'Please don't speak my name, cat snapper,' Hamish said angrily, 'my ears feel tarred and feathered.'

'Tempting,' Johanna said bitingly.

'Johanna!' Bruce said, horrified.

'Do you always make your patients feel safe this way?' Hamish drawled.

'Right, right…' Bruce said hastily, 'let's—'

'Please. I do not wish to stay here. Lest I wake up tarred to the bed and lightly feathered. Please keep your psychopathic psychiatrist away from me. She doth not understand,' Hamish said tossing his dreadlocks over his shoulders.

'Doth…' Bruce repeated, looking at him quizzically and then writing something down. Hamish couldn't see what, but as a picture of Shakespeare grew out of the note Bruce was making, he thought it must be a reference to the language he just used. *Fuck!* he thought; he'd never met anyone so literal.

'See. That bothers me,' Hamish said, upset. 'You concentrated more on my use of an old English word instead of my fear of cat snapper there ordering me tarred and feathered on my bed.'

'It's not going to happen,' Bruce said tiredly, again taking his glasses off and rubbing at the lenses with a tissue. 'Such punishments went out of social disciplinary methods many, many years ago.'

'Let's get to the root of the problem, Hamish,' Golu said, leaning back in his chair, crooking his elbow and resting it on the back of his chair, as he'd done earlier. 'Where the Bipolar Disorder you are experiencing, started.'

'With tree rot,' Hamish said bluntly.

'Tree…rot?' Bruce asked.

Hamish was silent for a minute.

'The family tree,' he said quietly, bowing his head and smothering his face with his hands.

9

Hamish sat on the bed in his ward, depressed at its tightly tucked-in white sheets, grey flannelette blanket, and white pillowcase stretched tightly over a flat, hard pillow. *Bedding which leaches out dreams*, he thought, staring at it in misery. The type of bedding he saw in movies about concentration camps: the grey stiff blanket like the misery of dying skin, the stiffness of regime, the facial sterility of Nazi captors.

He did not know what to do in this sterile little coffin. No window in his room; just white smooth walls, plastering his mind.

He wondered how long he would have to stay in this tin can of a room.

'Hamish?'

Hamish looked up to see her standing in the doorway.

His beautiful Justine.

Her eyes regarded him steadily and certainly. And just like every time his eyes met hers, his mind stopped burning with the thousand different implications of objects around him and impurities of people he met. Nor did words sinew through his mind, growing veins and arteries of stories, twisting his mind up like an ivy vine in a hot house.

Justine's tree-like solidness stopped those shifting fields of people, places and objects passing through his mind. Sometimes, he lay awake all night, his mind hit by rapid tides of ideas, none of them belonging to just one ocean; he had the tides of the Pacific, the Indian, the Atlantic and the Arctic all riptiding into each other with nothing separating them out. No landmass, like Justine there, beside him; so the riptide waters could not rip apart his mind.

Sometimes, he drowned and burned at the same time.

He did not know how to stop it.

But there was something in Justine's eyes that did.

Hamish looked at her speechlessly, his eyes filling with tears.

'Can I come in, Hamish?' she asked, her eyes softening.

Hamish nodded, unable to speak as silence fell across his room. The mental noise from all the shifting people and places and objects through his head, had died the minute he saw her.

Relief flooded him, as the silence spread through his mind.

'I got lost in here, trying to find your room,' she said offhandedly, walking into his room.

'You never get lost,' Hamish said broodingly. 'Your foot *always* steps one in front of the other, in a long straight line.'

'There was no long straight line in this place to put one foot in front of the other,' Justine said as a matter of fact, gesturing out the door. 'There were corners everywhere. Left then right, then left, then right, then these big locked doors—'

'It's like a labyrinth in here,' Hamish interrupted. 'Did you run into the psychiatry beast?'

'The…what?' Justine asked, looking at him in dismay.

'The psychiatry beast. The Minotaur in the middle of the mental health labyrinth, here.'

Justine took a serious tone. 'Now, Hamish. You know there are no such things as Minotaurs living in mental hospitals. They belong to fairy tales. And you are older than that.'

Hamish looked down at his bed sheet, picking it up, scrunching it and dropping it down. He didn't know what to say to her. One look in her eyes and all his Batmans and Darth Vaders just sat down in his head and didn't fight and avenge anymore; not with him, not with each other and not with others either.

'You're better than medication, Justine,' he said, still looking down at his sheet, embarrassed that she, his altar, his sun, was seeing him in a mental health ward. 'You are the Valium of all women, my luscious Tinkerbell, taking me out of my lost places, leading me by the dick—'

'Hamish!' she said, shocked.

Hamish looked at her, distressed. 'I didn't mean that, Justine. It just came out of my mouth,' he said apologetically.

'Well, that's a problem, Hamish. Things just coming out of your mouth and those things are not of the Church, or from what you learnt in school. Just…strange things. I may be able to help take you out of those…what…lost places, because I'm studying a Bachelor of Counselling; but the strange things? That's why you are in here, Hamish.'

'I need someone calm to talk to,' Hamish said. 'Those shrinks in there, they are fucking my head up even more with their peculiar disorders manual and faces tight as a fist. They are pissing me off, and I need someone nice and calm, like you, to talk with.'

Justine said carefully, 'Distressed people like talking to calm people. Who can, as you said, help take them out of lost places; through discussion Hamish, *through* discussion…I don't want to hear about—'

'Cocks,' he said bluntly, 'peculiar disorders manual and shrinks with disorders of normality.'

Justine clapped her hands over her ears. 'I don't want to hear it,' she mouthed silently at him.

'Sorry,' Hamish mouthed at her, taking her hands gently away from her ears. He looked at her soft white hands in his large clumsy ones and bit his lip. 'I can't seem to get all this mental shit out. And the other mentals in here, I've tried talking to them, but they have more mental shit than I do. So, we sit there, like dung heaps, talking about whose dung heap fucking stinks more. See, you're not a dung heap, Justine. You are the bleach, the disinfectant, your thoughts have the clean thinness of tissues. You talk straight, no mental shit. You just are.'

'You make me something more, Hamish,' she said, troubled, removing her hands from his, 'than I actually am.'

'Well, that's why I'm in here, and you're not,' he said, his fingers bunching and stretching his dreadlocks. 'Implication is everywhere for me. You see and hear solidly. For you, it is, as it is. I see by implication. The ocean…it had cunt implication, it was a wide watery cunt all over the land; nothing phallic sticking out of it, and reminding me of…reminding me of—'

Justine held up her hand, looking alarmed. 'Hamish. Stop.'

His thought faded. Died in her certainty.

'Oceans don't have a sexual orientation, Hamish. They are genderless. It is just an ocean, with the functions of an ocean. And that's it.' She sat down on the edge of his bed and patted the spot next to her. He sidled up to her like a crab, scuttling and stopping, scuttling and stopping, uncertain how close she would let him be to her before her soft white hand stopped him. As he moved nearer to her, the faint rose scent of her perfume and the early morning garden smell of her hair grew softly around him, making him want to quietly lie down next to her and just be.

Just be in her, his mind thought immediately, *suddenly and unexpectedly.* His erection sprang out hard and fast at the thought of fucking her, and he covered it quickly with a pillow.

'Hamish?' She asked, concerned, 'Did you put that pillow there for a reason?'

His cheeks flamed as he clutched at the pillow, trying to stop his hands from throwing her down on the bed.

She looked at the pillow, realisation dawning in her eyes. She looked at his face, back at the cock-smothering pillow and looked away, appalled.

'*Please* don't go,' he pleaded. 'I need you. I need for you to be here, smothering me with roses and feathers and early morning gardens.'

Justine turned her head back to him, her eyes softening. 'Well that sounds better than the dung heap you were talking about.'

Hamish laid his head on her shoulder. 'You'll never be a dung heap, Justine. You were rose-born.'

Justine gently placed a hand on his hair. The quickening in his mind became slower and slower. Finally it stopped.

She was his shore, Justine. She was his shore.

When he woke some hours later, she was gone. He remembered blacking out on her shoulder. The insomnia which had burned through his mind, sending him mentally hysterical, finally dying and falling down. Nothing bright and burning behind his eyes anymore; just the coolness of her saturating his mind, like damp green moss, deepening down through hot sand.

Hamish's hand felt for where she'd sat on the bed, and he grasped it with his fingers, clutching the last of her presence with his hand. 'Justine,' he muttered, falling back down on the bed.

Hamish heard the door creak open, and sat up with a start. He looked up to see a fat Asian nurse with dark brown hair in a top knot standing threateningly in his doorway.

Like a big, fat, brown tarantula.

'Hello Hamish,' she said, the sharp little inflections in her voice scaring him. He looked in alarm at the spider legs growing out of her fingers, waving around with venomous little tips. *Fuck*, he thought, *Fuck! A mental health tarantula, here to poison me.*

'What are you?' he asked fearfully, scuttling back against the pillow propped up against the wall.

'I am a nurse here, Hamish. I've come to give you your anti-psychotic injection. You need one at least every two weeks,' she said.

'Don't be stupid,' he said bluntly.

She smiled patiently at him. With the patience of the spider fatly lurking in his doorway, waiting to spin a drug web all over his interesting cognition.

'We need to get the weeds out of your mind, Hamish.'

'You're the pesticide nurse, are you? Come to give me mental weed spray?' he asked unevenly. '*Fuck* off!'

'Hamish. It is medication to treat your condition,' she said. 'Don't argue.'

'I don't have a condition,' he said defiantly. 'I have allergies to systematic society.'

She looked patiently at him. It annoyed the fuck out of him; that patient, waiting, tarantula face.

'Hamish,' she said insistently, 'stand and pull your pants down.'

'What?' he asked in panicked disbelief. 'You want to fuck me?'

'No, Hamish, no I don't,' she said factually.

'Thank fuck for that. Fat Asian tarantula *really* isn't my type.'

Politeness slid off her face. 'Hamish. I need to put an injection in your bottom,' she said, her voice low and quiet; *the same quietness of funerals, when the coffin lowers into the ground*, Hamish thought, fear growing in him. *What if that is a lethal injection she holds in her hand?* How the fuck was he going to get out of that?

'What?' he said, still panicking. 'You want to stick me up the arse with a needle? *You* sadistic bitch, get the fuck away from me, brothel bitch. I *know* you want to fuck me. I know you do, brothel bitch, brothel bitch. She who pole dances with spiders, just get the fuck away, bitch, get the fuck away!'

'Hamish,' she said, her voice returning to mechanical patience, 'I need to put a needle in your bottom cheek. Not insert in your anus.'

'I don't *want* a needle in me,' he said furiously.

She lowered the needle a little. Venom liquefied in her brown eyes. He felt drugged, almost hypnotised by those tarantula eyes; eyes which made him feel like she was hanging him upside down, so he couldn't see the world the right way up. He rubbed at his eyes, trying to clear them of her tarantula magic. And he knew it was. His gift of truth manifested her as a fat magical tarantula hypnotising him into doing the will of mental health.

Those eyes hissed like acid all over him. Hamish stumbled back, trying to put some distance between them.

She was about to fang him.

Her voice travelled like a web thread and snapped against his ear. 'Hamish, you *will* have this needle.'

Hamish pressed as hard as he could against the wall, his knees shaking, 'No. I won't.'

Her lips pressed together in a hard line. 'I will get a straitjacket on you. There is a compulsory medication order on you. You have no right to refuse.'

'Why not?' he asked, his voice trembling, 'Why the fuck not?'

'Stop asking me questions,' she said, her eyes flaring amber. 'This is fact. You are sick. This is treatment for it. There is no question.'

'Well, yes. There is,' Hamish insisted. 'My rights come under humane treatment. United Nations have principles on that.'

'It is law you stay here. You are out of control.'

'I know what you are. I know what you fucking are,' he said angrily.

Hamish turned his head as he heard the sound of footsteps slowing and pausing by the door. The fat, brown tarantula calling itself a nurse slowly turned, her fat, brown legs shifting into a wide stance. *The insolence of it*, Hamish thought, *standing like that. Aggressive bitch.*

His mind fell rapidly, flatlining into depression, as he saw physically and mentally skinny Johanna. She moved towards him, with a threatening sort of angularity, the sharp thrusts of her hips like falling blades.

Hamish shuddered and looked away from her.

'All done, Hotaru?' Johanna asked.

'Hotaru. Is that your fucking name is it? I will remember, Hotaru, I will remember. And then, it will be revenge of The Hamish,' he said warningly.

'I don't care, Hamish, what you remember. I just want your animal mind fixed up,' Hotaru said.

'That's not very professional, Hotaru,' Hamish said. 'It's in your own mental health law to treat me with dignity. I got the brochure when I got in here. You have insulted me, implying I have an emu for a mind.'

'I did not say that Hamish. I said animal.'

'Well, I live in Australia. So I give the animal an Australian name. Emu.'

'He thinks he is an emu now,' Hotaru said to Johanna. 'I tell you he is very sick. He also mistakes me for a gobble tarantula.'

'I did not say gobble tarantula,' Hamish said vehemently. 'I said *fat tarantula.'*

'I don't care if you said gobble tarantula or fat tarantula,' Hotaru said, 'you are very sick and you have to have medication.' She turned to Johanna. 'He thinks he has rights and refuses medication.'

Johanna gave an exasperated sigh. 'And how many of them think that?' she asked. She turned her attention back to Hamish. 'Look, Hamish. You are under mental health law now. And one of the reasons you are under mental health law is because you have no decision-making capacity…'

'Yes, I do. I just said no to enforced medication. That's a decision I made.'

'Only people who *have* decision-making capacity can lawfully refuse medication, Hamish. And only people with decision-making capacity come under common law. Mental health law is separate to common law, Hamish. And you come under that, not common law. Take the medication, Hamish. Or we'll get out the straightjacket and force you into it.'

'I have the right to dignity,' Hamish yelled, 'I HAVE THE RIGHT TO DIGNITY!'

'Not if you are a threat to yourself and the community,' Johanna insisted, her nasal voice twanging against his ears, making him want to murder her. 'And you are, Hamish. You are harming your own reputation by flipping it out at your delusion of a vagina ocean, calling it a cock teaser. By forcing you on medication, we are preserving what's left of your dignity. Because it *is* undignified to stand naked on clifftops yelling out delusional abuse. The next behaviour from you could very well be flipping it out at a community member. So, take the medication, Hamish. Or we'll force it into you.'

'You are advised to co-operate,' Hotaru said.

'Co-operate? *Co-operate?* Is that some mental health lingo designed to make your brain compliant? The new word medication?' Hamish asked sarcastically, 'And furthermore, *what* are you trying to make me compliant with?'

'I think you are reading too much into things, Hamish. *As* usual,' Johanna said dismissively. 'I don't know who invented the word co-operate, but it wasn't us.' She paused for a second, looking at him like he was a social termite.

'This is what you don't get, Hamish, despite your abnormally high intelligence and abnormality aside from that. Mental health, Hamish, is part of the social system that corrects deviations. You, Hamish, are considered a deviation.'

'And you must be the negative control mechanism,' Hamish said sarcastically.

Johanna's cheeks flushed. 'Careful, Hamish. You could get another month in here.' Her mouth twisted into a sneer. 'Just accept that society does not run off *your* ideas. It already has set systems in place. And you have registered as an aberrance in the feedback system society has.'

'You need a fucking new career,' Hamish said to her scornfully. 'You just don't have a way with people, do you? You talk to me like a fucking piece of living legislation. Fuck off, Johanna, you mentally evil insect, just fuck off. I'll find some way to spray you to death. I will,' he threatened.

'I have to go and put in a report,' Johanna said to Hotaru. 'He has homicidal intent towards me. Don't give him any more chances. Call Gary. Get the straitjacket. Lock him in first before you leave.'

Hotaru looked at Hamish, her brown eyes flickering amber. 'Should have played it smart, Hamish. You'd be out of here, with a community treatment order. But now? You will be here longer, for non-compliant behaviour and defiance of us. Your urge to kill Johanna, just earnt you more time in here.' Hotaru stepped closer to him. He flattened himself against the wall, as he saw her retinas flick venom into his eyes.

'Will you just leave me the *fuck* alone? You are doing my head in more,' Hamish complained.

Bruce stuck his head around the door. 'And read up on how to socially behave,' he advised kindly. 'It's a skill like anything else. You just learn the skill, just as you just learn the skill to drive. Because if you don't, you will keep ending up in here, time and time again. Most of you vigilante types fail on one key domain in our assessments. Social well-being. And you fail because you do not accept how society operates, nor do you make yourself useful to the community; and therefore are not valued by society. And because of that, you end up dumped in here.'

'So, you think I am useless to society as I am; want me to justify my existence and turn me into a social mannequin,' Hamish said sarcastically.

'Just a functional person, Hamish,' Bruce said, giving him a quick smile and leaving.

'Most people with anything to say are not social mannequins, Bruce,' Hamish yelled out as he left. 'Ernest Hemingway wrote naked, you know. The greatest writer of all time is not socially normative.'

'I don't care about that,' Hotaru said. 'You are my patient. Not Ernest Hemingway. From what you say, it is necessary for him be in mental hospital.'

'You don't get why he wrote naked?' Hamish asked.

'He wrote naked because he was inappropriate,' Hotaru said.

'No,' Hamish said, looking at her with scorn, 'he wrote naked because naked is the act of being bare. Just like writing is. It's a bareness.'

'He is bare because there is no thinking in his head,' Hotaru insisted.

Hamish said, exasperated, 'You really don't get it, do you?'

'What is there to get? His behaviour shows untreated mental illness. No one should write naked. Not anywhere. Not even in their own house. Write with clothes on. That is appropriate.'

'You don't get it,' he muttered. 'Let me think…'

'That is for people who are not sick in the head. Have treatment. Then you can think, safe. And then we are safe too.'

'You have to see the patient perspective. It's part of your job,' Hamish pointed out.

'Your perspective is called mentally ill,' Hotaru said, 'So I don't have to listen.'

'No,' Hamish insisted, 'my perspective is not mentally ill. Neither was Hemingway's. He just belonged to an eccentric culture. Let's see…writer Vladimir Nabokov specifically wrote in pencils tipped with erasers. Always. He did not write in ink, or by typewriter.'

'He has Obsessive Compulsive Disorder,' she said, 'and phobias about writing method.'

'No. It was just part of his writer persona,' Hamish said, exasperated.

'I don't care,' she answered. 'Just take the treatment.'

'You know what?' Hamish said accusingly, 'You are the one out of line here. You are a strange contorted tarantula, who is vigilante about conformity. You are displaying the same sort of thinking you are discouraging in others. You think I am defiant, yet you are too. You are defiant about those who dream and fight, those who want more for themselves than mannequin existence.' He leant forward, close to her. 'You are a mental health gestapo, you are,' he spat.

‘I do not understand what you are saying, Hamish. You are very strange. You think I am a Nazi spider.’

‘Mental health gestapos exist in the figurative sense,’ Hamish insisted.

‘There is no such thing,’ Hotaru answered. ‘You are *badly* mentally ill and need treatment. We do this for your own safety and ours too.’

Hamish turned his back to her. If she would not see his point, he refused to see her face. He stared straight ahead, as she repeatedly called his name; the cold white, corpse walls rapidly turning him into bones.

10

'Now, Hamish,' Bruce said, quickly checking his notes and looking at him with consideration, 'at our last session, you informed us the cause of your present problems was tree rot, which I am to believe is a less generic way of describing family dysfunction.'

Golu looked at Bruce impatiently. 'Rot is simply a term for something which has decayed within a family; rotted, gone off track.'

'There are a thousand different ways of describing the same thing, Bruce, if you are not comatose with systematic indoctrination,' Hamish said confidently, flinging his dreadlocks back over his shoulders.

'Watch that vigilante talk, Hamish,' Johanna warned. 'The so-called socially comatose people are the ones not in mental hospitals.'

'Ideological violence victims don't speak up, cat snapper. They don't get noticed enough to be admitted to mental hospital,' Hamish answered sarcastically. 'They are either too silent, or ideologically repeating themselves too much to be any threat to The Establishment with some revolutionary or original idea.'

'Right, right,' Bruce said absently, scratching his cheek. 'You are, in fact, implying that ideology is a form of psychological violence which batters the mind too much for some bright or world-changing idea and traumatises the victims into social submission.'

'Exactly,' Hamish said enthusiastically. 'I, The Hamish, and you, The Bruce, understand each other at last.'

'No, Hamish. I'm simply paraphrasing you,' Bruce said cautiously.

'Then you have one of those sad little minds punched out by the iron fists that rule society. Religion, law, tradition, education, philosophy, politics. *And* mental health…noooooo-relationship to self; just a relationship to the collective,' Hamish said. 'How fucking boring.' He leant forward in his chair, as he felt the fingers of those iron fists prod at his mind again; parables pinching his thoughts, the family threat of scissors on his dreadlocked hair, the model citizen gestating in his mind. He sat back in horror. He kept feeling it there like a mitosis division from his true self, The Perfect Hamish, growing in the mental health placenta.

He saw it. The mental health placenta joined between the fingers of the three psychiatrists, as they wrote their notes: growing fetal citizen Hamish, the Modified. He looked away, appalled, unable to speak.

'OK,' Golu said broadly, 'those systems you talk about, religion, law, education, politics and so on, exist as social controls, Hamish; however, people like yourself, with very high intelligence, who have a wild spirit, can sometimes find submitting themselves to social controls difficult. You have the right to be you, but you have to do it in a safe way, Hamish.'

'Yes, safety is agreed upon,' Bruce said absently, 'as it benefits us all. Now, let's get back to what you were saying…er…Hamish…'

'Hamish, here—' Johanna began.

'Well, I'm not anywhere else,' Hamish said pointedly.

'That is debatable,' Johanna said under her breath, writing a neat and concise note.

'Cattttttsnnnnnaaaapperrrr, how shall I count the ways you remind me of death tuna?' Hamish said, placing his hand mockingly to his heart.

Johanna's voice rose high and thin: 'What?'

Bruce looked at Hamish, bewildered. 'Death tuna…' he pondered, scratching his cheek again.

Hamish looked from Johanna, to Bruce, to Golu. 'Why is that a statement I should have to explain? It talks. I don't.'

'Let's get this discussion to the point we left off, which was the actual point,' Golu said mildly. 'Hamish was talking about a thousand different ways of describing the same thing.'

'Yes,' Bruce said, 'and I have a response to that.' Hamish looked away from Bruce, irritated at how he was studying him like he was paragraph five on page thirty-three in a psychiatry textbook.

'My response to you, Hamish,' Bruce continued, still scratching his cheek, 'on your thousand different ways of describing things, is that some of the less…er…spirited of us like to just use one word to describe one thing. In my profession, it makes things a lot easier if you do. You cannot call schizophrenia anything other than schizophrenia. It is the agreed name for that condition.'

‘I could think of a thousand other words for schizophrenia,’ Hamish said confidently, stretching out his legs and crossing one ankle over the other.

‘I don’t want to hear all your names for schizophrenia,’ Johanna said, her nasal voice twanging over each word.

‘Your name, said a thousand times,’ Hamish said, smiling insolently at her.

Johanna’s cheeks mottled their usual red, and she looked furiously at Bruce. He gave her a warning look.

Golu looked from Hamish to Johanna. ‘Ah…describing or reading things in more than one way, like Hamish does, is called polyvalent,’ he said, ‘as opposed to monovalent.’

‘Which means?’ Johanna said, her voice squealing over her syllables.

Golu replied coolly, ‘Polyvalent means Hamish can read something or someone in many different ways. If you are a monovalent sort of person, you just receive the communication and linguistically understand what it says, not what it symbolically means. A monovalent person just read texts and people one way through the facts, not through interpretation.’

Johanna looked at Golu scornfully. ‘I don’t think so. That’s just complicated talk for a man who is delusional.’

Hamish sneered at her. ‘It’s not complicated at all, cat snapper. I have the ability to read people, not just look at someone and just see the facts of them. The facts of you Johanna are, you are 5 feet 9 inches, skinny, brown eyes, and dark brown hair with white skin. That’s a monovalent reading of you. The polyvalent reading of you is a thousand different meanings of Bitch.’

‘Do something about him, will you?’ she hissed to Bruce.

Hamish looked in satisfaction at her pissed-off face. He just loved it when the arse-retentives of the world started losing it. Still grinning, he turned to Bruce. ‘And you, Bruce. You may read *The Diagnostic and Statistical Manual of Mental Disorders* as a manual of mental health disorders but that’s *not* what it is.’

‘Now, Hamish, that sort of talk indicates paranoia to us,’ Bruce admonished, his eyebrows drawing together.

‘We’ve been through this before, Hamish,’ Johanna said, her voice thin and impatient. ‘*The Diagnostic and Statistical Manual of Mental Disorders* is *not* called *Peculiar Disorders of the Non-Conformist.*’

Hamish looked at her scornfully. 'You have conformist eyes, Johanna. You are a blind mole in this already dark world. I can see with my non-conformist eyes what that DSM-IV manual is *really* about.'

'Ah...Hamish,' Golu said contemplatively, then paused, looking like he was considering what to say next. He continued: 'There are three of us in this room who all read the title in the same way, as *The Diagnostic and Statistical Manual of Mental Disorders*, and just one of us who reads it as *Peculiar Disorders of the Non-Conformist*. How would you explain these differences in visual perception, ah, Hamish?'

Hamish threw up his hands. 'Oh, what the fuck. I'm already in the screw house. A priest, Father Matthias, who ran all the Sunday masses I had to attend because of family obsession with normality. He says it is the Devil's gift to see and read the real story, and I had to pray to God to make my eyes normal; but he should have been looking in the other direction. I have Jesus' eyes, you know. I'm the middle word in his most common expression of *I am the way, the truth and the life.* And some people find this a threat, Bruce.'

'I thoroughly agree with your priest that your eyes need to be normal,' Bruce said, 'and, in fact, medically encourage normal vision as opposed to...er...delusional. But, in this case, let me assure you, Hamish, the source of your bipolar disorder is of biological origin, and not as you implied, of...er...non-conformist or Jesus origin.'

'Can we move on, please?' Johanna whined to Bruce. 'We've gone *way* past allocated time for this patient.'

'Another screwed-up offering to you, cat snapper. I'm here, in the room, not existing in your textbook as a phrase called "This Patient",' Hamish sneered.

'Your screwed-up offering is declined,' Johanna said, her nasal voice squealing through the room, 'since the word patient is, in fact, what you are called when you are in a hospital.'

'Hospital present, person absent...is that what you mean?' Hamish demanded.

'I don't want to hear your abnormal statements, Hamish,' Johanna said. 'You have to learn how to talk normal.'

'Let's move on, shall we...' Bruce said delicately, clicking his pen on and off.

Hamish winced at the sound, shifting in his seat irritably. He fucking hated that sound. Hated it. People repeatedly clicking their pens in his hearing sent him mental. 'Would you fucking not click your pen like that, Bruce?' Hamish demanded. 'It's just disrespectful.'

'What?' Bruce said, scratching his cheek in bewilderment.

'Pen clicking is offensive. It's an inane banal sound which annoys the shit out of the ordinary person, let alone someone non-conformist…'

'Now, Hamish, that's not what you are,' Bruce said firmly. 'You are, in fact, ticking all the boxes for bipolar disorder and your vigilantism is leaning dangerously towards paranoid personality disorder. You possibly have obsessive-compulsive disorder as well. Hamish, you seem to think that conformist society is out to get you; you are afraid of subordination; you don't like authority, or its representatives; and you are suspicious and scornful of mental health staff here, regarding us all as the enemy. We are just trying to help you, Hamish, get out of the dysfunctional focus your mind is trapped in.'

'Well, how can you tell this, Bruce,' Hamish said, 'since you can't actually *see* my mind. My head is not some clear goldfish bowl you can actually see my mind swimming around in, like a fat little goldfish for you to psychologically lust after.'

'Hamish. Are you accusing us of fish bestiality?' Johanna demanded, her cheeks flushing with anger.

'You're such a fucking literal,' Hamish said.

'Ah, Johanna. Can you see me afterwards?' Golu said, looking at her, concerned.

'What for?' she asked belligerently. '*He* is the one making delusional accusations. You need to put *him* back in the acute unit, you need to—'

'Johanna!' Bruce said, his voice resounding loudly in the room.

She fell silent at his raised voice, looking sullenly down at her clipboard.

'Right, right, let's move on with this, shall we?' Bruce said, glancing at his watch.

'Before we go any further, get Johanna out of the room. She is a *diseased* turtle,' Hamish said.

'The turtle part is questionable and possibly hallucinatory,' Bruce said pensively. 'I do understand, however, you are talking about how social systems form systematic thinking. And the reason I understand *that* part of your dialogue, Hamish, was because you spoke to me in plain, concise, logical language. You made the meaning very clear. The diseased…er…turtle is not so clear.'

'*Hello*. Turtle is a metaphor for *slow*.'

'OK,' Golu said, 'it's a *fairly* acceptable wording of a message, Hamish; turtles included or excluded. What you have said to me, Hamish, is you feel society does not allow for unstructured or unsystematic thinking.'

'Yes,' Hamish said blandly, tossing his dreadlocks over his shoulders.

Golu crossed one leg over the other, linked his hands behind his head, and regarded him with interest. 'So, you feel like you don't belong, Hamish.'

Hamish looked at Golu hopelessly. 'I ask too many questions. I think too many things. I can't call that a table; or that, a chair; or that, a desk. Everything has implication or meaning to me. The table, the chair, the desk: they elongate or balloon or project three dimensionally at me to show me the truth.'

'Hallucinations, Hamish,' Johanna taunted, 'hallucinations.'

Golu looked thoughtfully at Hamish. 'That sort of visual perception you just described could also indicate a perceptual disorder,' he suggested.

'I'll look into it,' Bruce said absently, writing some notes. 'It's possible it's a perceptual disorder, separate from bipolar symptoms.'

'Or, it could just be due to a general medical condition,' Golu added.

'A…*a general medical condition?'* Johanna asked in disbelief, turning and staring at Hamish. 'That?'

'Oh, excuse me,' Hamish said irritably. 'There seems to be something wrong with your perception of me, Johanna. You seem to think I am a demonstrative adjective, called *that*. Perhaps, it's you who have the perceptual disorder, cat snapper.'

'Well, well, well,' Johanna said condescendingly, 'it looks like someone did pay attention when in English class, after all.'

'Can you get your mental health bitch out of here? I mean, fuck! She's more occupationally suited to the Nazi Party,' Hamish said vehemently.

'Ah…Hamish,' Golu said, leaning forward in his chair and putting both elbows on his knees, a troubled look on his face, 'let's return to the subject at hand, about how you perceive things, Hamish.'

'Yes,' Bruce said firmly, giving Johanna another warning look. He clicked his pen and focused his attention back on Hamish. Hamish gritted his teeth, looking determinedly away from the pen.

‘I want to talk through with you, Hamish, about what happened that day on the cliff,’ Golu said placatingly, noticing his irritated face. ‘You, and witnesses there at the time, stated you seemed to think the ocean was a vagina, sexually tormenting you; and that the way it rolled and swelled reminded you of…er…’ he quickly glanced at his notes, ‘a dilating vagina; and this sight did, in fact, inflame your sexual frustration about a girl you want to the point you couldn’t stand it anymore.’

‘The ocean made me think of a big cunt all over the land,’ Hamish said rapidly. ‘Just one big cunt, singing to my cock like a big cunt siren.’

‘A big cunt…siren?’ Bruce asked bewildered.

‘A siren. They sit on rocks like slippery sluts, entrancing sailors to them with song, and shipwreck them.’

‘And that is the effect of this girl on you? You feel like she is shipwrecking you?’ Golu asked with concern.

‘She actually kept me very calm up to a point,’ Hamish said, leaning both elbows on the back of his chair. ‘Before that point, her eyes were like lullabies. They put me to sleep; stopped all the burning, brain wrecking thoughts I had,’ he leant forward, putting his forehead in his hands, rubbing at it.

‘And *still* have,’ Johanna corrected sarcastically. He looked up at her with red-rimmed eyes which felt grainy and dry from lack of sleep. Her eyes flicked over his face with dislike. ‘Perhaps, we should hire lullaby eyes to put psychotic patients like you to sleep. You might have to do something about *that*,’ she said, glancing down at the cock bulge straining at his pants, ‘before we let her in again to see you. These notes say it’s in a super stimulated state.’

‘Would you not look at my cock like that,’ Hamish demanded. ‘You just made it shrivel.’

‘Oh. Now I am responsible for cock-reductionism,’ she said nastily.

‘You are a national cock-threat!’ Hamish yelled, getting out of his chair, his feet hitting the ground rapidly, as he went towards her. She shrank back when his knee knocked her chair. He brought his face close to hers and said, ‘They ought to put your name in that fucking manual as a mental health disorder.’

‘Bruce!’ Johanna screamed.

Golu was there three seconds before Bruce, his hand landing firmly on Hamish’s arm. ‘Hamish! Sit down. Now!’

Hamish glowered at Johanna. 'You are an offence, cat snapper!' he said. 'An offence!'

Hamish turned away only when Bruce's hand landed on his other arm. 'Hamish,' Bruce said firmly, as he and Golu pulled him away from Johanna, 'we need to sedate you.' He turned to Golu, 'Lithium levels aren't high enough yet to reduce the mania. He's still highly irritable and will keep reacting like this if we disagree with him or inadvertently anger him.'

Hamish didn't remember much after that. Just a blur of slamming doors, a stab in the arm, and feet moving rapidly around him.

Then, it went dark.

11

The days turned into weeks, falling like a whiteness. Erasure. He felt it. A mental skinning of all the thoughts in his head. The reductionism of his soul. Another needle, another and another. His mind lost its humming and quickening; its unordinary ways.

Cave structures slowly formed in his mind, making him feel like his head was made of thick rock and dull musty spaces, slowing the quick flow of his spirit.

Who the fuck am I now? he asked himself, wrapping his arms around his knees and lowering his chin on them. He looked at the closed door of his room: cold, steel, morgue-like. His view of the door didn't produce anything in his head like it used to. No thoughts flew through his head about the door, pulling out implications, associations, or stand-tall ideas. It was a door.

Just a door.

And then it opened.

His father walked in.

His father didn't look like he used to. To Hamish, he was mostly a compilation of impressions; a caricature; a Catholic Church satire. But, now, Hamish could see him as just a man whose face looked tired and worn. Just a man who spoke Catholic thoughts and worked hard at his job at the local council.

'Are you cured of those homosexuality thoughts, Son?' his father asked tightly.

'Dad,' Hamish said, exasperated, 'I have no homosexual thoughts of being a man lesbian.'

'Now, see? That's not a normal term to use. Man lesbian.' He turned his head and yelled down the hallway. 'Nurse? I think he needs more medication. His sentences still aren't normal.'

'Dad. Some of those ideas you have about homosexuality aren't really normal either. It's not a mental illness, I think it's more a genetic thing. As much as you have brown eyes because of genetic heritage, I think there is a gay gene.'

His father's face reddened. 'God would not create gays, Son,' he hissed.

'Well, maybe there is another God, who does,' Hamish argued.

'Son. There is only one God. You know that.'

'I don't actually know that, Dad. That's just what I've been taught. Like most ideas in society that is a learnt idea, not a natural one. But I question it, Dad, I question it.'

'There is no question!' his father yelled, his voice resounding down the hallway of the mental hospital. 'It is a necessary separation of culture. It happened many centuries ago. Leviticus! It says very clearly: *You must not live according to the customs of the nation; I am going to drive out before you! Because they did all those things, I abhorred them...* God put his prohibitions down, banning Israel from practising the immoral practices of the cultures all around them. They were *pagan* cultures, Son. You think my attitude is about discrimination. But it's not. It is about a cultural practice, where the licensed sexuality is heterosexual, a *non-pagan* sexuality.'

Hamish's mind stumbled. 'I...I...' Hamish faltered, as his thoughts faded into a black hole and disappeared. 'I can't remember what I was going to say,' he muttered.

'Just as well,' his father said darkly, 'your thoughts are out of Catholic bounds.' He folded his arms, looking at him forcefully. 'It is *our* right, Hamish, to enforce the morality of our faith.'

'So, you have enforced it on me by bringing me to mental health hospital, because you think I have secret gay longings which not only violate the "morality of the faith", but determine me as mentally ill...and I...I...' he slowed, looking down, unable to form the next thought. Hamish looked up again, agonised. 'I...can't...think...'

'Good. Your head was turning pagan. That is why ideology was invented. To stop pagan parts of the brain becoming active. Evil *esoteric* parts, much better dead and buried, underneath proper papal thoughts. It is *our* right to enforce our faith, to protect our families and our Catholic community. And it is the *freedom* of religion to enforce our faith how we see fit to do so,' his father said firmly, thumping his fist on Hamish's bathroom door. His father gave him another hard look. 'Stop staring at me like a martyr, Son. You just don't qualify. There's too much leprechaun in you and not enough saint.'

'I do so qualify,' Hamish said, raising his chin and locking his gaze with his father's. 'Medication has made a martyr of my intelligence.'

'If medication kills your pagan thinking, that is a good thing, Son,' he said, 'because you talk all retarded with your pagan tongue.'

'I can speak the Hamish Word if I want to.'

'The Catholic word,' his father said, 'has the tongue of God through it; not the tongue of the pagan devil.'

'So, you think I speak with the tongue of the pagan devil?'

'*Don't* say its name.'

'Well, you just did.'

'As part of God's Catholic body, I can say its name in the safety of sanctity. But you have been amputated from God's Catholic body because of the nasty plague sore you are.'

'Well, aren't you just so good for my self-esteem,' Hamish said sarcastically, folding his arms and glaring up at the ceiling. 'Perhaps I can be part of God's non-Catholic body, who may not cast me out. Hello, are you there?' he said to the ceiling.

'I don't think so, Son. You are too low down. And I don't have to pander to your self-esteem, as ego is well decided as one of the seven vices,' his father said firmly. 'Giving you false vanity, Son, will only take that soul tumour of yours to a fatter actuality. And stop talking to the ceiling. It's just another form of queer you have.'

Hamish glared at him. 'Can you try thinking about me as a virtue then?'

'When you show them, Hamish,' his father answered.

'Right,' Bruce said brightly, appearing at the doorway, rubbing his hands together, 'are we ready?'

His father raised his chin, his face still storming with the Bible. 'We are ready to take the demon on.'

Bruce looked at him in dismay. 'You think this is about defeating a demon, Mr McColl?' he asked.

'They are all demon-possessed in here, Bruce. Give him the tablet. Give him many, until his secretive leprechaun is dead.'

'Right, right,' Bruce said, rubbing his chin, his eyes flickering with clinical analysis of what disorder his father could possibly have. Bruce turned to

Hamish. 'Come on, Hamish. This shouldn't take too long,' he said reassuringly.

'Long things are better than short things, Dr Beyer. Look at the Bible. What if God's faithful scribes took a shortcut on all of that? We would be leaner people in a state of soul poverty. Can you take your time with him please, with his endless leprechaun? It hides sometimes, making him look a bit normal. You have to make it talk.'

Bruce's look of dismay deepened. 'Mr McColl,' he began.

'I don't want...want...don't...want...*fuck!*' Hamish broke off, looking helplessly at Bruce. 'These tablets are fucking me up...they...tablet...don't want...tablet...*fuck!*'

Bruce gave Hamish a comforting look. 'The medication is acting on a neurotransmitter in your brain, which we think has been producing too much norepinephrine, Hamish. This neurotransmitter escalates arousal and lifts your mood. The problem is this particular neurotransmitter is too active with you, causing high levels of arousal and mania. The lithium we are giving you is changing your nerve impulses and slowing your thoughts down, out of that manic space. Your thoughts may begin to change in content as the mania reduces and this in turn will change your behaviour. At least, that's what we are hoping.'

Hamish held his hands up, giving Bruce an agonised look, 'There's shaking there. There is shaking and I never shake.'

'There shake in your mind,' Hotaru said firmly, coming into the room.

Hamish glared at her. 'That's called thinking. Shaking in the body is different. I feel like I've got body stammering...stammer...body...*fuck!*'

'Now, Hamish,' Bruce said, 'you have to train your mind not to react like that. It's in a habit of rapid reactivity, where you speak too fast and without thinking about what you are actually saying.'

You want me to be a cognitive pet, a mental dog on a leash. Sit, stand, fetch, obey...and...and... Hamish lost the thought. He looked at Bruce, his struggle visible on his face. 'You don't get it. There's no universe opening up in my mind anymore,' Hamish said. 'No...no...no...' his face flushed with rage, as the thought seemed to disappear. 'I *hate* this,' he said vehemently. 'I hate this.'

Bruce looked at Hamish sympathetically, 'If there is nothing huge in your mind anymore, then that's a good thing, Hamish. It means your thoughts are rationalising again, proportioning as normal.'

'See?' said Hotaru, reaching out and touching his arm. 'Don't you feel so better? Now you co-operate?'

Hamish angrily shook her arm off, 'No. I feel very strange you fat tarant…tarant…thing bitch, person.' He looked at Bruce in confusion, tears filling his eyes.

'That confusion will wear off,' Bruce said comfortingly. 'Your thoughts are still veering between dysfunction and function. You retrieved the right word, right at the end, to describe Hotaru. Person. Not fat tarantula. Person. That is a good thing, Hamish. And very heartening to hear.'

'Is he cured of his homosexual thoughts?' his father asked anxiously; his fists clenching and unclenching, clenching and unclenching. 'You know, those sorts of homosexual thoughts are against our faith. I can't have him in the family home if he's like that, sitting on seats, leaving hell's contaminate there to hang off our underwear. We can't have his secret leprechaun living at our address. It's got to go Dr Beyer.'

Bruce looked uneasily at him. 'Homosexuality is not in the *Diagnostic and Statistical Manual of Mental Disorders,* Mr McColl. And neither are leprechauns.'

'When are you going to put homosexuality in your manual?' his father demanded. 'It's a sexual and mental abnormality. A violation of God's laws!'

'Er…perhaps those are issues for a religious-based counsellor, to talk with Hamish about. It's not our role here, to…er… "cure" sexuality, which your faith determines as abnormal. It's a religious issue, not a psychiatric issue.'

'Good idea,' his father said firmly, 'I will arrange for a religious-based counsellor for Hamish. They are closer to God than your profession, who won't cure the true ills of this world.'

'Er…and that is?' Bruce asked tentatively.

'Those of the pagan occupations; homosexuals. Whores. Atheists. Trapeze artists who display their genitals while swinging across the tents. Those are the sort you need to be allocating the beds too. Not the ones with a bit of healthy depression.'

'Healthy. Depression,' Bruce repeated. 'Mr McColl. I am somewhat bewildered.'

‘It makes the person realise that something is not right with his spirit. And that is: his spirit is disconnected from God. But, Hamish here, what is in his head is not healthy, those homosexual thoughts.’

Hamish stared at him, dismayed. ‘Dad. I’ve already told you. I’m *not* gay. And I don’t need religious-based counselling for homosexuality when I am a heterosexual.’

‘There have been ominous signs, Hamish. No girlfriend, no dates with women, you are only friends with them. Not to be interested in girls at your age is a religious milestone you have missed,’ his father warned.

‘Er…Mr McColl. Homosexuality is really not the issue at hand here. Bipolar 1 Disorder is.’

‘And are you sure homosexuality is not part of that?’ his father hinted.

‘Mr McColl. There are heterosexuals that have Bipolar 1 Disorder, and there are homosexuals that have Bipolar 1 Disorder. In any case, the delusions and manic episode he had actually centred on a vagina, not anything to do with thoughts about sexual intercourse with men.’

His father looked broodingly at Bruce. ‘Can you just add this clause to his discharge plan? He can only come home if his discharge plan has an anti-homosexual behaviour clause in it.’

‘Dad…I…I…’ Hamish felt the thought drop off, and looked up frustrated at Bruce. ‘I hate this,’ he said, his voice trembling. ‘I…I…hate it. I can’t finish a thought anymore. It just stops.’

‘And that is the wisdom of medication,’ Bruce said serenely. ‘And, Mr McColl, we do not have anti-gay clauses in our discharge plans.’

‘Surely you have medication for aberrations like homosexuality,’ his father demanded.

Bruce sighed heavily, rubbing his chin with his hand. ‘Mr McColl—’

‘Dad!’ Hamish interrupted. ‘You are obsessed with me being maybe gay,’ he said, ‘like some sort of OCD…OC…OC…*Fuck!* It’s happening again.’

‘Maybe that homosexual thing might drop off too, like those thoughts do…’ his father said with rancour, looking at Hamish, dislike flickering in his eyes.

‘Can…can you treat him?’ Hamish asked Bruce, pointing a shaking finger at his father. ‘Please?’

‘Er…his thoughts are contextual to his religion, Hamish,’ Bruce said, ‘and I can’t treat him unless he is a patient here, which he is not.’

'His thoughts may be contextual to his religion, but they are obsessive.'

His father's face tightened. 'What you call obsessive is just reinforcement!' his father said forcefully. 'So you learn to think Catholic, not pagan. *I* am the head of the family. You are expected to obey instruction.'

'Dad. You are no family Jesus!' Hamish exploded. 'You are the plague rat, suffering from the Catholic plague of self-righteousness. I am not a heretic or a homosexual who needs mental treatment, just because I no longer believe the things you do!' Hamish felt his thoughts slow and bit his lip, struggling to form his next sentence. His eyes flared with rage at not being able to think quickly and rapidly, like he usually did. 'How am I supposed to survive like this, Bruce?' he asked, his voice trembling.

'You survive because you co-operate with us. And it not hare win race, it tortoise,' Hotaru told him, her face lifted in triumph as he gripped the edges of his bed, his legs shaking, his mind warping in, like a sound slowly coming to a stop.

'I *hate* clichés,' Hamish barely managed to say, clapping his heads over his ears. '*Do* not speak to me of them.'

'It fable, Hamish,' Hotaru said, still smiling happily.

'I don't give a fuck what it's called,' Hamish yelled. 'Fables are just literary dictatorship; just another social format, setting out social dictates for you to…live…live by…live…and…what…and…*fuck!*' he swore, biting his lip, his eyes filling with tears.

'OK. OK,' Bruce said soothingly, holding both hands up.

'That's it,' Hamish mumbled, 'surrender to The Hamish, Bruce. All fucking psychiatrists should.'

'Time to go!' Johanna said, striding into the room. She clapped her hands loudly, 'Come on!'

'Er…let's all proceed to the conference room, quietly and calmly.' Bruce looked at Hamish, 'OK now, Hamish?'

'No. I'm not fucking OK. And why do I have to go first?' Hamish asked belligerently.

'The psychiatric team have proceeded first in the past, only to have the patient run the other way. So yes, you do have to go first.'

'I like to have all my threats in front of me, not behind me,' Hamish said broodingly, feeling like all the cells in his body were gathering together, causing a darkening, a brooding within him, much the same way a storm did, when about to crack. 'And…*fuck!*' Hamish yelled, rubbing his forehead, trying to get his thoughts working again.

'And that is an example of Hamish's paranoia,' Hotaru whispered loudly to Johanna.

Johanna nodded thoughtfully, her eyebrows drawing together as if she was a scientist studying specimen *Type A* paranoia. 'Yes. I see what you mean.'

'Hel-*lo*. I'm still here,' Hamish hissed at Johanna.

'We talk psych language in here, Hamish. It's not meant to exclude you,' Johanna said casually. 'Although I think it should. It's a language for us only.'

'Try human language,' Hamish said sarcastically, swinging his legs off the bed and standing up.

'Are you going to the conference in *that?*' Johanna asked, looking horrified at Hamish's striped navy-blue and white pajama pants, and his bottle-green sloppy-joe stained with milk.

'Yes,' Hamish said dismissively, deciding not to explain why. Anything he said seemed to be contextualised to ten different mental health conditions, so he decided on a new strategy of using basic words like 'yes' or 'no'. He calculated that 'yes' and 'no' were words accepted in society, as normal language, and no mental health condition could be found, brimming like bacteria, in those words.

He caught Johanna looking at his clothing again, her distaste obvious. 'It's not normal or appropriate to wear clothing like that at a formal conference, Hamish,' Johanna told him.

'Oh, who fucking cares, cat snapper,' Hamish sneered, forgetting his new one-word rule. He felt his mind flush with lithium, the next thought slowing to a stop. Hamish looked around at the expectant faces, his heart sinking. '*Fuck*,' he swore. 'I forgot what…forgot that…forgot which…' he trailed off, looking at them miserably.

'Your mind is forgetting how it used to think because of the lithium, Hamish,' Bruce said soothingly. 'It's altering your nerve impulses into slower thinking. Your mind can't retrieve the ideas and thoughts you used to have because your nerve impulses have changed in frequency. You have to learn how to think with an altered mental frequency.'

'Fuck that,' Hamish said belligerently. 'You want me to become Alzheimer and forget how I think.'

‘Who cares?’ Hotaru said contentedly. ‘You lose your memory. That is a good thing. You forget how to be mentally ill. It is not in your memory anymore.’

‘That’s the strangest fucking thing I’ve ever heard,’ Hamish said.

‘Now, Hamish,’ Bruce said, gesturing him towards the conference room, ‘things will make more sense to you when the medication becomes fully effective.’

Hamish stumbled down the hall, towards the conference room, where dunny-flushers Bruce, Johanna and Golu would decide whether to flush him down the social toilet or not.

‘Now,’ Bruce said amiably, ‘why we are here today, Hamish, is to discuss a Community Treatment Order for you.’

Hamish looked at him suspiciously. ‘Are you organising the whole community to look after me?’ he demanded. ‘Because fuck that.’

Bruce smiled patiently. ‘Firstly, that’s not what a Community Treatment Order is about. It’s about you receiving the medical support and the care you need to be able to live in the community, without being too restricted.’

‘What?’ Johanna asked, turning to Bruce, shocked. ‘You’re going to let him out to terrorise the community?’

‘So says the Mental Health Terrorist,’ Hamish sneered.

‘Now, Hamish, please listen,’ Bruce said. He gave Johanna a warning look, with a small shake of his head *no*. Her lips tightened, her cheeks mottling red as they did so often.

‘The second thing you need to know, Hamish,’ Bruce continued, ‘is you don’t have the right to refuse a Community Treatment Order. It’s a legal order on you, made after reports by your family, yourself and medical reports.’ He tapped his pen on his clipboard, looking at Hamish considerately. ‘Hamish, you need others to care for you and make decisions on your behalf because of the impact of Bipolar 1 Disorder on your decision-making capacity. You are not in control of your own mind; your mental illness is. And please keep in mind, it was your mental illness which caused damage to your own reputation, by…er…’ he checked his notes again, ‘making you strip all your clothes off and screaming vitriol at the ocean…which you described as…let me check your statement here…’ Bruce adjusted his glasses, checking his notes again. ‘I quote: *her big wide watery cunt, spread all over the land.*’ Bruce lowered his notes, looking at him with compassion. 'That's not you talking. It's your mental illness.'

'Were you dick-sticking the ocean, Hamish?' Johanna goaded.

'Er…you are reminded to keep your language professional, Johanna,' Bruce said austerely, looking up briefly at her, from the notes he was reading.

Johanna looked fixedly out the window, as if she hadn't heard or was ignoring him. Hamish heard Bruce's loud exhalation, as if he was trying to calm himself, and turned away from looking at the cat snapper, the ugly face of psychiatry. His mother, sitting next to him, patted Hamish's arm. She had been doing that since he was in nappies, when she wanted to calm him.

'Let's continue, shall we, Hamish, with our discussion about your Community Treatment Order,' Golu said.

'Discussion. Is that what you call it, is it?' Hamish asked sarcastically. 'You've just told me I have no choice in it, as it a legal order.'

'What would you like to call this, Hamish,' Golu asked, 'considering your argument then?'

'Vengeance of psychiatrists on the non-conformist population,' Hamish pronounced, tossing his dark brown dreadlocks over his shoulders.

'Hamish. This is not about psychiatrists taking revenge on you. This is about you having bipolar disorder,' Bruce explained carefully and quietly.

'*How* has this happened?' his father asked despairingly, clutching at his shirt as if in grief. Much to Hamish's horror, his father stood up, looking up at the ceiling, tears running down his face, ripping at his shirt. 'I raise him in the Catholic faith and he turns out like this! Behold, my face of grief, Oh Lord!'

'Dad,' Hamish said exasperated, 'you're not Jewish. There is no need to tear your shirt like that.'

'You are like Joseph to me now, in the book of Genesis. You are the dead Catholic son, now the strange pagan,' his father wailed, ripping his shirt even more.

'Dad. Stop ripping your shirt! You're not Jewish!' Hamish said galled.

'Catholics come from the Hebrews,' his father said mournfully. 'So, I do the Kriah on you, and mourn you the ancient Jewish way, in the Catholic time of now. I have lost my Joseph,' he said in anguish, tearing at his shirt again. 'I have lost my Joseph!'

'I never had that many colours, Dad. To qualify as your Catholic-Jewish Joseph.'

'That's one of the saddest things I ever heard,' Bruce said, looking at Hamish, deeply moved.

'And I am the saddest parent in the world,' his father said, lifting his face to the ceiling again.

'What exactly is a Kriah?' Golu asked, leaning forward, looking puzzled from Hamish to his father.

'Kriah is a word from the Hebrew language, meaning "tearing". The tearing of clothing is a Jewish custom, which symbolises the loss of a dear one,' Bruce explained to Golu.

'I didn't know you were so familiar with religious customs, Bruce,' Golu said interestedly.

'I'm not,' Bruce said, looking up briefly, from writing his notes, 'but I have had some Jewish patients and families pass through here.'

'Probably being pack-hunted by Nazis,' Hamish said sarcastically.

'Now, Hamish,' Bruce said warningly, 'that's your paranoia talking…'

'It's well-known that Nazis hate Jews,' Hamish said. 'That's just fact, not paranoia. They hated them so much, they sacrificed them to their Nazi Gods in concentration camps, making them suffer and suffer, until dark power was produced and—'

Bruce held up his hand. 'Enough,' he said quietly.

'Where does he get such thinking from?' his father yelled. 'His sick, strange leprechaun is talking through his mouth again. I tell you, you must medicate him more, to shut it up.'

'Mr McColl—' Bruce began.

'Dad! It was in one of your books up the back of your bookshelf. Those concentration camps in Europe for Jews were arranged in a pentagram shape and the Nazis were making Jews suffer in them until they produced enough dark power to power up that pentagram. It kind of contradicts Father Matthias's hammer argument, which argues we must all suffer to produce a great soul.'

'Hamish,' Bruce said, his voice, even quieter, 'enough.'

'Suffer ye the little children, so dark power is produced for satanic wankers out there,' Hamish said argumentatively.

'My God, my God, help me,' his father wailed, looking up at the ceiling with tear-filled eyes. 'My books. They say no such thing.'

'As I have already explained to the mental health gestapo here, I can see the truth,' Hamish explained. 'I see it in books, I see it in people, and I see I am here today, because of it.'

'Now, Hamish,' Bruce said, 'we have already been through this. Firstly, you are in here for taking off your clothes and screaming delusions at an ocean you thought was a vagina. Secondly, your claim to be able to see the truth is simply you hallucinating different words and titles than what's actually there on or in the book.'

'See? He has Pan disease,' his father moaned, clutching at himself and rocking back and forth on his heels.

'What?' Bruce asked.

'The pagan sight,' his father answered. 'He sees like a pagan.'

'Mr McColl,' Bruce said firmly, 'what Hamish sees is the result of his bipolar condition. Nothing more, nothing less.'

'You are a mental health heretic,' his father said firmly. 'You do not understand these things.'

'Er…let's return to what our purpose here today is. Mr McColl,' Bruce said, 'would you sit down, please.'

Hamish's mother tugged hesitantly at Hamish's father's shirt sleeve. 'Please…Wallace…sit down…'

Hamish's father shook off his mother's hand, looking resentfully at her.

'Please. Mr McColl,' Bruce said firmly, 'hear us out. We want your son's future to be as normal as possible, just like you do.'

His father turned towards Bruce. 'You have a tablet, that can return him Catholic?'

'Er…no, Mr McColl,' Bruce said mildly. 'However, we can work on some goals, that will contribute to Hamish having the opportunity to be a valued, functioning member of the community. And, I think your Catholic faith values that same principle.'

His father sat slowly down, gripping the arms of the chair.

'Just make him normal, Dr Beyer. Pull that diseased leprechaun out of him. So I don't have to hide my face from my good friends in the Catholic community.'

Bruce looked at him considerately. 'It's possible some of Hamish's antagonism towards your family, is because, er…let's see, how can I best phrase this…Rebellion can happen when there is a contradiction or discrepancy in ourselves, created when new beliefs form. This can cause an insurgence in self, making the person hostile toward the belief system they held in the past.'

'Self-mutiny, he is talking about,' Golu explained to Hamish's father. 'You revolt against who you were in the past.'

'His rebellion is so long, Dr Gupta, he has been defying us since he was two,' his father said, pounding his fist on the armchair. 'He'd throw his nappies off in the back yard and run around naked. And I've asked every Catholic priest in the district: did my wife lie with the Devil one night to bring this Son of Pan into our family?'

'Wallace,' his mother said, her voice trembling, 'I am a good Catholic woman. I would never, never, be a consort of the Devil.'

'Er...listen, Mr and Mrs McColl. It's clear that aside from the Bipolar Disorder, your son is also working through some things that...well...could take some time to—'

'How old do you have to be,' his father interrupted angrily, 'to know what is conscionable and what is not? I teach him the seven sins and the seven virtues as a child, and here he is, trying all the sins out. I ask you. What do I do?'

'It's not what *you* do, per se, it's what *he* does,' Bruce said, looking at Hamish.

'A reminder from Hamish, that Hamish is still here,' Hamish said, looking up at the ceiling, refusing to look at the mentally contorted shrinks because of their casual disregard of his personage. 'So, please, stop referring to me in the third person, as if I am *not* here.'

'What I'm saying to your father *is*,' Bruce said emphatically, 'is that it is what *you* do which will make the difference in your state of mind, and how *you* behave, not what your father does.'

'I already teach the sour little leprechaun the right state of mind,' his father said insistently, 'but he thinks he knows best. This is why he talks about strange things, and inviting the ocean in with his penis, instead of a nice Catholic girl. I tell you Mr Beyer—'

'Dr Beyer,' his mother gently reminded him, touching him on the arm.

His father shook her hand off. 'Don't contradict me, Josephine. Corrections are for me to do, not the woman. Remember your place.'

His mother hung her head, twisting her fingers together. His father looked determinedly at Bruce. 'Dr Beyer, I tell you. Hamish. He goes outside Catholic boundaries, and he finds himself spiritually dead. I mean, look at him,' he said, gesturing at Hamish in disgust. 'With his pagan hair and unwashed devil's body. What am I supposed to do with him? I have a son of Pan now, not a son of God.'

'Er…that's not perhaps the way to make a difference in Hamish's state of mind,' Bruce said, 'through comparing him with personas not approved by Catholic society.'

'The way to a good, sound mind is good, sound Catholic theology,' his father argued.

'Er…Mr McColl,' Bruce said considerately, adjusting his glasses, 'your opinion will always be challenged by that somewhat keen, but unstable, intelligence in your son.'

Hamish cheeks flamed red. 'It's not just a keen intelligence. I have a 159 IQ,' he said hotly.

Bruce looked at him doubtfully. 'Now, Hamish, how do you know that? I would have put you at around 130 maybe, but 159 is climbing up near Einstein. And even with all that high intelligence, your mental illness is destabilising it. You can't focus your high intelligence properly, because your thoughts are so rapid and delusional in content. This is what possibly led to you failing your Higher School Certificate.'

Hamish looked at him confidently, flipping his dreadlocks back over his shoulders. 'I *know* my own IQ, Bruce, because I had myself tested. *After* I failed the Higher School Certificate. So I could challenge the Board of Education. So I could…I could…*fuck!* It's happening again! Turtle thought…*fuck!*'

'I think secret homosexual longings were disturbing his concentration and that's why he failed his Higher School Certificate,' his father said darkly.

Bruce looked decidedly away from him. 'And…er…what was the result of the Higher School Certificate challenge?' he asked Hamish interestedly.

Hamish looked broodingly at Bruce. 'The Board of Education would not accept my argument.'

'Which was?' Bruce prompted.

'My argument was that the HSC markers who marked my papers had lower intelligence than mine. Therefore, they were marking my answers at their own intelligence level and not at the superior 159 IQ level of myself. I mean, I would rate their thinking level at 50 to 60 IQ points maybe; based on the responses I got from them. Some of them bordered on moronic.'

'Hamish,' Johanna said, her nasal voice pricking at his senses, irritating him. He ground his teeth together, trying to stop the riptide she was causing in his mind.

'Hamish,' Johanna said again, her voice twanging in his head like an out of tune guitar note. 'It is highly doubtful that the HSC markers had learning difficulties. I really don't think they would have had *three* HSC markers, all with learning difficulties, marking your Year 12 papers.'

'Unless you shot them first, Hamish, giving them a head injury, which caused difficulties,' Golu said. 'And I might have felt like shooting them too, had I failed my HSC.'

Hamish did not smile at his joke. He did not want the mental health gestapo to think they were on his level, joking and talking with him like they were in his IQ range. He tossed his dreadlocks back over his shoulders again, lifting his chin. 'Don't try that sympathy: *I'm on your side,* sort of stuff. I know all about it. I have read novels and books with such techniques listed.'

Golu smiled generously at him. 'What I meant for you to know, Hamish, was gunshot wounds to the left side of the head can cause mental impairment. I thought you may find that of interest.'

'It's very clear that the left sides of their brains were collapsed already,' Hamish said sarcastically.

'I don't think that's possible, Hamish,' Bruce said.

'*Fuck!*' Hamish said, lifting his eyes to the ceiling and staring at it, 'you are the mental health condition of literal, Bruce.'

'Now, Hamish,' Bruce said seriously, 'no such mental health condition is listed in the *Diagnostic and Statistical Manual of Mental Disorders*.'

Hamish shook his head, still staring at the ceiling.

'Let me clarify this, Hamish,' Golu said, his voice bemused. 'You think you were marked unfairly because the HSC markers had lesser intelligence than you; and because of that, did not recognise the insight and brilliance of your responses.'

'Exactly,' Hamish exclaimed, 'exactly!'

'And what happened after that?' Bruce asked cautiously.

'I...well...' Hamish looked away from him.

'Well…' Bruce prompted, leaning forward and looking at him intently.

'Hamish didn't get into university despite his appeal,' his mother said quietly. 'He was *very* upset about it.' She turned to him, giving his hand a gentle squeeze, 'Weren't you, Hamish?'

Hamish looked down at his hand resting limply in his mother's soft hand, feeling some strange sense of childhood comfort there. His mind struggled against that childhood relief. That limp acceptance of what he had been raised in, not knowing he should challenge his religious indoctrination; learning it as he had learnt the alphabet: a way to read the world.

There had been nothing in his childhood or teenage years to provide any shade from that hot sun of religion. No other view allowed to make mutiny in his mind—it was full of stern virgins, parables which snapped over his thoughts like oyster shells, and the face of Judas appearing in the many faces of people in his life. Thinking in Church archetypes made his mind hot and fixed as the sun. He thanked his own obsession with things that fly—butterflies, dragonflies, birds, bats—for lifting his mind out of stone.

And now here he was, surrounded by a mental health Stonehenge. Circled by more stone.

Nothing flew in here. Not even a fly struggled through the room.

'And what was it you hoped to study at university, Hamish?' Bruce asked, his voice becoming more gentle.

Hamish bowed his head. 'Teaching.'

A laugh escaped Johanna's mouth. Bruce looked up at her warningly.

Hamish's hand slipped out of his mother's, and he looked darkly at Johanna. 'Do you treat the dreams and hopes of all your patients with such disrespect? I mean, you just sat there and laughed at me when I let it out about my sadly passed-away dream.'

'I just can't see you as a teacher, Hamish,' Johanna said, laughter shaking her voice. 'You'd disagree with every page of the educational curriculum. It would hit the wall within five minutes.'

'Watch *Dead Poets Society*, cat snapper,' Hamish snapped. He sat back, irritation crossing his face, as he felt his mind slow again. He searched slowly around in his head for more words. It was like fumbling around in the dark, suddenly unfamiliar with the room you'd always lived in.

He looked at Bruce, trying not to cry.

Bruce encouraged him sympathetically, 'Go on.'

Hamish slowly put one word in front of the other: '*Dead Poets Society* is about an anti-curriculum teacher who stood on his desk and gave his students wings, not anchors,' he said unevenly. 'Taught them to think outside The Establishment, outside The Accepted, outside The Wingless.' He leant forward, linking his hands together and resting his head on them. 'There is, now and then, a greater spirit present in humanity.'

'Yes. And they usually get lynched,' Golu said.

'Some of them live,' Hamish said, 'but always in struggle.' He paused for a second. 'You know what some of the greatest leaders in the world have in common?'

'What?'

'Gandhi,' Hamish answered.

'I don't understand,' Bruce said. 'How is Gandhi common to these great leaders?'

'They all followed Gandhi principles. Nelson Mandela, the great leader of the South African people; John Lennon, Beatles revolutionary; Albert Einstein; Al Gore; Steve Jobs; the Dalai Lama...They all caught the Gandhi elevator up and landed on the top floor.'

'Interesting,' Bruce said. 'I didn't know that.'

'You don't know that because your principles come from that,' Hamish said, pointing at the psychiatry textbook then tapping his forehead, 'and that. And not...not...' He struggled for words again. 'Here,' he said, pointing at his heart, 'where the great spirit lives.'

'Our jurisdiction is not spiritual leadership, Hamish; it's psychiatric care,' Bruce explained patiently.

'Whatever,' Hamish said, bored, looking up at the ceiling.

Bruce looked up. 'Is there something...you're seeing up there...Hamish?'

'Just another barrier to the open sky,' Hamish said morosely.

'Hamish,' Johanna said, her voice twanging in his ear. He leant forward, putting his forehead in his hands; hating the sound of her voice. 'You should really start thinking of things in functional terms. A ceiling is what protects us from rain, hailstones and storms. I mean, it's not meant to be perceived as a barrier to the open sky.'

Hamish looked at her in disbelief.

Johanna folded her arms, her expression smug. 'And I have seen *Dead Poets Society*, Hamish. And, what I noticed about it was that the stand-on-the-desk teacher also had a very promising student, who decided to do some desk standing and went on to commit suicide. What do you have to say to that, Hamish?' she asked belligerently.

Hamish looked long and broodingly at her. 'You didn't watch it very well, did you? Some people, once their eyes open to the truth around them, don't *want* to live anymore.'

'And are you one of those people, Hamish? Do you want to kill yourself?' she asked with clinical interest.

'Every time I look at you, I do,' he answered sarcastically.

Johanna's cheeks mottled their habitual red. 'I'll get a code 4 on his bipolar disorder coding, Bruce, if he continues to speak like that to me.'

'A what?' his mother asked anxiously. 'Is that dangerous?'

'Bipolar disorder has a diagnostic code of 296. Specifiers get added to that code depending on what state the person is in. Code 4 means…' Bruce flipped the page of his manual, 'severe with psychotic features,' he read out and closed the manual, placing it on the table.

'It's for dangerous people,' Johanna said, her cheeks heating. 'Like Hamish,' she said, her breaths shallow, as if trying to calm herself down. 'Mr and Mrs McColl, your son is out of control.'

'And *that* is what happens when you leave the Church,' Hamish's father said, gratified.

'The Church was no mental safety belt, Dad,' Hamish said sarcastically. 'It was more like a mental penitentiary. One thought out of line and it got Joan of Arced. Set on fire by some priest lavish with God's intelligence.'

'Right, right,' Bruce said absently, finishing his notes. He adjusted his glasses and looked up at Hamish. 'Hamish. You have a…somewhat…interesting way of putting things.'

'Delusional, more like it,' Johanna said sarcastically and turned to Bruce. 'Are his lithium levels high enough? He was slowing down, but now he seems to be speeding up again.'

Hamish glared at her. 'Can you get that bitch out of here?' he demanded of Bruce.

Bruce held his hand up, giving Johanna a warning look before she could respond.

'I don't think cat snapper's strange personality is going to yowl to a halt at your psychiatric hand signal,' Hamish said sarcastically.

'Er...Johanna. It may be best if you...er...leave the room,' Bruce suggested delicately.

'Yes. Lessen the mental pollution, by all means,' Hamish said.

'Hamish,' his mother said tenderly.

'*What?*' he said aggressively. 'She's pissing me off.'

'Love your enemies,' his mother reminded him gently, touching his arm.

'They're not the Mills and Boon type in here, Mum,' Hamish said sarcastically.

'That's *not* what I meant, Hamish,' his mother said earnestly. 'You must love your enemies, no matter how much they hurt you.'

'Shall I still love them from my grave, then?' Hamish asked her.

'Oh, *Hamish*,' his mother said, tears filling her eyes.

'Try *not* to think of us as the...er...enemy, Mrs McColl,' Bruce told her, 'we are here trying to help your son.'

His mother looked at Bruce hesitantly. 'He seems...to be seeing you...as...well...'

'Evil vultures,' Hamish said darkly, 'staring at their mentally convulsing prey.'

His mother bowed her head. 'Hamish, sometimes, puts things a little...well...differently...' she said, her voice low and meek. 'Try not to take offence,' her voice lowered even further, 'it's just his way of talking.'

'His way of talking is delusional,' Johanna said, standing up, looking forcibly at his mother. After a minute, she turned and said to Bruce, her face tight and angry, 'I'm telling you; those lithium levels *aren't* high enough. He's talking too fast and too strange.'

'Fuck off, cat snapper. You are Hamish diagnostic code: x-files,' Hamish bit out.

Johanna glared furiously at him and slammed the door behind her. He caught a glimpse of a red, bloody knife in her back.

Just as he suspected, he thought, nodding to himself.

A backstabber.

Another face of Judas.

Hamish realised his thoughts were sinking into church arches and Bibles again, so he turned his mind away from Judas backstabbers. 'Perhaps, you should put personality criteria in your employment interviews,' Hamish said irritably to Bruce. 'Cat snapper is the worst person–environment fit I've *ever* seen. She must drive patients mental with that herpes-sore personality and if you *don't* do something about her, your patients will become infected by her.'

'Herpes-sore personality…infected…' Bruce mused, '…no, no. It's just a…well…personality clash.'

'Perhaps, you should do some qualitative research on this, Bruce,' Hamish said, linking his hands on top of his head and staring at the ceiling. 'Because you will find many patients feel like she's the banging saucepan in their heads.'

'Right, right,' Bruce said thoughtfully, giving him a concerned look. 'Let's get back to the Community Treatment Order, shall we?'

'Yes,' Golu said, relief crossing his face. 'Let's.'

'Now. Hamish,' Bruce said firmly.

'What?' he asked belligerently.

Bruce smiled patiently. 'I would like to work in with your high intelligence, Hamish, to get some positive outcomes in your life.'

'How to feel like an equal in society,' Hamish said sarcastically. 'Let someone of higher social status plan your life and tick and cross the boxes.'

'Hamish,' Golu said thoughtfully, 'try to think of it this way. It's exactly the same as if you have broken your back and you need a rehabilitation team. Except, this is your broken mind we are talking about. And it is your mind which operates everything. So, it is important you get your mind back up and running.'

'You better stop people like Johanna being on those rehabilitation teams,' Hamish said, giving the door she had exited through a disgusted look. 'Every bone in my mind will be broken.'

Bruce tried not to smile. 'Er…yes, let's get on with this.'

'Yes, let's…' Golu said, linking his fingers together and waiting patiently for Bruce to continue.

Bruce clicked the end of his pen, making Hamish flinch, and neatly turned the page over on his clipboard; flicking more decibels in Hamish's ear, scraping at his mind, irritating him.

'Now. Hamish,' Bruce continued, 'you mentioned you wanted to be a teacher. Why don't we work towards that?' He leant forward, putting his hands together in a steeple under his chin. 'See, one of the problems here I see with you, *aside* from your bipolar disorder, is you have too much time on your hands just to wander around, play guitars and do what you want to do. Those wandering traits may be part of your persona, but it has also affected the patterning in your mind. Your mind has established itself in these wandering patterns and because of that, you also have wandering thoughts, not focused thoughts. So, what we need to do, Hamish, is some cognitive behaviour therapy with you, so you can learn to think and act differently. And you need to do that before you do any course, or you will set yourself up for failure, with your mind and body wandering off like that.'

Golu held up his hand. 'I think we also need to include a disability liaison officer at the university to work in with him. You will be setting him up for more failure otherwise, because he needs assistance with more than just focus. He's been in...ah,' he glanced discreetly over at Hamish's parents, "disadvantaged circumstances".' Golu leant back in his chair, folding his arms, nodding to himself. 'You don't throw a patient in the water without teaching him skills in how to swim.' He nodded at Hamish. 'We are going to teach you mental swimming, huh? Then you won't drown in all that academia. And panic at the water level being too high for you.'

'I kind of like you,' Hamish mused. 'Even if you do have the diseased occupation of psychiatrist.'

'A disease?' Golu asked, giving Hamish a bemused look, 'In what way?'

'In the tumour way. Psychiatry can give people spirit cancer.'

'Cancer? That's a bit strong,' Bruce said indignantly.

'*No,* it's not,' Hamish retorted. 'No, it's *not.* This medication is like a cannibal eating my spirit. You and your team are putting coffins in the minds that could solve global warming or civil wars. Minds like mine think outside your recommended social thinking design. We are in the sadly declining 15 percent of the innovative population who do not obey conformist commandments which 85 percent of the population follow: *Thou shalt agree on one version of events only.* You keep seeing patients because you can't solve the mental illness issue. You can't solve it, because you keep putting on medication the people that could solve it.' He leant back in his chair, flinging his dreadlocks back over his shoulders. 'Your patients keep coming back because you're not solving the problem with your so-called acceptable thinking. You're adding to it.'

'Er...Hamish,' Bruce said. 'Although that's a very interesting theory, I don't think you can argue that; a lot of our patients go on to live very productive lives.'

'I will argue anything that stops you from killing my native ways and native thinking,' Hamish said belligerently.

'I see,' Bruce said, leaning back and crossing his arms. 'You think you are losing your native ways and fear becoming…well…'

'Colonised with invader thinking,' Hamish said.

'Er…' Bruce said, lost.

'I think, those ways you call native,' Golu said thoughtfully, 'were the result of a brain dysfunction in the *first* place, Hamish. So, you see, those ways are not native to you at all. Those native ways are a *product* of the dysfunction in your brain. We need to change that. So you can have all the social and personal opportunities that are out there for you to access. Your *own* mind is damaging that. Not anyone else, Hamish. It's your *own* mind. There is a saying about it, which goes something like, "Your mind…it can be your worst enemy or your best friend."' He leant forward, looking at Hamish intently. 'The question I have for you, Hamish, is…are you going to shoot at your mind, or hold hands with it?'

12

'There will be no elimination of the Hamish,' Hamish said warningly to Hotaru, as she stabbed his bottom cheek with a needle. 'Oh no, there won't.'

'Now, Hamish, I think you are being dramatic about this,' Bruce said, standing in the doorway of his ward room.

'Would you mind not watching me in my playboy patient pose?' Hamish demanded.

'Now, Hamish. You are being very dramatic today,' Bruce said warningly.

'If you said anything about playboy patient pose, Bruce, it would be reasonable. If I say it, I'm guilty of Dramatic Shakespearean Disorder,' Hamish said.

'I don't think we have pills for that Mr McColl,' Golu said, walking into the room.

'Fuck! What is this? You've come to watch as well?'

'We are just doing a final supervision before you leave, Mr McColl.' He looked at Bruce. 'I think his lithium levels need increasing more. He's still very spirited.'

'Would you *not* call me Mr McColl? That is some tie-knotted version of me I'm just not ready for.'

'Perhaps, it may be an idea to learn to be like that, Hamish,' Bruce said. 'Tie-knotted, as you have termed it. You would not struggle so much with yourself, and other people, if you operated within conformity. It's a social measure, you understand, to keep people safe.'

'Conformity is *not* a social measure, Bruce. It's a form of strangulation. And look what happened with your Nazi bastard, Herr Hitler.' He pulled his pants up hurriedly, as Hotaru pulled the needle out of his bottom. 'Adolf Hitler was the biggest dictator of conformity ever to exist. And his Nazi soldiers all had the mental disease called conformity. Did the genocide on the Jews, without questioning it or thinking about it? In fact, they stated they were just obeying orders. Bruce. You think I'm some sort of a social amputee, right? Because I don't go around just conforming, submitting, and obeying; because it's a dangerous thing to do. I, too, could end up a dangerous conformist, ordering genocide on vigilantes because their thinking takes the form of a question mark, and not a Church. Or the political commandment, that sailed over on the first fleet: *Thou shalt learn to be a model citizen.* You just remember, Bruce. Conformity is how dictators…or cuntators…rise to power. No one questions them because they are taught *not* to question authority.'

'Now, Hamish, being a model citizen is not a bad thing,' Bruce said comfortingly. He turned to Golu, lifting his hand up several times, glancing at the needle, indicating more lithium was needed.

Hamish, seeing this, glared at Bruce. 'Conformity. It's a mole system, Bruce.'

'A what?' Bruce asked, bewildered.

'A mole system. For people who have blind beliefs, Bruce. Those people who stumble around in that darkness, blowing out their own lanterns.'

'Yes. Well. Society without its "mole system" is *how* we got the free love generation and the VD that went with that attitude.'

'Are you implying freedom…leads to VD?' Golu asked, looking at Bruce doubtfully. 'I don't think that's good wording.'

'It's an example of what can happen to a free society without rules,' Bruce explained.

'I have to wear a social condom; is that it?' Hamish asked angrily.

'OK, OK. We need to talk further with you about your discharge plan, Hamish,' Golu said.

'Is it called "Get Me the Fuck Out of Here Now?"' Hamish answered.

'No. No. I'm afraid not,' Bruce said. 'Definitely not.'

'What? I'm stuck here?' Hamish yelled.

Bruce looked at him, alarmed. 'We need to get that lithium level right for you, before discharge. So, you have functional mental capacity out there.'

'I've never had a Ferris wheel for a mind, mechanistically going round and round in the same place,' Hamish said. 'I talk and act from my spirit.'

'Yes. That's why you are here. You don't think before you speak. You talk from some delusion you call "my spirit",' Johanna said patronisingly, appearing in the doorway.

‘Another one here for mental health porn,’ Hamish said, tucking in his shirt and glaring at her. ‘You’ve missed the bare arse show. And the way you say things, Johanna, makes you a *really*, *really* bad psychiatrist.’

Johanna glared at him. ‘That’s not for you to judge.’

‘You judged me,’ Hamish retorted.

‘From my skills in clinical analysis,’ she answered, ‘not from a mental illness.’

‘You are a G-string, bitch,’ he snapped.

‘A what?’ she said, looking at him like he was one year old.

‘You’re thinking line is up your arse,’ Hamish told her firmly.

‘Hamish—’ Johanna began, her voice shaking with anger. ‘I—’

‘Uh…I think we better call a close on this…’ Bruce said hastily, gently touching Johanna on the back and lightly pushing her out the door.

13

Post-discharge from Black Crag Mental Hospital.

Sydney, NSW, Australia

September 2007

Hamish wandered around Circular Quay, wondering what to do next. The ferries, tied up at the docks, creaked loudly from side to side. People pushed past him, blurs of skin and colour. Their mixed scents of sweet, sharp perfume and spicy aftershave stung the air around him.

Conversations slapped loudly at his ears, as the crowd pushed past him. Transience. It was all around him. People, pets, boats, clouds, quickly passed him by. Nothing stayed with him. Nothing wanted to.

Strangely, Hamish wanted to reach for the solidness, the lasting texture of things. Not songs which lasted five minutes, or thoughts that went through his head like comets. Or people that slunk off after five minutes of conversation; sometimes five seconds.

A flier flapped on a pole nearby, and he stopped to look at it, newly attracted to plain, thick lettering and precise presentation. It appealed to a new mental lens of exactitude opening like a small round ship window in his head, giving his thoughts a new method of travel instead of mania or depression.

Hamish walked over to the flier and picked up the bottom edge, holding it still. *Old Politics, New Society*, it read. He found his mind examining the phrase before he could stop it; noting thematic contrast, oppositional phrasing, his thoughts sparked with excitement and rapidly climbed. Clawing out information from his memory, faster than a dog digging dirt with its hind legs. Hamish felt the lithium slow his mind again, clearing spaces to actually think his thought. He waited until his mind felt calm and looked at the sign again.

Old Politics, he ruminated. He took to mean the past governance system of top level down to ground level. *The Submit and Obey system...submit...submit and...* his thoughts petered to a stop. His mind searched slowly for the next phrase of the flier. After a minute, he recalled it: *New Society.* He supposed that meant changing old politics through social activism. So, a new society came about.

It was still old politics, old society to him. Just shifted to the next generation.

Hamish tried to stop his mind pitching angles, as he had a long habit of changing the straight line of a statement by mentally bending it to another meaning. Whether it was true or not didn't matter. He just liked thinking about the one thing from many different angles, putting together a mental mural he could hang in his mind.

His eyes strayed towards a man painting at his easel. The ferries in the painting appeared as blurs, had lost their exactness and the lines which contained their definition. The lines of the ferry defined it as a ferry, yet as a blur, were an interpretation, a shapelessness, which left literals floundering and non-literals quietly confident.

Name it as it was. Lose the blur.

It was going to be very hard.

Hamish looked grimly at the floor in the office of his GP, Dr Frances Jodhur, trying to stop his past-thought that his GP looked like a walrus with his drooping grey moustache, and squinting brown eyes. His short, fat body was tightly held in a white shirt straining at the belly, with navy blue trousers buckled over his swelling stomach. 'You are doing the right thing, Mr McColl,' his GP said to him, his signature emerging under the firm strokes of his pen. He handed him the prescription. 'Bipolar disorder is hard to live with, one in 50 people have it. You may as well take what help you can, without being proud about it. Medication will help keep you level and cautious, and not like a racehorse.'

His GP flipped the pages of his file, pausing to read something. He looked up at him, concerned. 'You really don't want to be standing naked on the edge of a cliff, screaming at the ocean about your sexual torment. Those sorts of thoughts are outside normal cognitive functioning. See, the problem you are having at the moment is those sorts of dysfunctional thoughts are mixed in with highly intelligent thoughts and you are going between a state of reason and a state of delusion. My concern is that reason and delusion will eventually become the same thing for you. So, stay on your medication, Mr McColl.' He paused to give Hamish a sympathetic look, then continued, 'You are very wise to want to think about things concretely. It eliminates the possibility of abnormal thinking.'

'Well, that's what I want to do. Concretely think. So, I can just be like other people, and have the things other people have. And not scare women away.'

'You scared a woman away?'

'She heard some things. Wouldn't say what.'

'Things outside normality scare people, Mr McColl. So, you are very wise to want to be normal; otherwise, you may end up friendless and alone and without the social privileges the rest of us enjoy.'

Hamish looked at his GP wistfully. 'I've had too many years of being the social scarecrow. And I'm unemployed, living in a hostel, busking on the streets, without family or a lover to hold. The people I meet, never last long. They just pass through my life. The only permanency, the only thing that is always there, is my fucked-up head. And I want to change it. I figure, if I change my fucked-up head, life will change. Because I'm not acting from fucked-up thoughts and screwing up all the time.'

'Don't write yourself completely off, Mr McColl. You do have a very high IQ. You just have to focus it. Without medication, you may be able to give a highly critical and intelligent analysis of a subject but you can also process visual or auditory input in a delusional way. So, you are getting abnormal thoughts, and impressions and perceptions of things. It's not your fault,' his GP said, looking in a kindly, fatherly way at him. 'It's a biological fault which can be addressed with the right medication, and some therapy.'

'I *want t*o think normally,' Hamish said, finding it hard to talk about, since he had always abhorred the concept of normality. 'I *don't* want this anymore.'

'If you learn to think normally, your behaviour will follow,' his GP said, giving him a pat on the knee and tearing a prescription off the pad. 'You will think a perfectly normal thought, like, I have to set my alarm at 5 am. And a person watching you do it would think nothing of it. It would register as normal action. However, a person watching you stripping off naked and abusing the ocean, would register this as an abnormal action. And it's an abnormal action because it comes from an abnormal thought, that the ocean is a penis-teasing female.'

'I...don't want to really talk about that,' Hamish said hastily. 'It was something I was interviewed about for weeks by mental hospital staff members. Over and over again. *And why do you believe the Pacific Ocean is a cock teaser?* I mean, fuck. I don't have logical explanations. It was just an impression.'

'Yes, well. Impressions are part of perceptions, not facts. You have to address these perceptions you have on a psychological *and* biological level. Find and resolve the psychological part first. Why you feel the ocean is a cock-teasing female. And, the second part is changing your reaction or behaviour with some biological remedy, like medication and some cognitive behaviour therapy, where you consciously change the way you think about things,' his GP told him, adjusting his glasses and peering at him.

Hamish looked away. 'I have always thought in impressions,' he managed to say, 'not actuality. Normalising myself is going to be very hard.'

His GP gave him another pat on the knee.

'Mental hospital is harder,' he said.

14

Black Crag University. Sydney, NSW, Australia September 2008

Hamish sat at the front of the lecture theatre, twiddling his pen on his paper. His mind struggled with what his lecturer, Warren Brown, said; his head felt as heavy as lead. *The medication is turning me into a mental corpse*, he thought, irritated. His mind no longer surged and sparked on hearing certain words, no longer found an implication in something.

His biggest fear had happened.

There was nothing interesting in his mind.

He was boring.

There was only cold fog on his mental landscape. No High Distinction material. *You just have to pass,* one of the Community Mental Health Outreach Team had told him earnestly, *you just have to pass.*

Passing wasn't good enough for him. He knew he was capable of much more; but his mind couldn't reach his intelligence level in the slow and fumbling state medication had left it in.

It's humiliating, he thought miserably, missing the quick comets of his thoughts. *At least people, objects and the environment around me are now normal, and not ballooning out at me or integrating with my mind the way they used to. Or showing otherworld things crawling around the place.*

Nothing moved in paintings anymore to show him the truth.

No secret words in books appeared to let him know the real story.

No secret aspect of people, like Hotaru's fat tarantula self, moved out of their secret spaces when he looked at them.

People were just people.

Trees were just trees.

Paintings were just paintings.

The truth he used to see, had gone.

'Hamish,' his classmate Rebecca whispered to him, pulling a couple of times at his shirt.

'What?' he asked absently, trying to find a solid point in his mind he could fix his thinking on, as opposed to no point.

'Deanna's at it again,' she mouthed near his ear, pointing at the front of the classroom.

Hamish looked at the front of the classroom, where Deanna was wheeling herself in her wheelchair, towards his lecturer. She smoothed her long-dark bob, cut just above the collarbone, and stared seriously at the lecturer, her glasses glinting in the light. She wore a diagonally zebra-striped jumper and blue jeans; they hung loose over her thin, wasted body slumped in the wheelchair.

'You're wrong,' Deanna said insistently, her brown eyes staring unblinkingly at the lecturer. 'You're *wrong.*'

'You've come all the way up to the front to tell me that?' the lecturer asked coolly.

'I'm not in school, where I have to put my hand up to speak,' Deanna said sarcastically.

'True,' the lecturer said, his voice detached, 'you don't. And getting yourself noticed in front of a whole lot of people, isn't always a bad thing.'

'That wasn't the point,' she said. 'This is.' She angrily waved a piece of paper. 'How could you even *list* this as recommended reading?'

Hamish could see himself in her; who he used to be, anyway. Questioning, belligerent, demanding to know the answers.

'Is there something wrong with the argument in that paper?' the lecturer asked dispassionately, glancing at the title of the article and its authors.

'That you even have to *ask* if there is something *wrong* with the argument, is somewhat shocking to me,' she said.

'What…was your name?' the lecturer asked.

'Deanna Scott. Why don't you know that?'

'Deanna…' the lecturer said, trailing off.

'Deanna,' she repeated.

'Deanna…'

‘How many times do we have to say my name?’ she said belligerently. ‘I was very clear about it, the first time you asked.’

The lecturer smiled thinly. ‘Deanna. What’s the problem?’

‘The problem *is* the cultural acceptance of Aboriginal people as some sort of plague on this country. I mean,’ she checked her paper again, ‘this paragraph says here, that Aboriginals were categorised as animals under the “Flora & Fauna Act” until the 1960s.’

The lecturer sighed wearily. ‘That paragraph is a reference to a particular myth going around in the 1970s. It was never proved as fact.’

‘So, Aborigines…’

‘The correct term is Indigenous Australians,’ the lecturer said coolly.

‘Same thing…’ Deanna said.

‘It’s not actually,’ the lecturer contradicted her, folding his arms and staring coldly at her.

‘Look. The point is *Aborigines*,’ she said forcefully, ‘are not having their *human rights* recognised because they are thought of as animals and not *humans.’*

‘Exactly,’ the lecturer said dismissively.

One of Hamish’s classmates, Joe, looked suspiciously at the lecturer. ‘Do you hate Aboriginals?’

The lecturer stared coolly at Joe. ‘Again. Wrong word. Indigenous Australian is the respectful word to use.’

‘Hey. You.’

Hamish turned to see his Aboriginal classmate, Jindardie, looking at the lecturer with dislike.

‘Are you talking to me?’ the lecturer asked Jindardie coldly.

‘I’m lookin’ at you. So, I’m talkin’ to you,’ Jindardie answered.

‘My name isn’t “you”.’

‘I know what your name is. But I want to show you the same disrespect you just showed me.’

‘I’m…not sure what you are saying or what you even mean,’ the lecturer said coolly.

‘No. We think in different languages,’ Jindardie told him, his brown eyes sparking with anger. ‘You think about meaning in white man language, putting me under the title animal. I think in the sacred language, which puts me in sacred meaning.’ He leant back in his chair; his hot, intent eyes drawing up a mysterious power Hamish couldn't name. 'Your language puts me under the word "animal". My language puts me under the word "sacred". Why is that?'

The lecturer looked at Jindardie, his face grim. 'Your past and present social status is because of social codes in this country.'

'I have to be a white boy?' Jindardie asked. 'Or make sounds like an animal? Because that's the only two choices you give me and my people. White or animal. You ignore that we are sacred people.'

'It is and always has been a political matter,' the lecturer said testily.

'Well, what's the point of going into politics if you can't change things?' Deanna asked scathingly.

'You're not in politics to *change* things, you're in there to preserve the status quo,' the lecturer said dismissively.

'Depends if you are right or left,' Deanna said, sneering at the lecturer. 'I thought you as a lecturer would know that.'

The lecturer gave another thin smile. 'You've learnt to read, I see.'

'Fucking arsehole,' Deanna muttered under her breath.

Hamish hesitantly put up his hand.

'Yes?' the lecturer said cuttingly, staring in dismay at Hamish's wild hair and his hemp shirt.

'Why are elections being held if Parliament is simply preserving the status quo and…' Hamish asked, the rest of the sentence trailing off; his next thought lithium-bombed.

The lecturer waited for him to finish his sentence.

Hamish struggled to find the next sentence in his mind. His cheeks flamed, mortified that his once quick mind had come to this. A struggling, stumbling creature that couldn't find its way around. He looked about from face to face, all staring at him, and found one sympathetic face—a woman: overweight, with short blonde hair, an earring in her nose, and a tight white T-shirt that had *Heterosexual free zone* written in red letters in a red circle, with a red diagonal slash across it. The woman looked at the impatiently waiting lecturer and then at Hamish.

'I…' Hamish said, stumbling over his words, 'I…'

The lecturer looked at him silently. More minutes turned over.

'Ah, look, I think what that guy is trying to say is that we have election platforms based on issues to *change* things; yet, you are saying politics is about preserving the status quo,' the woman said.

Hamish looked at her, grateful. Heads turned towards her and then the lecturer.

'Yes,' the lecturer said mildly, 'a particular party's election platform is about cancelling the other political party's status quo and then putting their own political party's status quo platform in.'

'That's wrong,' the woman said.

'Why is it wrong?' the lecturer asked coolly.

'Because it's not the point of a political platform,' she said. 'A political party platform is about showcasing that political party's goals in a way that interests the public. Not about political parties endorsing their version of the status quo and presenting it to the public; just another way they must submit, comply and obey to the bulldogs that rule this country.'

There was a smattering of applause in the classroom.

The lecturer smiled thinly again.

'Both the Labor Party and the Liberal Party in Australia endorse neo-liberalism. And in doing so, they have, both, complied with the non-democratic spirit now rampant in this country,' the lecturer said.

'So, you are saying social democracy in this country has given up its ghost?' the woman asked.

'It was always a ghost,' the lecturer said drily. 'As it was never solid political flesh.'

'Oh great. Social democracy is only a rattling skeleton in Australia's policy closets. More hope for those of us who live in the side alleys of society,' the woman said.

'I don't get it!' Deanna bellowed.

'That's because you haven't made it to lecturer yet,' the lecturer said matter-of-factly. 'Please, sit down.'

Deanna wheeled away reluctantly, sulking. The lecturer folded his arms, looking superciliously at her departing back.

'Would anyone else like to question the lecturer?' he challenged.

'You may know things up here,' Jindardie said, tapping the side of his forehead, 'but you don't understand things here,' he said, holding up his bare, brown foot.

'I'm not sure what you are referring to,' the lecturer said dismissively, looking at Jindardie's bare foot with hostility.

Jindardie lifted his bare foot higher. '*Bare*. Moves natural,' he lowered his foot. 'You got shoelaces on your mind. It's all squeezed in tight.'

'If you want natural movements, go study horticulture,' the lecturer said coolly. 'This is a class for thinkers.'

'You think because I'm an Aboriginal, I don't think about stuff?'

Hamish looked up startled as an Aboriginal man sitting next to Jindardie stood swiftly and turned around, pulling his pants down, flashing his arse at the lecturer.

'Pull your pants up now!' the lecturer thundered.

Jindardie looked at the lecturer coolly. 'He's showing his *boonga* at you.'

'What?' the lecturer said, wiping his brow and reaching clumsily behind him to steady himself against the desk.

'*Boonga*. Flashing our bums at colonisers was the highest insult we used to give them. The bum is the filthiest part of the body, so we show it to them. And to you.'

'Class suspended!' the lecturer bawled.

15

Hamish stood up, looking around nervously. It was his first normal speech ready to be presented to the class. He so wished for Justine: *The relief of her nearby; the soothing paleness of something without volatile emotion, without the breeding of wasps. It's what I so love about her, that absence of maliciousness, her clean mouth, her angel hair, her—the...* his thoughts cut out again, as medication stoned his mental electricity.

He missed her. He'd seen her around the university, pale pink dress drifting in the wind, the milk whiteness of her skin startling between the charcoal buildings.

Hamish was too embarrassed to talk to her after she'd seen him in the mental hospital like a limp, paralysed, helpless child with no control over himself or anything else. Lying there in a social coma, newly rebuilt into psychiatric linguistics.

A Bipolar man.

Hamish looked up again and saw the lesbian woman who had come to his defence, leaning forward and looking anxiously at him.

'Hamish?' prompted his lecturer, his eyes cool.

Hamish's knees started shaking. He never used to suffer from nerves like this and he felt frightened; nervousness could just take him over without any stops in his brain or body; to keep it out of himself. Nerves ran through him, quick as water, and made him feel just as fluid without the brute strength his mind used to have: the mental muscles of his 159 IQ. Now, he was mentally skeletal, just bones of his own magnificence, he thought sadly. His hand grasped the edge of the desk, trying to control his shaking. He was so mentally thin, he thought, trying not to cry, he could barely comprehend the class readings or stand the dry language. His mind felt so blurred.

Nothing spoke to him anymore. The rain running down the bark of a tree no longer spoke any story to him; no history books opened ghosts in his mind, howling their stories to him through ink, line after line.

Hamish startled as he heard the loud cough coming from the back of the classroom. He looked towards the direction of the cough, to see an older classmate of his, George, tapping at his watch and staring at him meaningfully.

Hamish focused his mind on his speech and took a deep breath. 'Social policy today,' he said, his voice stumbling. He took another deep breath to calm his speeding heart. 'Gone are the days of social democracy,' he began.

'Wrong assumption. The Labor Party is still alive,' Deanna interrupted.

Hamish looked uncertainly at her, then at the lecturer.

'This is where *you* actually say something, Hamish,' his lecturer said coolly, his eyes unyielding. 'Get in the Bear Pit.'

'Objection,' Hamish said weakly.

And then couldn't think of anything else.

'Objection not taken any notice of,' Deanna said doggedly.

Hamish looked at her uneasily. The woman reminded him of a bull with her flaring nostrils, her lowered chin and stubborn stare. He almost expected her to run her shoe backwards and forwards a few times, like a bull did with its hoof. His thoughts cut out again, warning him that his so-called so-delusional thinking was kick-starting again. His brain no longer approved of his comparisons. A nose was a nose, a mouth was a mouth, an ear was an ear.

There was nothing more to it.

'Gone are the days of social democracy,' Hamish began again, and rushed on before the class bull came at him again. 'We compete with each other now, not help each other. We look at each other in marketable terms. What can I get out of you? What product do you have that I can gain from?'

'But—' Deanna interrupted.

His lecturer held up his hand. 'Let him continue.' He looked at Hamish dispassionately, as if he considered him a class specimen of illogic, necessary to examine.

'With the loss of social democracy,' Hamish continued, trying to keep the shake out of his voice, 'has come the loss of human value. We are as commercialised as a supermarket when it comes to making personal choices. The question is, how am I going to profit from this? And not, how much do I love this person?'

Silence fell.

'Go on, Hamish,' the lecturer said distantly.

'Our thinking about people has become capitalist because we have become a capitalist society,' Hamish continued.

'Look. Just vote for the fucking Greens,' the lesbian woman called out.

'Well, that's the only party you qualify for anyway,' George said, 'as they are the only party which actively support a gay...thing.'

'What did you just say?' she asked. 'What did you just say?'

'You heard,' George said.

'You called me at thing. *A thing!*'

'Excuse me,' George said stiffly, standing up and walking out of the classroom.

'Prick!' the woman called out hotly.

All heads turned and looked at her.

She looked at them ferociously. 'What?'

'Continue,' the lecturer said, giving Hamish a curt nod.

Hamish's cheeks flushed. 'I can't,' he said, looking down at his feet. 'This is where my thoughts cut out and I couldn't write anymore.'

The silence went on and on. If Hamish could measure it, he was sure it would have been seven miles of silence.

Finally, his lecturer spoke. 'If you fall short of the required time for an oral presentation, this is where you are required to do more readings, to fuel more thoughts and produce more material for your presentation.'

Silence swept through the lecture theatre again. No talk, or fiddling with pens, or shifting in seats; just a tight silence where nothing moved.

'I...I...' Hamish stumbled over his words.

Hamish saw the lesbian woman stand up. She began loudly clapping him.

His throat tightened as he tried not to cry at this one person standing up out of the oil, out of the plastic.

'Are you OK?' his one supporter asked him, shading her eyes from the sun with her hand.

Hamish looked up at her miserably, hunching in further against the wall, wanting to disappear into the shadow, not to be seen by anyone in this condition...this stupefied, mentally dyslexic condition. He rested his chin on his arms, wrapped around his knees.

'No. I'm not OK,' he said despondently.

The woman squatted down in front of him.

'Can I do anything to help?' she asked, her face creasing in concern.

'No,' Hamish said, his voice cracking, 'my brain's fucked up and I'm in love with a girl I can't have.'

The woman turned around and sat beside him, drawing her knees up and wrapping her arms around them.

'That's fucked, hey,' she said sympathetically.

'You've no idea,' Hamish said, 'what it's like to lose your Einstein *and* your princess.'

'What did you do to lose your Einstein?' she asked interestedly.

'I agreed to become sane,' Hamish said mournfully.

'Oh, you bit the tablet' she said. 'Mate. That's the same thing as biting the bullet. Dead intelligence.'

He smiled at her, not feeling as lost or ghosted.

'My name's Leanne Cruxton,' she said. 'And I've bit a few bullets too in my time. It's not like I can change my sexuality to fit the heterosexual design recommended by the powers that be. This is my world and it's one not recommended by the fingers that sign the papers, mate.'

'I don't think I've ever known a world of my own,' Hamish said despondently. 'Anything in my world was transposed with Apostles, the Last Supper, and the Pope staring sternly from the wall. Nothing was ever as it was. A fridge. A wall. A door. A bed. It all had Catholic meaning.'

'That sucks. Hey,' Leanne said, 'you either be part of the system design, or be part of the plague. Either way, there are social systems that deal with you.'

'I don't think you're part of the plague,' Hamish said, turning his head to look at her interestedly. 'I think you could kick a few traditional heads in, though. You, and your fuck-you attitude and your army boots.' He paused for a minute, his mind carefully searching for words; they seemed to be receding like a tide, any time he said or thought anything his lithium-flooded mind considered abnormal. 'You know, I think the plague is more *them*—whatever you want to call them: The Establishment, the shut-up population, the sleepwalkers.'

Hamish saw a drift of pink dress and sunlit blonde hair, milky white skin. The scent of sun-warmed roses drifted around him, filling his mind with longing for her.

'Ex…excuse me,' Hamish said hurriedly, getting to his feet. 'I just saw someone…I know…and…I have to…I have to go.' Hamish slung his bag over his shoulder, looking at Leanne apologetically.

'Alright, see you around,' she said casually.

Hamish lifted his hand clumsily at her; a move which could be construed as a wave, if anyone was good at interpretation. He bowed his head as he walked towards Justine, distressed; his quick, deft movements were gone as well. He hadn't even thought about the gesture of waving before. Not until now, when everything natural and easy had to now be retrieved from memory; and even then, his motor movements were awkward and clumsy, difficult for him to co-ordinate.

Medication had fucked up his natural flow.

Hamish supposed he was presenting more normally with his new clock-like personality, which just moved from one hour to the next, without the arms of self rapidly spinning.

16

Reasoning kicked in as he saw her face. *Rationality*, he thought, *otherwise known as: The Justine Effect*.

Would she want to see him? His cheeks still stained at the thought of himself in the mental hospital, fetal-like in her steady arms, unable to grow any taller for her.

Taller or smaller, he couldn't stop the strange force which kept pulling him to her. She was the presence which was the absence in him. A beautiful blonde swan, with white-feathered skin, drifting in light pink, and blue eyes that spoke of calm lakes, and swans gliding.

Justine was looking at a textbook, one leg neatly crossed over the other. Her light pink dress draped down over her knees, falling softly around her ankles. Hamish looked at her lightly painted pink toenails in their light-brown leather Jesus-sandals, and thought Jesus should wash her feet, they looked so angelic. *Hail Justine, full of grace, the Devil is not with thee,* he thought, looking at her reverently.

Hamish briefly felt annoyed with the scratching of Catholic thoughts on his mind again and looked instead at her pale hand resting around the brown paper coffee cup; her pink-painted nails like little half shells.

He wondered if he should clear his throat, but it felt too clichéd. Like something out of a bad B-grade movie. Then again, he thought, he might have better luck with women if he stuck to B-grade scripts and not his own clumsy lines.

Hamish hesitated, still feeling his helplessness and shame from when he was collapsed in her arms in the mental hospital. His strength had come from his mind and in mental hospital he was just floating weakness all over; no comets shooting through his mind, no ideas honeying his mental stamens, fertilising his spirit.

He had become like the conformist clutter of leaf people, all the same shape. The same colour and all hanging off one place, whatever you wanted to call it: religion, law, tradition, education, politics.

Hamish's thoughts slowed and stopped and he let them be this time, because thoughts were what had stuffed his whole life up anyway. Mental atrophy might bring him better luck.

Hamish drew in a deep breath.

'Justine?' he asked, his voice stumbling. He could never produce the sound of certainty anymore; that confident sound of people using their own intelligence, not intelligence inoculated with ideology.

Justine looked up, showing no surprise at the sight of him. She regarded him steadily with those cerulean-blue eyes, waiting for him to speak.

He couldn't. He was still caught in an image of himself, weak and helpless in her arms.

Justine waited patiently for another minute.

Finally, she smiled, and said, 'It's so good to see you here at university, Hamish. How are you finding it?'

Hamish waited tensely for an answer to come into his mind, but there was just sleepiness and words like *helpless* and *weak* and *strange* tattooed there. And a big, black hole, pulling him into it.

'Hamish?' Justine prompted.

He felt her like warm blood going through the empty veins in his mind. His cheeks flooded with warmth.

He finally scraped up some words, 'I…well…it's different to what I'm used to.'

Justine laughed. 'You mean it's normal.'

He looked at her, offended.

She smiled at him affectionately. 'Hamish. You are usually in eccentric states, which don't quite fit this world. But now, look at you,' she said, her smile widening, 'in all this normality.'

Hamish scratched his head. 'You think so?' he asked, looking around. 'There's some people with some pretty strange ideas, here.'

'You think it is strange because you are not used to being around normal people, having normal conversations and expressing normal thoughts. It's the best thing for you, Hamish.'

'Growing…normal. I'm cold, Justine,' Hamish said, '*cold*.'

'Think about how warm you'll be out of that mental hospital, which might become your new home, unless you grow normal. Uni is your chance to become normal and get the normal things of life: a job, a house, a car, money in the bank…and you won't have to rely on anyone else, or depend on anyone else, because you worked hard to be normal.'

He looked at her, alarmed. 'I don't know if I will ever get to that, you know. Normality leaves me mentally cold and stumbling around trying to find my place,' he said.

'Find your place here, Hamish. Then you won't have to stumble around, lost and confused.'

'I can't find my place because I see things as they are now. Not an interpretation or a—' he broke off, looking away.

Justine's voice reached him, comforting and steady: 'That's a good thing, Hamish. Just seeing things as they are.'

'You've never seen the inside of something, have you?' Hamish asked, his voice wistful.

'I'm not sure what you mean, Hamish,' she said, lowering her eyes and turning the page of her textbook.

Hamish sat down on the red lounge, diagonally opposite her. 'Haven't you ever looked at someone, and seen more than what there is?'

'No,' she said, looking at him carefully. 'I haven't. And it's thinking like that, which will put you in mental hospital.'

Hamish hung his head, his cheeks flushing again.

'Hamish,' she called, her voice softer.

Hamish looked up at Justine, seeing regret briefly cross her face. 'I'm sorry, Hamish. I didn't mean to upset you. I just don't want to see you back in mental hospital, so miserable and not quite right, you know? I'm so pleased to see you here, using your brains the right way. You are a smart man, Hamish. But the way you see things, it lets you down, you know.' It was what he liked about her. She was the one person he knew who was honest with him. She just told him, instead of smiling tightly at him or saying nothing at all.

'Well, at least I never have to try and read you,' he said. 'You are, as you are. A sentence on the page, in black and white print and—'

'Hamish,' Justine said sternly, 'you are calling me a sentence on a page, when I am as I am.' Her eyes softened. 'I am as I am, Hamish, that's all there is to it.' She paused, looking at him thoughtfully, as if debating whether to say anything more. 'I saw your dad the other day.'

Hamish felt every muscle in his body tense, at the mention of his father. Every day, he was trying to mentally get out of what his father thought was wrong with him. His so-called anti-Catholic Disorder.

'And?' Hamish asked, trying to sound as casual as he could.

'And he would like to see you again,' she said encouragingly.

'I don't want to see him,' Hamish said tightly. 'He's a bigot who doesn't understand me.'

Justine lowered her book, looking at him with concern. 'Hamish. You've got to get out of those sorts of thoughts.'

'Those sorts of thoughts are all he left me.'

Justine gave him a sympathetic look. 'You've had it hard, Hamish. But it's because of the sort of mind you've got.'

Hamish looked at her helplessly. 'It was the mind I was born with,' he explained.

'No,' Justine corrected, 'it's not. Your mind. It's a product.'

'A what?' he asked.

'A product. It's full of things you've read, and ideas from people you've talked to and experiences you've had.'

'So, my mind is like a carton and inside it is the milk of everything I have suckled on,' Hamish said and then the thought cut out, as it usually did when his newly medicated mind detected something out of logic.

'I didn't say your mind is like a breast, Hamish,' she said, 'I said it's like a product.'

'So, do you suggest I find a new tit to suckle on? To turn my mind into a different product?' he asked.

'Hamish!' she said, exasperated.

'OK,' he sighed. 'OK, I will call it as it is.'

She looked down at her textbook again, and he looked at her downcast eyes in despair. Justine would never love him like this, with his tit-suck talk and long dreadlocks, which she tried not to look like she had an aversion to, but did. She liked clean things, Justine. Clean, straightforward, uncomplicated. He was messy, he realised; he was just so messy. 'I'll…see you around,' Hamish said, turning away in despair. He realised she saw him as some sort of bat brain, something dark and cave-like she didn't want to share space with.

‘See you around...somewhere...’ she said indifferently, turning another page of her textbook. Hamish closed his eyes briefly, anguish washing through him; her casualness, her dismissiveness, her nonchalance with him, meant she did not regard him as anything but a friend. A somewhat peculiar friend. That’s when he decided. He was going to be someone. Someone outside peculiarity. Someone outside of bat brain. Someone clean with an A plus from society.

17

Hamish slumped slowly down against the brick wall outside his next class, next to Leanne who was reading an article from *Politics Today*.

'What's up?' Leanne asked, looking at him, concerned.

'Woman trouble,' he answered miserably, lowering his chin on his knees, wrapping his arms around them.

'Me too,' Leanne said despondently, looking over at a woman with fair hair closely cropped to her scalp and cat-like blue eyes. She was talking and laughing with a pale thin man, who had longish, tumbling dark hair, and nervous hands; so nervous the fliers he held shifted rapidly in and out between them, like a pack of cards.

'You love her?' Hamish asked tentatively.

'Yeah, I do,' Leanne said softly. 'Problem is, she's bisexual and for conformist reasons is choosing dick. That thing. How could anyone be attracted to it?'

'Some people like the penis look,' he said defensively.

Leanne stuck her fingers in her mouth, as if she was about to vomit. 'Disgusting.'

'Some may say so, some say not,' Hamish said, sensitively.

Leanne scrutinised him. 'Are you bisexual, Hamish?' she asked bluntly.

'No,' he said, 'my father would have shot me at birth.'

'Ah. You're from the strictly Penis and Vagina family,' she said sagaciously.

'Yeah. Something like that. No. Definitely like that. Dad put me in mental hospital for suspected gay longings, and my suspicions that the ocean was, in fact, a disguised vagina.'

'It could be,' she said, looking at him appraisingly, 'it could be.'

'I have since been informed by people that oceans don't have genders or sexualities.'

'Well, whoever told you that is not seeing things other ways, are they?' Leanne said. 'In poems and myths, oceans can be as sexual, or male or female, as they like.' She paused to scrutinise him again. 'So what's your woman trouble?' she asked.

Hamish lowered his eyes, his face falling. 'I've loved this girl since I was fourteen. I mean *really* loved her. She's so stable, you know. Like a rock. Just always steady and the same. Like a refuge you can just walk into when everything is falling apart,' he said firmly.

'So, what's the problem?' Leanne asked, yawning.

'The problem is she doesn't love me. I'm too wild for her, too all over the place, too much of a social nit. She'll never love me.'

'Do you love you?' she asked.

'Not like this,' Hamish said despairingly. 'Catatonic on medication. But I take it, so I don't have a mind in riptides. But, me being on medication doesn't change the impression she has of me.'

'So, change the impression,' Leanne said offhandedly.

'What do you mean?' he asked, shading his eyes from the sun, as its rays came sharply through a scudding cloud, crossing his face.

'Change the impression,' Leanne repeated. 'She's had the social nit impression of you since you were fourteen, right?'

'Right,' Hamish said, picking at some grass unhappily.

'So, she's a social conformist. And you're a social renegade. And there's nothing wrong with that. It's how society changes, mate. Or tries to. But be a social renegade in the right way. You can't go announcing your secret suspicions about the ocean being a vagina to your intended, because she sees things in a different way to you. You see things in a lyrical sort of way and she sees things in a concrete way. And there's nothing wrong with that either, if you're not harming anyone. Mind you, concrete-phobes who hate gays and lesbians won't be put up with, mate.'

Hamish looked at her uneasily, 'Are you telling me to be a social conformist? To appeal to her? Because I already decided to be someone society would give an A plus to; but does that mean I have to be a social stiff?'

'No, mate, no. Just be a social renegade in the right way. You've been doing your renegade stuff through social defiance, right? The hair, the clothes, the attitude of "Fuck the lot of you", and "I'll do and say what the fuck I want".'

'Yeah. I did,' Hamish admitted, 'I didn't see why I had to wear my hair in a certain way, to be perceived as normal. You know, short front, back and sides. Or a blue collared shirt, buttoned right up to the top, with a starch collar, that says without a word, *I fit society*. I mean if I was walking down the street in a ripped AC/DC shirt, with nose studs and a tattoo on my face, I would fit back alley society. Yet, that same AC/DC back alley person could have the intelligence of Einstein. It's just that no one bothered to find out or talk to him because of his off-putting social and personal presentation.'

'Yet, you could conform to the socially recommended look and be a dumb-arse who does not how to reason or think; just poos on with clichés and generalisations. Nothing specific or original. Just the same old shit,' Leanne mused.

'Yeah. You got it,' Hamish said despondently.

'For a lesbian and a straight, we strangely get on,' she said.

'Both been through the same shit,' he said, 'called marginalisation.'

Leanne looked at him thoughtfully. 'You know, I don't think your church princess has been hit with the same shit you have. You're looking at different levels of understanding, you know. She's never been mental, has she? Or depressed, or marginalised?'

'She knows how to act socially,' Hamish explained. 'Knows the right words to say; knows what to wear; knows how to act; and as long as I've known her, has always been very stable.'

'Look, Hamish,' Leanne said carefully, 'I don't think you should parrot her thing. You know, become *like* her, just to get her love and acceptance. I think you *should* be you. But, people like your church princess, Hamish? They don't understand, because they haven't been on the receiving end of the shit out there and that's because they've been socially conditioned and accepted by society.' She paused, smiling at him comfortingly. 'Social renegades are seen as trouble, you know. And it's not always in the message they are trying to tell the world, *this is wrong, this is an abuse of human rights.* That's all true enough. It's the way it's presented in riots that makes it look dangerous and anything you say, whether true or not, gets perceived as a threat in that sort of social presentation. You have to put what you want to say, in a non-threatening way. You can't just get up on the podium and steam away.' Leanne looked at him thoughtfully. 'When you give a speech, Hamish, tell a story. People like listening to them, mate. Stories, analogies, quotes, move and inspire people.

Like Martin Luther King's *I have a dream*...I mean, who fucking doesn't? He took that one wistful thought, that everyone has, and appealed *en masse* to all. I mean even a killer has a dream—of murdering somebody.' She paused, looking around at other students. 'Martin Luther King was clever, *very* clever, to use that one word that everyone carries with them: *dream.'*

'I don't think Martin Luther King would have wanted to encourage killers with a murderous dream,' Hamish said doubtfully, a frown crossing his face.

'Thousands of people know what it's like to suffer and be denied their dream, Hamish. So, mate, you stick to Martin Luther King language. It'll take you further than the "Fuck You" sort of language, which will eyeball you in social misery.'

'You've inspired me, you've *so* inspired me,' Hamish said fervently, feeling so relieved he could feel something.

'A lesbian inspiring a straight,' she said speculatively, raising an eyebrow. 'Mate. I thought, at first, all we had in common is we both like vagina. But you and me, mate, we both want acceptance in this world. I don't get it because I'm a lesbian and you don't get it because you are a social nit. We're not status quo material.'

Leanne looked longingly at the blonde-haired woman again, now standing near The Greens stall.

'No chance with her then?' Hamish asked, reaching out to touch Leanne and then hesitating, as he remembered she was anti male flesh.

Leanne shook her head. 'No. No chance. Not unless she loses her fear of social stigma.'

'Does she know how you feel?' he asked thoughtfully.

Leanne lowered her head, her eyes downcast. 'No. There's no point unless she's open to ditching dick. I don't want to share her with a man.'

Hamish leant back on his hands, looking broodingly at an empty bench in the university courtyard. 'I have the same problem,' he said darkly. 'Justine's not open to a relationship. I talked to her once, about my feelings and...well...she didn't want to know about it. Said she'd heard some things, but wouldn't say what they were.' He looked down and resumed picking at the grass unhappily.

'Things might change, you know, if you say your words the right way,' Leanne said encouragingly. 'Use a bit of Martin Luther King language. *I have a dream, Justine*...and tell her she's it...Hamish...Hamish...will you...Hamish... I don't usually ask men to look me in the eyes, but I'm trying to tell you something important...Hamish...'

Hamish looked up finally.

'Hamish. Justine is older now. She might be able to look at what she heard about you, with more perspective. *And*, she's doing a Bachelor of Counselling, if this is the same Justine I saw you with before?' Hamish nodded. Leanne continued, 'So that will give her a different take on you as well. You should talk to her again. At least you will be able to shut or open the door on her. No use leaving the door halfway open, mate. It will just put you in a position of suffering.'

'Yeah, OK,' Hamish said, 'the halfway door is pissing me off.'

'Now another bit of advice to you, Hamish. About your Martin Luther King dream of politics. You've got the social ideals, Hamish. *And* you're intelligent. You've just got to get your political platform right, you know? No singing in the mall, with your wild caveman look, or talking publicly about the secret vagina ocean. If you poetically see the ocean this way, it's best to put it in a poem, not in a public speech. In a poem, mate, it's literature. In a conversation or a public speech, it's a mental illness. It's all in how it's presented Hamish, an acceptable medium for your particular type of thought.'

'I get it. Thanks.' He frowned. 'Perhaps, I should have become a writer.'

'No, mate, no. You may really tip your brain off the edge. Stick with a political platform. Put your social ideals into politics, and leave vaginas posing as oceans out of it.' Leanne got up and reached out her hand. 'Don't usually hold hands with—a man. But you've got no-one else to pull you up out of the shit. Come on.'

He took her hand and she pulled him up, quick and fast.

'Ow,' he said, shaking his arm, 'that's one hell of a grip you've got there.'

'Social muscle, mate, social muscle,' she said, letting go of his hand and wiping her hand on her red baggy pants.

Hamish rubbed his arm. 'Got to get me some of that.'

Leanne pointed at the small table in the university courtyard, with The Greens poster taped on the table, flapping in the wind. A group wearing The Greens T-shirts were busy handing out fliers to students; stepping back as one student scrunched up the flier handed to him, and threw it back in their face. '*Do you think I fucking need more to think about?*' the student yelled.

‘That’s where to find social muscle, mate,’ Leanne said decisively, ‘at that table. The Greens. They’re for disadvantaged people, and for the crippled environment. They’re all about stopping violence between people and bringing democracy back. Sadly, democracy’s living in the back alleys with the fish bones.’

‘Crippled…environment?’ Hamish asked, bewildered, flopping back down on the grass and leaning back on his elbows.

‘All the housing complexes and mines, mate. Human constructions have crippled the environment,’ Leanne said resolutely. ‘It’s this simple, mate. We should go back to cave man–woman, or cave woman–woman days, mate. Not, who has the best economy, the best house, the most socially correct partner.’ Leanne sat back down. ‘The social ladder, mate. You are judged by what rung your foot is on.’

‘*And*, the social ladder ignores people in wheelchairs,’ Deanna said nearby, wheeling herself over to them. ‘There’s a social ladder, but no social ramp.’

Leanne looked pointedly at her wheelchair. ‘You are not from the race of perfection; Hitler’s blessed ones. They don’t believe in modification. You get neither ramp or ladder,’ she muttered.

‘Just as well,’ Deanna retorted. ‘I would hate to be held up as an ideal by the Ultimate Gasman.’

‘What’s your name again?’ Hamish asked.

‘Deanna. Deanna Scott,’ she said. ‘Yours?’

‘Hamish. Hamish McColl. The Imperfect.’

‘You suffer from Imperfection Syndrome too?’ she asked bitterly, her hand gripping the edge of her wheel.

Hamish tapped the side of his forehead: ‘I suffer from it up here.’ Hamish held out a long, dark brown dreadlock. ‘And I suffer from social misfit syndrome, as well.’

‘Leper hair,’ Leanne agreed.

‘I don’t think it’s any danger of falling off his head, Leanne,’ Deanna said matter-of-factly, looking at his hair. ‘It’s too firmly knotted.’

Leanne gave a long-suffering sigh. ‘It was *just* a way of describing his hair. As it rates with the socially elite.’

Deanna looked hard at Hamish. ‘If you want to get taken seriously in politics, you can’t have that hair, Hamish. A Prime Minister with leper hair has never been seen.' She sat back in her wheelchair. 'Every politician. You look at photos of them: short back and sides hair.'

'Yeah, it's a bit like uniform requirements for school,' Leanne said drolly. 'The political uniform. Short back and sides hair. A crisp, starch-sprayed shirt, usually white or pale blue…'

'Yes. I have to say that's true,' Deanna remarked, nodding her head. 'I've never seen a pollie in a magenta shirt…'

'No. Magenta is not a toe-the-line shirt,' Leanne said deprecatingly. 'People trust that white shirt look, because it speaks of a certain behaviour. Behaviour that is crisp, starched, with not a wrinkle in the words. Magenta shirt behaviour is quite different to white shirt behaviour. Magenta shirt wearers may chain themselves to a tree or be found screaming at social stiffs.'

'I don't know about white-shirt behaviour only for politicians,' Deanna said practically. 'You mustn't have seen a parliamentary session in full swing.'

'Yes,' Leanne agreed, 'Some of them claw at each other: *hisssss, rrroooowwww, scratch.*'

'They were probably wearing red that day,' Hamish said.

'Bear pit speech, it's called,' Deanna said.

'Shirt behaviour and politicians and the strange but extraordinary connection…let me get this straight,' Hamish pondered.

'Yes. You do have a few too many knots around your head,' Deanna said, with a concerned look at Hamish's dark brown dreadlocks.

'Oh, leave off,' Leanne said irritated. 'He uses his dreadlocks to swat social mosquitos, don't you, Hamish.'

'Social nasties, you mean,' Deanna said, 'as there's no such breed type as "social mosquito".'

Leanne sighed impatiently, 'Yeah. Those. So, what did you want to get straight, Hamish? And you should never use that tragic word around gays or lesbians.'

Hamish scratched his head, 'What?'

'Straight. Don't use the word *straight* around us,' she explained patiently to him.

'Oh. I get it. Straight is not a gay sort of word,' Hamish said sensitively.

'Oh *please.* That's…a bit—'

'It was a joke, Deanna,' Leanne interrupted impatiently. 'I use the word myself.'

Deanna ignored her. 'Hamish. You must get it straight about politics and political etiquette before you get out there in public. Because that's what Leanne is getting at, with her white shirt talk.'

Leanne looked at her, annoyed. 'Getting at? I thought I was very clear.'

'No, you weren't,' Deanna said definitely. 'There were a lot of comparisons, but little conciseness there.'

'*Fuck!*' Leanne said, shaking her head and looking at the sky. 'I'll make it clearer then. A doctor will talk to you in anatomy language, right?'

'Right,' Hamish agreed.

'And the doctor has a certain look, and a dress code, right?'

'Right.'

'Well so do pollies, mate,' Leanne said confidently. 'And if you want to make it to the Bear Pit, get the language and the look right…but put your own ideas in there.'

'Why aren't you a politician, Leanne?' Hamish asked, drawing his brows together, puzzled.

'My sexuality is not a carbon copy of what is culturally accepted in this Judeo-Christian established society, mate. They all wear the heterosexual, mate. And you don't find too many gay or lesbian or transsexual politicians in the Bear Pit, either.'

'But you could do politics, Leanne. Social code or no social code. You make people laugh so much; they'd vote for you straight away. People like people with a sense of humour. Puts them in the sun for a while,' Hamish said, looking at her affectionately.

'I could, Hamish, I could,' she said casually, nodding her head. 'But my social defender persona may get in the way of my humour if I had to face a bigoted crowd. It would be, *Fuck you*. You *have* to have a certain persona in politics, mate. Can you be one thing in public, and another thing in private, Hamish? You have to look at that.'

'I'm pretty much the same, all the time. Screwed up,' Hamish said deprecatingly, again picking unhappily at the grass.

'You have to stop thinking of yourself like that, Hamish,' Leanne said, slapping him on the wrist. 'The "I'm so screwed up" self-belief won't get you anywhere. Mate, you've got to find your mental muscles. What makes you feel strong. It may be swimming 20 laps in the pool; or going trekking in the Himalayas; or meditating with the Buddhists in a Tibet temple; or running in a 20k marathon. Start thinking from what makes you strong, not from what made you screwed up.'

Hamish looked away, his gaze falling on the rubbish bin, bits of screwed-up wrappers and food falling out of it. 'My mind is always thinking from the screwed-up position, because many, many people have *told* me I am screwed up.' Hamish looked at Leanne bitterly. 'All I get is "Hamish. You think wrong" or, "that's not normal thinking, Hamish".'

Leanne looked at him affectionately. 'You don't think wrong, Hamish. You just think differently. Most people do not sit down together and talk in elevated conversation like you do, mate. You know, mental pot. Your sort of thinking and talking, Hamish, is in a different mental space than ordinary society. But your social ideals wanting to change society, and get it out of status quo mothballs, that puts you here with us. In our language and our thinking. So, stop pot-smoking your speech, and talking away in a language most ordinary people just can't understand. Start talking Martin Luther King language of *I have a dream*...I mean, your dream is not sitting in front of a mental health tribunal, trying to explain yourself, is it?'

'No. No,' Hamish said hastily, looking down, and pulling at his dark brown pants, with tassels on the ankle hems.

'I think you'll find that the girl you want so much will look at you in a different way, if you stop thinking of yourself as screwed-up, Hamish. You think of yourself like that, she will too,' Leanne advised.

'You are a guru,' Hamish said reverently, clasping his hands together as if in prayer, and bowing his head at her.

'I could do that,' she said, 'be the Lesbian Guru. Not used to being a pin-up for a straight man, Hamish, not at all...'

'You are a lesbian super girl, rescuing the socially smashed,' Hamish pronounced.

'A lesbian super girl saves a straight man. Don't think Hollywood will buy it, mate,' Leanne said caustically, leaning back on both hands.

'It may become the new social script one day,' Deanna remarked.

'No, mate, no. The Australian Constitution preserves the colonial ideologies Australia was founded on,' Leanne said definitely. 'Which is why the same issues and arguments keep repeating through the eras and never changing. Society is designed *not* to change. It doesn't matter how much you wave posters, crowd chant or riot about rights. Our society was designed a particular way and is preserved by our governing laws. Mate, people like me, or that Aboriginal over there, or that Asian standing in the queue there, were never in the original Judeo-Christian design of this country.'

'So, it's survival of the constitutional fittest,' Hamish said, biting his lip, looking appraisingly at the Asian man and then at the Aboriginal woman.

'It's just survival, full stop, Hamish. The Constitution mentality, mate, it's in the very cornerstones of society. You would have to undo whole towns, build new ones to get rid of it. I don't belong in old towns. I'm not what gets respect, mate. That Christian priest over there handing out Bibles is. And so is that white, heterosexual, well-dressed university lecturer, with his brown leather briefcase, walking past the university science lab.'

'Will you accept respect from a mere social nit?' Hamish asked, looking at Leanne pleadingly.

Leanne laughed. 'Respect is respect. What face it wears doesn't matter.'

'Well, it does,' Deanna said pointedly, 'I mean, I wouldn't want any respect from the local paedophile.'

'I don't think the local paedo would respect you anyway, for your non-paedophilic views,' Hamish pointed out.

'Can we move off...that...please?' Leanne said, 'I hate talking about that sort of stuff. It makes me want to get out my shotgun and shoot the bastards up the arse.'

'I'll be in the paedo shooting club,' Deanna volunteered.

'Can we move on...please...' Leanne said, grinding her teeth together, her fists tightening.

'OK, OK, I won't ring Derryn Hinch and tell him we've got a new shame, shame, shame corner in Sydney,' Deanna said, disappointed.

'Yeah. Let's get off that agenda. I have to get past my university agenda first,' Hamish said resignedly. 'Pass.' Hamish handed his marked paper to Leanne. 'You've got to help me with this.'

Leanne looked at the P+ and back at him. 'You passed. What's the problem?'

Hamish looked at her miserably. 'The problem is, I *know* I can do better.'

'I get it. You know you don't have an L-plater brain and you're pissed off at the low mark,' Leanne consolingly.

'Well, yeah. My brain got off its L-plates at two years old,' Hamish said brashly, 'but this slow lecturer doesn't like my ideas. See?' He pointed at the essay. 'There's slash marks all over it; he's *murdered* my essay. He's committed academic homicide on me, he's…' the thoughts in his head faded, as the words he was using registered as illogical in the new coma posing as his mind.

'I think that's taking it a bit too far, Hamish. Here give it to me,' Leanne said, stretching one hand out, and using the other hand to hold her salad sandwich.

Hamish gave Leanne his marked paper, pondering the salad sandwich in her hand. 'Healthy,' he ventured. He could almost feel a green tick mark, in his mind, at the use of a relevant word, in the right context. Then, that imagining faded into his lithium-soaked mind, drowning with all the other imaginal forms at the bottom of it.

'Leanne avoids sausage rolls, because they are phallic-shaped,' Deanna said matter-of-factly.

'That's just stupid,' Leanne muttered.

'You're a lesbian. It's not stupid at all,' Deanna said.

Leanne shook her head, muttering something under her breath, and turned a page of Hamish's assignment. 'Look, mate. From what I can see here, your statements are not backed up with facts. A bit of hyperbole. Opinion based. Emotional…' Leanne stopped as she saw the woman she loved in the distance, standing at The Greens table, laughing with some other members.

Leanne looked at the woman miserably, her eyes lingering on her face.

'Leanne?' Hamish said, looking from her to the blonde-haired woman, 'Leanne?'

Leanne said irritably, 'Shut up, would you. I'm in a state of sad yearning and lesbian lust.'

'Well, at least you're honest about it,' Deanna said.

'As-it-is sort of girl. No mental hidey holes with me.'

'Have you…finished…yet?' Hamish asked, looking impatiently at the blonde-haired woman and at Leanne.

'No,' Leanne snapped, as she continued to look at the woman.

'What's her name?' Deanna demanded.

'Torment. Tease. Orgasm,' Leanne said caustically.

'Yeah. Well I've been in that place too,' Hamish said miserably, picking at the grass again.

'Mate. That place has locks around it you just can't break,' Leanne said. 'If she doesn't love you, she doesn't love you. There's no magic key that's going to break that lock.'

'Yeah. I know,' Hamish said. 'I met Justine when I was fourteen years old and I'm now twenty; and my heart's still hammering for her.'

'What is that woman's real name?' Deanna demanded. 'And I don't want to hear anything called orgasm. Just her name.'

'Donna,' Leanne said, her voice softly catching on her name.

'Is Donna part of The Greens group? Or does she just hang around them?' Deanna asked.

'Yeah, Donna's a member,' Leanne said, leaning back on the grass with both hands. 'Mining is her particular concern. She's worried we'll become a third world economy, with the mines here sitting on top of the food bowls.'

'Advance Australia Skinny's. No,' Hamish said, worried about this. Thoughts of rationed food started going through his head, followed by a flood of lithium.

'Hamish,' Deanna scolded, 'that's inappropriate.'

'He's just having a bit of a poetic go at things, aren't you, Hamish?' Leanne said.

'Yeah. I am,' Hamish admitted.

'If you want to go into politics,' Deanna said, her face forbidding, 'you can't use strange poetry to describe the effect of serious Australian issues.'

'By the same token, he doesn't have to be a political corpse, either,' Leanne said reasonably.

'Medication has already turned me into a mental corpse,' Hamish said worriedly. 'Having to take political correctness as well would be like taking social lithium.'

'You're not entirely dead yet, Hamish,' Leanne said. 'There's still a bit of spunk there; it's just not the psychotic spunk that can scare people.'

'And the term "political correctness" exists for a reason, Hamish,' Deanna added. 'Our social structure is built on it.'

'And racism and discrimination are part of that good, solid and stable society,' Leanne said sarcastically.

'That children's writer, Enid Blyton, got in trouble for writing about a golliwog thief, didn't she?' Deanna asked. 'There were those who felt she was having a go at black people. Terrible, really. I read that the golliwog characters all ended up replaced by white goblins in the revised edition of those stories.'

A look of disgust crossed Hamish's face. 'The colonial times are still happening, as savage black toys get replaced with the more cultured, elegant white goblin.' He stopped, inordinately pleased he could describe outside practical terms once again.

'You know, I read on some website, there was trouble over Humphrey B Bear as well. He was not considered politically correct, as he wore no pants. The pissed off fundamentalist Christian wrote on the website that pants-less Humphrey was lewd and exposing himself to kids on television, with his no pants look and seductive poses,' Leanne said solemnly.

'Playboy Humphrey B Bear,' Hamish said doubtfully.

'Toys will be subject to political correctness testing, before making it off the factory line,' Leanne said sardonically.

'And tagged. With, *This is a politically correct toy*,' Deanna added.

'As if the child would give a fuck anyway,' Leanne said, shaking her head.

'Can we get back to my murdered essay,' Hamish asked plaintively, '*please*?'

'Alright, scarecrow,' Leanne said good-naturedly, looking down at his paper again. 'Now, where were we?' Her eyes quickly scanned the last paragraph. She frowned, glancing up at him and looking down at the paper again. 'No,' she said, shaking her head, 'no.'

'No, what?' Deanna asked irritably.

'Hamish's concluding statement about Terania Creek: "The tree chainers are to be revered for their defence of vulnerable rainforest trees, skeletal with fear".' Leanne looked up kindly. 'Hamish. No…you'd be better off rewriting that, to…go ask the lecturer,' she advised.

'My lecturer doesn't like me,' Hamish said unhappily.

'He doesn't like what you're *writing*,' she said, handing the paper back. 'Get him to sit down and explain it to you. You've taken personal offence at his comments, see? It's not personal, it's academic.'

'Well, his so-called academic comments were rather sarcastic,' Hamish complained. 'And he's not exactly a fair man to speak with. He's a fucking academic Nazi…a…can't think…a…*fuck!*' he swore, as the lithium blasted his mind again.

'I wouldn't go that far,' Leanne said reasonably.

Hamish looked suspiciously at his marked paper again. 'He is lowering my marks. And I know it's because I have a non-subservient mentality to The Establishment.'

'No. Hamish. No,' Leanne said realistically. 'You're not respecting his PhD status. You're just writing your own thing and ignoring what he is telling you to do.'

Hamish looked at her in disbelief. 'You want me to be a puppet. On the academic marionette?'

'Mate? The ones all sitting up at the top? They've learnt from others, or they have found someone who knows what they don't. That's how they get to the top. It's not about academic puppetry; it's about finding the right answers. Right across the social spectrum. From lecturers through to doctors through to parents. Finding the right answers is how you don't fall into the quicksand and sink yourself.'

Now Deanna looked at her in disbelief. 'I've seen some pollies at the top with quicksand-covered legs.'

'That's *after* they got there, mate, after they got there.'

'How reassuring for us all,' Deanna said sarcastically.

'Can you just get my assignment out of quicksand?' Hamish asked, looking at it in shame.

'Go and see your lecturer, scarecrow, for triple 0 assignment rescue. Deanna and I will work on the rest of you.'

'The rest...of me? What the fuck does that mean?' Hamish asked, his face furious. His rage died just as suddenly as it started, swept away by another lithium flood through his mind.

'Mate. We are going to turn you into our new policy mouth,' Leanne said decidedly.

'What?' Deanna asked alarmed. 'There are strange things coming out it.'

Leanne ignored her. 'Hamish,' she said, looking intently at him, 'you've got what it takes. Social ideals, high intelligence and the suffering of someone who doesn't fit in. You've seen a few walks of life, Hamish, and that always helps when trying to appeal to the broad public.'

'I don't think my social nit look appeals to the broad public,' Hamish said, fingering his dark brown dreadlocks, and glancing down at his tasselled brown pants and bare feet.

'If you're a social nit, then I'm a sexuality nit. The Church doesn't like us because we don't fit into their reproductive scheme or cultural specifications. I'm like the female ET, you know, the X-Files of woman they consider strange and paranormal to biblical standard.' Leanne rearranged herself, so she was sitting cross-legged, 'And then, there's the traditional man that women like me have to step around, because they think there's something wrong with me, because I don't fuck or suck penis. I love the same way you straights love,' she said passionately, looking wistfully at Donna. 'Straight from the heart.'

Hamish caught sight of Justine, on her way out of the university café. He looked at her desperately.

'Ohhh... That's your lady love, isn't it?' Leanne asked, looking at her with a critical eye.

'Yes,' he said desperately.

'Not really my type,' Leanne said, scrutinising Justine. 'But I can see how that peaches and cream, Bambi-type of look appeals to you.'

'It's not just that,' Hamish said mournfully. 'It's her strength. She's got a strength I don't have. She's got, like, this wing under her foot, which stops her becoming a social Titanic like me.'

'You're not that bad, Hamish. Really. You're not,' Leanne said comfortingly. 'And if she comes from feather world, maybe she's better suited to the Jesus man. And another thing. Calling yourself a social Titanic? Hamish. You won't get far in politics looking directionally at the bottom of the ocean. No one likes the arse-end of a shark for a policy platform, mate.'

'You got any ideas on policy, or what you would like to politically promote, Hamish?' asked Deanna.

Hamish didn't know, really. He used to see people as just representations, sketches, satires. Now they were suddenly…more…real…and coloured in. He now had to get to know people in a different way. Hamish looked at Deanna thoughtfully. 'Policy platform? How about being different and socially paying for it?'

'Can you put that in political terms, Hamish?' Deanna asked, her face thoughtful, her hands gripping the wheelchair arms tighter.

Hamish searched for the right words. It used to be so easy, fast and snapping, but these days, his mind was learning to jigsaw words together, so he made sense instead of sounding like a racecourse announcer on speed.

Finally, it came to him.

What he meant. Exactly what he meant.

'The Other,' Hamish said.

'We are all The Other,' Deanna said matter-of-factly. 'You've got to come up with something better than that.'

'What I mean by "The Other" is something different than the recommended citizen. By "The Other" I mean disadvantaged people in society: the gays, the mentally ill, the poor, the uneducated, the single parent, those who have a disability, the indigenous, the black person...there's so many really,' Hamish said.

'Well, *yeah,'* Leanne said as if condemning him for only just noticing this, 'there's a lot of social anger about so many people in the side alleys, while the perfect get the main road with the well-lit areas.' She scrutinised his face. 'So you've got your social justice theme, now what are you going to do about it?'

'Build a political platform for an inclusive society,' he said. 'That you don't have to be White or Heterosexual or Patriarchal or Judeo-Christian to qualify for.'

'Mate. Listen,' Leanne said resignedly, 'some of the higher levels of society have been frantically shutting out anything that looks "Other" since colonial times. Look at what happened to the Indigenous people, mate. No one wanted to see their faces showing in the streets, reminding them of something existing outside their culture. And how are you going to include *inclusion* in their thinking?'

'Giving them things to think about?' Hamish volunteered. It sounded weak, even to him, and his voice faltered and fell silent.

'Nah,' Leanne said, picking at fallen dandelion fluff on her baggy red pants. 'The non-marginalised already have *set* thought. It either fits or it doesn't. You've got to give them *stories*, mate, things that make them *feel*. Not think, *feel*. Break the colonial in them, mate.'

'Alas, I have been sentenced by mental health into a carbon copy of the model citizen, and don't have stories in me anymore,' Hamish said despondently, drawing his knees up, wrapping his arms around them and leaning his chin on his knees.

Deanna looked at him, then Leanne, her face bored. 'Can we move into some action? You've got no idea of how much we've got to do. We've got a council election coming up, and no candidate.'

'Why?' Hamish asked intrigued.

‘The candidate we selected pulled out,’ Leanne explained. ‘Found it too hard to fight the plastic, you know?’ She shook her head sadly. ‘Tragic.’ She scrutinised Hamish more closely.

‘Hey,’ she said.

‘No, no,’ Deanna said, gripping her wheels and wheeling backwards. ‘No.’

‘Hamish,’ Leanne drawled, ‘wanna be the new sunshine coming out of The Greens Party arse?’

18

'Now,' Leanne said firmly, looking Hamish over critically, 'where do we start? As much as I hate conformity, you've got to look presentable and hide the nuke inside you. A disguised vigilante.' She paused, picking up a dreadlock. 'Don't usually touch men, mate, but that hair...I had to feel if it was real or not. Is it?' she asked, lifting it up higher and squinting at it.

'Yes,' Hamish said defensively, 'it is.'

Leanne dropped the dreadlock and wiped her hand on her green baggy pants. 'Mate, listen. The caveman look isn't going to pass the social ballot. You look too rough. You need a new look that carries social power. That social nit look you have is more of a "fuck you" look.'

'It's hair that speaks of who I am,' Hamish said defensively. 'Speaks of...speaks of...hair doesn't speak,' he reminded himself.

'It's a hair look which says disturbance of the peace,' Leanne said drily. She gave his hair another scrutinising look. 'You want to be taken seriously in politics, Hamish. Remember, scarecrow, our society is conservative based. With that hair, you'll appeal to a few marginalised hippies, disillusioned artists, a few poets here and there, who appreciate your hair. Anyway, politics has enough knots in it, scarecrow, without your hair adding to it.'

'Oh, this is going too far,' Deanna said.

'No, it's not. Poets, artists, hippies like reality out of its safety pants,' Leanne said, leaning back on her elbows.

'Oh, that's even worse,' Deanna said, 'nude reality.'

'That's...not what I meant,' Leanne said. 'I meant that those sort of people like reality out of its conformist pants, so they can play with it on the canvas; you know, interpret it.'

'Let me get this straight,' Hamish pondered, 'I have to lose my metaphor hair, and get church-hair.'

'Church-hair?' Deanna scoffed. 'No. Socially recommended hair for men.'

‘That means short back and sides,’ Hamish said glumly, hanging his head.

‘Short back and sides. That *is* church-hair,’ Leanne pointed out. ‘There is no difference between socially recommended hair and church-hair since the Church decides society, including what sort of hair is acceptable.’

‘I’m surprised I was let in the church door so many times, with my unacceptable hair,’ Hamish said, baffled.

‘Perhaps you were a potential candidate for the lost sheep program,’ Deanna suggested.

‘Did they expect a hairdresser to find him?’ Leanne asked sarcastically.

‘No, Leanne,’ Deanne said seriously. ‘Jesus is pictured with long hair. My point is that short front, back and sides hair for men is the sort of hair worn by conservative male society. Whether that’s conservative church-men, conservative politics-men or conservative law-men or conservative family-men.’

Leanne reluctantly acknowledged her point. ‘Yeah well, short front, back and sides hair speaks of cleanliness. Of well-groomed minds, of hygienic thoughts.’

‘I don’t think I can do it,’ Hamish said worriedly, shaking his head.

‘Fuck those leprechauns in your head off, mate, that your dad talked about,’ Leanne counselled, giving his hair another speculative look.

‘You think I have leprechauns in my head as well?’ he asked despairingly.

‘That’s what I said, mate. That’s what I said. Little head-fuckers who speak the fairy to you. You need more of Pine O Cleen in your head, OK? Not little head-fuckers.’ Leanne gave him a measured look. ‘Now. Go get a haircut. Lose your leprechauns. Pine O Cleen hair. Bring it on…’

Leanne wasn’t the only one who referred to him as a scarecrow. Justine had once told him he reminded her of a scarecrow as well, scaring people away with his long, dark-brown dreadlocks. Bristled hair around his face, his wide, staring brown eyes and his tendency to threaten people’s psyches.

Bye-Bye, Scarecrow, he thought as he walked out of the newsagent with some men’s magazines. He quickly flicked through some of the magazine pages as he walked along, studying the conformist male look. Parted on one side, combed flat against the skull and neatly trimmed above the neck.

Dismayed, Hamish closed the magazine and walked the remaining three blocks back to the hostel. He walked slowly up the two flights of stairs, made his way to the end of the hallway, and opened the door to his small room.

Hamish sat on the end of his bed, holding a long dark-brown dreadlock in his hand. *I could weep,* he thought, *weep.* It had taken him years to grow his hair. He dropped the dreadlock, trying to think of excuses to keep his tribal hair: the socially clawed politician? The politician less travelled? He didn't know if the public would buy it. Father Matthias hadn't bought his church-explained hair, giving him a long, suspicious look when Hamish had sneakily said he was modelling his hair on the Bible character of Samson.

Father Matthias's stare had been the length of the Bible. *Don't try and pass off your wild hair as biblical,* he'd warned him, *we all know that's just your cleverness speaking, your mind indulging in devil's trickery. You want us to understand your hair in the religious sense, or to accept your hair by making it religious. We all know here, that's not the case. It's a defiance of order. And it's a nit invitation.*

The hairdresser looked at Hamish's hair, grieving as she lifted the first dreadlock to be cut off.

'Are you sure?' she asked, upset.

He nodded grimly. 'It has to go,' he said.

Hamish ran his hand over his newly shorn head. In a way, he did feel like Samson, like he *had* lost his strength. His long dreadlocked ropes of hair had signalled to conformist society that he was dismissive of social plastic. That he was confident enough in who he was, not to be concerned about what people thought of him. He had always been contemptuous of people who fit into one of the collective identities of a social system. Sacrificing their uniqueness to a collective belief system just to fit in or be accepted. And here he was doing the same thing. Sacrificing his uniqueness. Peddling the socially acceptable male look discreetly recommended on mannequins in storefronts.

Being a hypocrite.

'Well?' he asked Leanne, looking down, feeling ashamed; yet at the same time, tired of being scorned and marginalised.

He could hear splutters of laughter, quickly contained. 'Hamish,' Leanne said broadly, 'you are on the first rung of the social ladder already. From metaphor hair to mannequin hair.'

Hamish touched his head gingerly. He desperately regretted it already.

'There's the second rung,' Leanne said, pointing at the actual male mannequin in the window front.

Hamish stared with fear at the male mannequin with a crisp white-collared shirt on, neatly pressed khaki pants and plain brown leather belt. He looked down at the plain, brown leather shoes and brown leather briefcase placed discreetly nearby. Classically cut, plain, *sensible.* How he had always hated that word. *Sensible.* The word was a taped-up little box, which just didn't fit in with his mental warfare of words. He had liked words splintering like wood; words which bled meaning in his mind, bit at his thoughts; back-snapped the unmovable.

And now, here he was. About to live behind the glass window. Yet, this was what attracted a normal life. Another word he hated. *Normal.* Another taped-up little box, from the social museum on how to behave. And words like *normal* prescribed for collective behaviour. These Church beliefs are *normal.* These political beliefs are *normal.* These laws are *normal.* These family practices are *normal. Words like "renegade" make you social graffiti*, he thought, miserably. *You are the ugly word in society. The ugly name in your family. The ugly word in politics. The ugly word in law. The ugly word in religion.*

Renegade.

Just ugly.

As was anything that deserted the conformist cause, for the non-conformist cause.

And that's what he thought about a lot lately. How not to be socially ugly. How not to black sheep people. Because they always looked uneasily at him, smiled tightly and put him under the social guillotine. He was often cut off after one or two sentences and left there standing alone. People did not want to hear what he had to say. It was always somehow offensive. Justine tried to explain it to him once: *'It's not just what you are saying, it's how you are saying it. There's no...well...softness or thoughtfulness there. It's coming straight from your brain out of your mouth, without any filter.'*

'You want me to be cautious?' Hamish had asked her. *'Because cautious people never sit there and tell you the truth. They are selectors, putting together a careful conversational arrangement; a safety belt conversation you are never going to crash in. Falling trees like me don't belong in careful conversation. And, Justine, I don't know how to stop that motion of falling. I don't know how to be plastic.'*

Justine had looked at him with her characteristic steadiness. *'It's nothing to do with people being plastic, Hamish. It's to do with people being careful of each other.'*

Hamish had looked at her, his eyes struggling. *'With caution, there is no progress of society; just a maintenance of status quo.'*

'Maintaining the status quo keeps society functional, safe and predictable,' Justine had said to him, *'I don't know why you are so against status quo.'*

The words had spilled rapidly out of his mouth: *'Social reliability isn't always a good thing; you cut out your Beethovens, your Einsteins. What if they had all decided to live by the status quo, never confess to the world what was in their soul?'*

Justine had looked at him, as if the Beethoven option was something she would never consider. '*That's the world of the mad, Hamish. Up and down people. They are people the ordinary, everyday person, just can't understand.'*

'Why do you want people to be ordinary and everyday?' Hamish had asked.

'Because that's how everyone understands each other,' she'd said patiently, *'in simple, common language.'*

She put her hand over his, and he felt soothed, as if his mind was being bathed in hot water, making him feel lulled and sleepy.

'Justine,' he'd said drowsily, *'strangely one of the things I like about you, almost...'* He'd hesitated, wondering if he should say the next word, speak to her about it. The word he was going to use might produce a red traffic light between them. He might not have been able to move towards her again. Or her to him. But he'd known that unless he said that word, it would bushfire his soul until he got it out.

Justine had looked at him, her eyes patient. *'What were you going to say?'*

Hamish had stumbled over his words, *'One of the things I...'* He'd taken a deep breath and said the word: *'love...about you, is your granite. You are an unchanging person. And people like me, people whose minds toss around, rabidly questioning things, need granite like you. Something unchanging, something already answered. I...'* He'd looked at her fearfully then. *'Do you think you can love me, Justine?'*

Justine had looked at him, her eyes quiet. *'I can't...I...'* She'd stopped, carefully considering him, *'I've heard some things, about you.'*

'What?' he'd asked, reeling back from her.

'I…don't think we should talk about this any further,' she'd said firmly.

'Are you not even going to let me defend myself?' Hamish had demanded angrily. *'You've been told things, which you've just believed. Without talking to me about it.'*

'I didn't need to talk to you. It was a certainty. The person's reputation was impeccable.'

Hamish had felt a strange cracking in his soul. His pain and betrayal had shown on his face. *'I don't want to be with someone who doesn't question such certainty,'* he'd said and walked away.

'Hamish? Hamish?' Leanne asked, peering at him. 'Are you talking with those little head-fuckers again?' she asked.

Hamish looked at her broodingly, his spirit still storming with Justine's lightning crack.

'Your mind is wandering again, scarecrow,' Leanne warned him. 'Focus, Hamish. Focus.'

'Do you know how hard it is, to keep my mind to the tiny point, called focus?' Hamish complained.

'It's even harder in mental hospital, because your mind wanders over anything and everything,' Leanne said pointedly.

'Yeah. OK,' he said, looking unhappily down at his bare feet.

'*Don't* slang it, in politics,' Leanne warned. 'No "yeah". Your language must be culture wrapped around a missile.'

'I've heard pollies slang it,' Deanna said casually. 'Bob Hawke was a "crikey" man, wasn't he? And Kevin Rudd, "a fair shake of the sauce bottle" man.'

'Well, yeah. They were both Labor men,' Leanne said dismissively. 'The Greens candidates are composers, scientists, civil engineers.'

'You want me to become caviar?' he asked cagily.

'You could nominate Cinderella as your campaign manager,' Leanne said comically. 'She knows a few tricks about getting out of the dunny.'

'You want me out of the dunny and…and…' He looked at her, frustrated. '*Fuck!* I'm losing my words again.'

'You're losing the words you used to have, mate, because you've lost the thinking you *used* to have. That's what your meds are doing. And now you've got to lose your dunny language as well. OK, mate?'

'That leaves me with no speech,' Hamish said, distressed.

'People can learn Japanese, people can learn Greek, people can learn Italian. So, you have the innate ability to learn caviar speak already. You just study a few caviar people and learn that way. You'll have to study a few salesmen too, to learn how to sell your message. Quickly.'

'Yes. Some politicians are deliberately vague with their messages,' Deanna said suspiciously. 'So the real issue is hidden away, or not dealt with.'

'Yeah, mate, don't hide any issues up your arse,' Leanne agreed. 'There's a lot of people with disinfectant out there ready to clean out ugly political bums.'

'Yeah, OK,' Hamish said, 'no ugly bum hidey hole.'

'Lose the *yeah*,' Leanne reminded him.

'You say it all the time,' Hamish said defensively.

'That's my lingo, my persona, my way of being in this world,' Leanne drawled. 'You? You've got to find a new way of being. Which brings me to something.'

'What?' he asked uneasily.

'It's about your part-time job as a busker.'

'What about it?' Hamish asked fearfully.

'It has to go,' she said firmly.

He looked at her, horrified. 'What? Why?'

'It's not the done thing to sit there and yodel constituent complaints,' Leanne explained.

'Yes, Hamish,' Deanna agreed, 'busking is generally the job of the political protestor, not the politician.'

'But I like it.'

'Busking is part of your old persona, mate. Lose it.'

'Can't I just have one more time? Just me and my guitar, soul wandering together?'

Leanne turned her face away from him. 'Lose that cow-meander language. It's even worse than the slang.'

Hamish looked at her, pained, until she looked at him again. She looked away, then looked at him again, annoyed.

'Oh, for fuck's sake,' she relented, standing up and brushing grass off her zig-zag black and white baggy pants. 'Go have it off with your guitar one more time.'

‘We never got to the point of being sexual,’ Hamish said seriously.

‘Oh, for fuck’s sake, Hamish,’ she said rolling her eyes and walking away. ‘It was just a mouth-off.’

‘I’ve forgotten how to mouth-off speak,’ he called out after her. ‘I am R.I.P. drowned in lithium.’

There was no answer.

Hamish headed back to his hostel room to get his guitar, his head hanging down. Giving up another part of his life, as a part-time busker, was going to be hard. There had been so much freedom in it; sitting on a milk crate, strumming his guitar, releasing his soul to the crowd, trying to stir something in their tight little souls with songs about freedom.

Not many repent of their tendency to stay within the lines, he thought sadly. Those people with minds which did not like to imitate the motion of waves, lifting them up out of their flatness, and staying just for a tiny second at the highest point. Otherwise known as the Epiphany, he mused, grabbing his guitar, his milk crate and heading back down to the mall to busk; still thinking about epiphanies and what happened after experiencing that tiny second at the highest point; the descent down, the call back to drowning. That’s what epiphanies often did, he mused. Filled your mind with water and made you drown in all the uncertainty.

Hamish stopped a minute, startled at how clearly and smoothly all those thoughts came to him. He wouldn’t go as far as to say lithium was the Christ that saved him; but it had at least been the pesticide that killed the weeds in his mind.

In any case, lithium is no longer the enemy it was, he thought, thinking about Golu’s final words to him, about making his mind his best friend and not his enemy.

He wasn’t going to die in some side alley, *R.I.P. social nit after all*, he thought, placing his milk crate down and opening his guitar case. He pulled out his guitar and began strumming.

Hamish stopped as he saw her.

Justine.

Her blonde hair was shorter now, cut sharply just beneath the ears, in a bob. Her startling blue eyes were heavily outlined in kohl, and thickly lashed with mascara. Her pale skin gleamed with good health; a light flush of pink dusted her cheeks; her long, soft pink dress brushed over her light-brown sandals.

His guitar fell out of his hands, smashing on the ground. Like a lost song. A lost song he was staring straight at.

Justine turned her head, her eyes connecting with his. She looked at him with that cerulean certainty of hers, her mouth turning up in a slight smile. There was no smile in him to give her. The loss of her had hit him hard, cracked his mind, hurled him around in a mental tsunami.

'Justine,' Hamish managed to say.

Pity washed through her eyes, as she saw his milk crate, and the guitar case open at his feet. She lifted her hand politely. He felt something drown in him, at that distant politeness, drown and die as she turned her head away and kept walking.

He saw a man approach her; with hair black as the crow, light olive skin and brown eyes. His black business suit was sharply and cleanly cut; the trouser and wrist lengths a precise fit. His white shirt was buttoned up to the neck, the two planes of the collar stiffly starched and neatly folded down. His red silk tie was neatly knotted, and ended at exact lengths. The man smiled widely at Justine, his white teeth flashing, as he stopped in front of her and kissed her cheek.

Hamish watched as crow man talked briefly with Justine, his eyes holding hers in a warm, steady gaze. His eyes held a confidence and easiness Hamish had never known. His own eyes had always searched and brooded and stumbled looking for answers to the many questions that crossed his mind. This man already *knew* the answers.

He heard Justine laugh and pain tore at his soul. The renunciation of Justine still hurt. He *loved* her. He loved her more than anyone else. But he just couldn't have anyone in his life who did not question things, or was so casual with him, to the point of dismissive.

More pain seared his soul, as he watched crow man put his arm around Justine's shoulder. He leant closer to her, saying something. Hamish watched, pained, as Justine turn her head towards the man, smiling. It was the smile of a woman in process. A woman reaching to move past the unsaid, the lengthening looks, the silent knowing which exists between a woman and a man.

Justine was looking to tighten, to get things said, to acknowledge what was there between them. Hamish could see this in the way Justine was standing so close to him; she was wanting to close off the silence. She had never done this with him, Hamish. She mostly kept her lovely body kilometres apart from him.

The closeness of crow man's body to Justine, and that last bit of politeness of hers to him, closing him off, stung him hard.

He loved her. He loved her so much.

And he couldn't forget her.

Hamish let his smashed guitar fall into the ocean; watched the amber wood and thin strings, which sounded his soul, sink under water. He would not be full of those sounds anymore. Those sounds of variance which scaled his mind at different pitches, keeping him falling and rising. Sometimes, his mind sounded at a higher octave, like an A note resounding things like clouds and operatic thoughts. Sometimes his mind sounded at a lower octave, like a lower B note, and his mind became like the closed darkness inside bells; brooding and silent and waiting for something to strike.

Hamish did not want this variance inside his mind anymore, or the different pitches of thought. The rocks he had once renounced with their solidness, their thick texture, their dull colour of thinking; leaving him fixed, solid, stable.

He wanted that. Anything else left him in pain.

19

'Right, Hamish. You now have socially acceptable hair. And you don't moon around with your guitar anymore, singing with a dog's petulance when denied a bone. Now for the socially acceptable look…' Leanne said, looking slowly over his tie-dye shirt and orange bohemian pants. 'Mate, you look like a hung election, the political death. It's not the sort of image you want to present in politics.'

'I'm hanging myself now through compromise. I've given up my social nit look, for Pine O Cleen, and I'm no longer the majority rule on myself. Everyone else is,' Hamish pointed out.

'Mate, there's no way out of it,' Leanne said inconsolably. 'Society has been built by the powers that be and you are trained to fit into it from when you are in nappies. In this way, you don't get The Hung Parliament Effect, where everyone obstructs you and passes you in on the negative.'

'When was the last hung parliament?' Deanna asked frowning. 'I can't quite remember…'

'We had a hung parliament in Australia in 1940, which ended up with Curtin in power. Now. Hamish. Let's get back to hanging that clothing of yours. Yes. Those clothes must go, they speak of marijuana. Clothes, they speak, Hamish, they speak. They hint to people what you're about. People who wear casual clothing, tend to be casual people. Girls with short skirts and long thigh-high black boots, think their vaginas will take them further in life. So, you can't have your social nit look anymore, Hamish. It says *Fuck you* to everyone.'

'Sometimes you speak such rubbish, Leanne,' Deanna said critically. 'Clothes cannot speak.'

'You are such a literal, Deanna,' Leanne said, annoyed. 'Don't think of becoming an artist, will you? You would be fired by the muse for incompetence in interpretation.'

'I have no idea what all that meant,' Deanna said irritably. 'Let's just get on with it. Hamish. You look impoverished. And that's not the sort of image you want to present.'

'You are a bit skinny,' Leanne agreed, looking him over. 'Are you eating, scarecrow?'

'Noodles, rice, lentil cakes…'

'No. No,' Leanne said. 'You'll have to change your diet as well. A lentils man. No. Can't have it. The Asian trade with Australia would plummet. They just *love* our beef.'

'Beef or not, the main thing you need to know, Hamish, is that people want to know you can control yourself. Then will then trust you with control of the country,' Deanna said pointedly.

'Yeah that's right, Hamish. Don't blow up the sharks. Smile at sharks. Doesn't matter if they don't smile back or bare their teeth at you. Who cares? Getting past the shark without a grenade going off between you is the important thing. You've got to sugar the shark,' Leanne said definitely.

'Just a small point…' Hamish said tentatively.

'Cut that language out immediately, Hamish,' Leanne scolded, 'small things are not in political vernacular.'

'Children are. Childcare policies. Things like that,' Deanna pointed out.

'I meant the word "small" is part of mentally skinny political talk,' Leanne said irritably. 'You need to be a bit of a blowfish, Hamish. Fatten that mouth of yours with big, fat, strong words.'

'You speak the way you want to,' Deanna said, 'yet, here you are telling him he has to speak another way.'

'He *has* to, Deanna,' Leanne said impatiently. 'He's got to become a new social self; not keep his old social self where he talks as he wants to and does what he likes. He has to become an actor, perform the political personage. Or the political script. So, to speak.' She paused. 'He's got to be a nuke, wrapped in an Oscar.'

'A nuke? In an Oscar? What do you mean this time?' Deanna snapped.

'You know. A performance award. He's got to act the part, *then* release our policy weapon.'

'Which is?' Deanna asked, alarmed.

'A policy weapon against status quo society, the preservation of tradition, the marginalisation of people like myself. Hamish won't be able to launch the policy weapon for us if he's standing up there, on the podium, looking like a scarecrow on pot. He's got to look like the boy next door.'

'Don't forget his blonde, ponytailed wife with her full skirt, tight top and vacuum cleaner,' Deanna said sarcastically.

'Are you interested in that sort of wife, Hamish?' Leanne asked, giving him a scrutinising look.

'No,' Hamish said politely.

'You will be,' Leanne said comfortingly.

'No,' Hamish said more firmly.

'Your sweetheart over there,' Leanne said, nodding towards Justine, talking with some friends by a tree, 'she's blonde, she wears long feminine skirts, has little pink apple cheeks. You just have to stick a vacuum cleaner in her hand, and you will have the perfect political wife.'

Hamish looked over at the woman he so desperately loved. 'I wouldn't want to monotone her like that.'

'What do you mean?' Deanna asked sharply.

'Justine's steady and calm and practical. But she's not the 1950s type of woman who speaks the language of saucepans and vacuum cleaners.'

'I think you have the wrong idea of a political wife, Hamish,' Deanna scoffed. 'Some of them are in very high-profile positions. *Very* high.'

'The high-profile political wife *doesn't* appeal to women in ordinary or struggling circumstances,' Leanne said pointedly, 'where she's scraping up her last dollar to buy a loaf of bread for the kids. Or living in her car with three kids, because she can't afford to rent or buy and there's a countrywide Bible-length list for public housing.'

'Yeah. My mother knew a family who had to live in a car for months because there was no public housing or rentals available,' Hamish said.

'And what did your mother say to that?' Leanne asked.

'She said it was because they weren't Catholic, no-one would help them. And God wouldn't either as the family never prayed.'

'Your mother's a fucking fundamentalist, mate,' Leanne said. 'No wonder you stumbled so much wearing her Catholic high heels. And as for Hamish scoring a high-profile political wife, I agree a bit of she-plastic hanging off his arm won't help his cause as champion of the disadvantaged.' Leanne looked over at Justine, now sitting with her group of friends at a picnic table under the tree, her legs and feet neatly together. The skirt of her pink dress drifting in the wind. 'What did you say she's studying?'

'Counselling,' Hamish said. 'She's almost through her Bachelor's. She had a head start on me, educationally speaking, as I wandered around busking for a couple of years and she just got straight down to business, as she usually does.'

'No fog in her head then,' Leanne said.

'No. Not one to become lost,' Hamish said regretfully.

'A counsellor for suffering people will go down well with the public, Hamish,' Deanna commented, looking at Justine approvingly.

Hamish looked down, staring dejectedly at his feet. 'She won't look at me like…' he broke off, biting his lip, 'you know…that way a woman will look at a man, if he's not considered platonic.' He looked hopelessly at Justine. 'I don't think there's any chance of her becoming my political wife.'

'Would she be able to handle it?' Deanna asked interestedly. 'Being a political wife?'

'Justine can handle anything,' Hamish answered, looking over at Justine again, deeply craving her.

'Then that's what you want,' Deanna said matter-of-factly.

'I'm not what *she* wants,' Hamish said miserably. 'I saw her the other day, with a man who looked like straight out of Wall Street.'

'Ohhh. One of those. Crisp, clean, banker types. Walking starch,' Leanne said.

Hamish hung his head. 'Yeah, one of those,' he said despondently.

'*Yes,* not yeah,' Leanne corrected. 'It's all syllables go, boy next door.'

'Next, you'll be wanting him to move to England and go cantering in breeches,' Deanna said. 'You seem to be speaking a lot of hypocrisy lately, Leanne.'

'I am not,' Leanne said indignantly. 'In front-row politics a certain amount of Pine O Cleen talk is expected. In the back row of politics, where I am, the placard waver, the grounds person, I am *expected* to speak Aussie dialect.'

'Ocker language, you mean,' Deanna said.

'Whatever you want to call it. It's a language that exists among those who speak in plain speak, not the talk of the political Devil.'

Deanna and Hamish spoke in unison: 'The what?'

'Political Devil,' Leanne said, irritated as if the political Devil was common knowledge and why didn't they know about him.

'What? Do you mean pitchfork language?' asked Hamish warily. 'Or is hell ruling this country without voter consent?'

'Don't be stupid, Leanne. I never saw "Vote 1: The Devil" at the polling booth,' Deanna said, annoyed.

'I don't think the terms of the Australian Constitution allow for the election of the Devil,' Hamish said solemnly. 'The government has to be elected by the people. And do the will of the people. I don't think that includes the Devil sitting in Parliament; unless the voter was a hardcore Satanist.'

'What a joke!' Leanne scoffed. 'Doing the will of the people…The government are *not* doing the will of the *people*; they are doing the will of some mothball pollies, who wrote the Australian Constitution. The will of the people has nothing to do with it, since most of us are subjected to the ideology which rules our country.'

'So, it's not hell ruling our country after all, it's whiteness,' Hamish said cuttingly.

'Some people see that as the same thing,' Leanne said nonchalantly.

'What? Hell and whiteness? The same thing?' Deanna asked, looking at her as if she had suddenly developed a mental illness.

'White Australia is the Devil's way of thinking, Deanna. Creating division, subjection, pitting people against each other; that sort of thing.' Leanne leant back on her hands. 'The Devil rules white heterosexist people, Deanna.'

'I think you need to think about taking medication, Leanne,' Deanna said bluntly.

'Don't be stupid,' Leanne said.

'Can we please get back to why you think political language is the language of the Devil?' Hamish asked. 'Because I may not go into politics if that's the case. I had God talk all my life. Devil's talk may put my mental health at risk as well.'

'Well you know, the Devil is in the details. So is politics,' Leanne said knowledgeably.

'Like…?' Hamish asked.

'Like a really specific word. A detail word. Like "fiscal". Who the fuck, in plain-speak world, is going to understand that? The first time I heard it, I thought the pollie was referring to a type of fish. That the word was economically related, was something I found out later on.'

Deanna gave Leanne an annoyed look. 'Fiscal policy. Only two words were needed for that whole bewildering speech.'

'Whatever,' Leanne said, equally annoyed. She turned to Hamish. 'Now, what happened with your girl and her fiscal looking banker?' Leanne asked.

'What happened? What *happened?'* Hamish said, his words tumbling out the way they used to, when he was upset. 'That thing that happens between a man and a woman who know each other and want more. And he looked very skilled at getting the more part out of her. I've been trying since she was thirteen. I was always met with a sexually absent look.' He sighed.

'You just want to take her to bed?' Deanna asked in disgust.

'No. I desperately love her,' he said miserably. 'But it's a one-way street called platonic with her. Full of stop signs.'

'Maybe she's responding to you like that because of what you're presenting to her,' Leanne said, looking at him speculatively. 'They're not the things that attract her, Hamish. At the same time, women know if you're putting it on; they know if you're pretending to be something you're not, just to impress them. So, my advice to you, Hamish, is present yourself to her in a different way. She's not getting the full story of you, mate. Too many closed chapters from the way you have been brought up.' In a firm voice she said, 'Start opening some of those closed chapters, mate, you may find the one you kissed her in.'

20

'You look bare of social defiance,' Leanne said to Hamish, as he sat down in front of her.

'Yes,' he answered. 'I now look like the shut-up citizen.' He ran his hand over his neatly cut hair, glancing down at his buttoned-up shirt. 'I feel like I've swapped one mental illness for another.'

'Normality is not a mental illness,' Deanna said firmly to him.

'Conformity could be considered a mental illness, Hamish, as it indicates an inability to think for oneself,' Leanne said comfortingly.

'Well, why the fuck are you turning me into this for?' he asked, pulling at his white buttoned shirt and his neatly ironed, light-khaki pants.

'Remember, the right social packaging on the outside and the nuke hidden within,' Leanne reminded him.

'Most pollies use sales language or rhetoric, Hamish,' Deanna told him, 'so you'll have to downsize that mouth of yours. It'll never pass like that.'

Leanne looked at Deanna sharply. 'Many a would-be voter has fallen asleep at political rhetoric. Put a bit of dragonfly in your words, Hamish.'

Hamish remembered then: *It was only when he watched things that flew, he remembered his mental wings. Dragonflies, butterflies, fireflies, words containing yellow and fire…*

Hamish looked at Leanne, his face struggling. He missed the speed and spitfire of his thoughts, his mind now in lockdown. 'I used to think in dragonfly, but I can't seem to…' he broke off, looking down, trying not show his anguish. 'But I can't seem to think like that anymore.'

'I know, mate. I know, the meds,' Leanne said compassionately. She touched his arm. 'You might not be able to *think* like you used to. But you can still write a dragonfly speech. It's dragonfly behind your social justice principles.' She leant back on her hands. 'Ancient lore says when the dragonfly appears, flying around you or darting out from behind trees, it's time for change. Time for transformation. Time to look at things from a new angle. That's what you need to take into politics with you, mate. Change. Transformation. New angles.'

'The dragonfly is medicated to death, Leanne. Dead on the floor of my mind,' Hamish explained sadly.

'Hamish. Resurrect your dragonfly *outside* of yourself. In what you *do*, not what you *think,'* Leanne said encouragingly.

'Let's get back to how we are going to get Hamish into politics,' Deanna said, looking Hamish up and down. 'You pass the first social test,' she said, looking at his khaki pants, his white buttoned shirt, light brown loafers and neatly shorn hair.

'I still can't quite look at that,' Leanne said, glancing at his clothing and looking away. 'I kind of miss your social nit look.'

'Talk like that isn't going to help him,' Deanna said. 'You are trying to get him to socially conform, to get him into politics; yet, here you are, mooning around about his lost self.'

'First social test,' Hamish said to Deanna. 'What do you mean?'

'Well, there's a first,' Deanna said, 'you asking me what *I* mean.'

'What *do* you mean?' Leanne asked irritably.

'I mean, you get judged first on your appearance. That's the first thing people see.'

'And yeah,' Leanne said scathingly, 'then you get slotted into ugly, mildly ugly, fucking ugly, that's unspeakable *or* beautiful, I want to fuck you gorgeous, or you are my goddess on the mountaintop. Anything in between ugly and beautiful is pretty much dismissed. You know why? Because people have strong reactions to either ugly or beautiful people. Reactions to the in-between population barely register.'

'No. I don't think so,' Deanna disagreed, 'I think that's just how you see things because you're a dismissed lesbian.'

'By you, maybe,' Leanne retorted.

'Um,' Hamish said, then trailed off, looking uncertainly from Leanne to Deanna.

'Oh, we're old friends, Hamish,' Leanne said off-handedly, 'we just tell it as it is to each other.'

'OK. If you want to offend each other, I won't get in the way of that,' Hamish answered circumspectly.

‘It’s not like that Hamish,’ Deanna explained. ‘Really, it’s not.’

‘Can…we get on with this…?’ Hamish asked tiredly. ‘I need to progress from social nit to social puppet.’

‘A social nit you may have been. But now…’ Deanna paused, thinking.

‘Now we can call you a cultured arsehole,’ Leanne declared.

‘You’ve put me in a social binary,’ Hamish said fearfully.

‘A what?’ Deanna asked him.

‘A social binary. Cultured on one end, primitive on the other. A social plus or a social minus,’ Hamish said despondently.

‘Become a social neutral then,’ Deanna said, yawning.

‘Making neither choice is worse,’ Leanne said. ‘I mean what if you chose neither; to be good or evil? You would passively endorse both good and evil. Just say some poor kid gets raped. You’re going to do nothing about it because you are neutral instead of good, where you take out your gun and shoot the bastard or bitch. But, *if* you’re evil, you say “good on her or him, a kiddie rapist has wrecked another child”. By not intervening or preventing evil acts because you’re neutral, you are saying it’s alright to do that to kids.’ She leant back on her elbows. ‘I don’t think of evil as something with horns and cloven feet. I think of evil as a kiddie rapist.’

‘I read a quote about that once,’ Hamish recalled. ‘It said: “The darkest places in hell are reserved for those who maintain their neutrality in times of moral crises.”’

‘Dante Alighieri wrote that,’ Deanna said. ‘He’s the guy who wrote *The Divine Comedy*. And that quote, has been quoted by people everywhere, from JFK to Martin Luther King.’

‘It’s a quote for the pissed-off population,’ Leanne said casually.

‘What?’ Deanna asked, irritated. ‘Talk English, would you?’

‘JFK and Martin Luther King…’ Hamish pondered slowly. He looked up at Leanne. ‘Didn’t they both get shot?’ he asked nervously.

‘Yeah. They did. Both in the 1960s,’ Leanne said bitterly. ‘Both visionaries. We’re lucky we’ve got a lot more global support for visionaries now. People no longer get shot for talking big talk.’ She paused, looking at Hamish kindly. ‘I don’t think you’ll get shot on your bicycle, Hamish, for talking about the need for peace or dreams, or hunting idiots who smash both.’

‘Can we get back to Project Hamish?’ Deanna asked, exasperated.

‘You’re turning me into a project?’ Hamish asked in dismay.

'Yes. We now pronounce you Corporate Hamish,' Leanne announced.

'Fuck!' Hamish swore. 'I hate the corporate world. It's so…mechanistic.'

'It won't be that bad,' Leanne said, smiling affectionately at him.

'I feel like I'm selling out on myself,' Hamish said uncertainly. 'Losing my social nit self to corporate self.'

'You're not really losing anything, Hamish; not if you remember what you originally built that self on,' Deanna said, staring hard at him. 'The mental illness persona…'

Hamish's cheeks flared red. 'My way of thinking was not mentally ill,' he denied. 'I could just see the world differently than others because of my high intelligence range.'

Leanne looked at Hamish speculatively. 'Hamish, I think you built your past self on everybody else. What your mother thought, what your father thought, what your priest thought. How to be head-wrecked, mate,' she said sympathetically. Leanne patted him on the shoulder, and quickly withdrew her hand. 'Mate, trade it in.' She shook her hand. 'Got to get that maleness off my hand,' she said, shaking her hand again and rubbing it on her pants.

'You need to change your walk as well, Hamish,' Deanna advised.

'My walk?' Hamish asked, confused. 'What's wrong with it?'

'Your walk,' Deanna said impatiently, 'is strange, Hamish.'

'Well, how is it strange?' Hamish asked, upset.

'You sort of lope along, Hamish,' Leanne explained more kindly.

'Yes, that's it,' Deanna said. 'If you look at how an emu walks, it's like that.'

'An emu?' Hamish asked, staring at her belligerently.

'Lope…' Leanne explained, looking at Deanna warningly, and then kindlier at Hamish. 'You lope as you walk, with your knees bent. They don't straighten out after your foot hits the ground. And you walk fast. Almost well…'

'Manic,' Deanna pronounced.

'I wasn't going to say that,' Leanne said. 'I wasn't going to say that. Deanna. You don't talk about people's mental illnesses in front of them.'

'You just did,' Deanna said pointedly.

Hamish cheeks flamed again. 'Can we talk about something else?' he asked angrily. 'I don't want to be emu blasphemed, or DSM-IV discussed.'

'Just practise walking slower,' Leanne said kindly, 'and straighten your legs. Have a practice walk.'

Hamish got up and tried shortening his stride, while stiffening his legs.

'No. No. Hamish,' Deanna said, dismayed, shaking her head. 'You need to learn to walk like a prince if you want to give the impression of confidence.'

'More chance of getting your church princess, too,' Leanne said comfortingly. 'With a bit of prince confidence.'

'Or other princesses,' Deanna said matter-of-factly, 'besides church princesses.'

'He prefers virgin-type princesses,' Leanne said, 'don't you, Hamish?'

'She's the only woman for me,' Hamish said vehemently.

'We know, we know, we know,' Leanne said. 'The Church Princess and the Social Nit. Our ears are still weeping.'

'Try again a bit later, Hamish,' Deanna said. 'When you are more…her social type.'

'Yeah, mate. Grow a few more inches socially,' Leanne added. 'Then have a go. Make sure you have a strategy to get past her chastity belt psyche.'

Hamish turned on his heel and tried his new walk again. It felt strange and awkward, like his legs were made of tin. 'What social size do you think I am now?' he asked warily. 'And when can I stop strutting?'

'Now,' Leanne said definitely, putting her hand to her mouth and looking away. 'That penis thrust in your new strut makes me want to vomit.'

'To answer your question, Hamish. If you were measured socially, you would be about a size one,' Deanna said bluntly.

'Just out of nappies, then,' Hamish said dismayed.

'Yes. And we have to socially toilet-train you,' Deanna said.

'You don't want to sit in the wrong place, mate,' Leanne said warningly. 'You may miss the shit catcher.'

'Social outcasts are always sitting in the wrong place,' Deanna reminded her.

'A shit-catcher is a toilet…or a potty…?' Hamish asked uncertainly, looking at Leanne, then at Deanna. He hated how he could no longer instantly understand nuance or implication, and had to ask for concrete explanations. Meds. He *hated* the negative effects of them.

'You have to learn how to sit on the social potty, mate. Can't throw your dirty nappy around in politics. No shit flinging,' Leanne said kindly to him.

‘Have you watched Question Time lately?’ Deanna asked caustically. ‘Because there are some mouths out of control there.’

‘The Bear Pit has gone a bit feral,’ Leanne agreed. She turned to Hamish, giving him a warning look, ‘You don’t want to be flung out the political bum as diarrhea.’

‘No danger of that,’ Hamish said despondently. ‘I have a constipated self with this medication…and…and…I can’t think of what I was going to say after that; because my brain is now registering my constipation statement as strange and incoherent.’

Leanne exploded with laughter. ‘You’re honest, Hamish,’ she said, wiping tears of laughter from her eyes. ‘And that’s what people will love about you in politics.’

21

'Ready, Hamish?' Leanne asked, giving him a nudge, her voice sparking with excitement.

'Ready,' Hamish lied, looking around at the room full of people, barely able to breathe; his lungs felt small and tight. He could see their notepads with all their questions written down; some people flipping over their notepad pages, re-reading information. His glance skittered to the empty podium waiting for him like the cupboard he'd read about in CS Lewis's Narnia books, a doorway into the new land of politics.

Hamish hoped, to whatever was called God these days, that there was a lantern on a post, glowing in the Parliament snow, in his new political Narnia.

He decided relying on possibilities was unsafe and he himself had to become the lamp in the snow. Shine on the people.

Hallelujah, brother.

Hamish frowned at Church language entering his mind again and unhappily admitted to himself that shining on people was going to be difficult; he barely had enough light within him to shine on himself, let alone thousands of voters.

Hamish stood slowly up. Everything seemed slow: the people turning to look at him, the clock on the wall ticking to the next point, the beckoning hand of the host.

'Go on, Hamish,' Leanne said encouragingly, giving his back a push, 'go up on the stage there and take your seat.' She wiped her hand on her pants, as if trying to take away his male imprint.

Hamish stood motionless, his heart becoming louder, and the people around him slower.

Become the lamp, become the lamp, become the lamp, he told himself.

'Go on,' Leanne hissed, 'fuck off up there.'

Hamish's hand tightened around the piece of paper he'd written his speech on. A speech he'd spent hours agonising over, trying to find both words and courage.

He had to be the white Martin Luther King *and* the Political Poster Boy Next Door. Without getting crowd shot.

Tonight, he would lose his social nit self, Hamish thought, caught between panic and hope as he walked slowly up the aisle, trying not to look at the people around him. The sight of so many people gave him a type of social vertigo, making his head spin from too many different types—religious, political, legal, family, marginalised.

They all had a core interest in common: preservation.

Hamish reached the podium.

The host to the political forum moved aside, waving him towards the seats at the back of the stage. 'Have a seat, Hamish.'

He glanced at the three political candidates sitting there; his eyes skidded quickly away, not wanting to take in any detail. He would only panic or feel inferior to them.

Hamish walked over to a seat, refusing to look at them, and sat down. He closed his eyes, feeling as if his heart was hotwired to a revving engine. He didn't even hear what the other candidates had to say, his heart was gunning so much.

'Hamish,' the community host called out loudly.

Hamish startled, opening his eyes. 'Now?' he asked, his voice rising in panic.

'Now,' the community host said kindly, beckoning him up toward the front of the stage.

Hamish got up awkwardly, forgetting his well-practised political strut and stumbled towards the podium. He saw Deanna cover the side of her face, looking away in embarrassment.

Hamish's cheeks flamed red.

'All yours,' the community host said cheerfully, handing him the microphone. One of the political candidates leant forward. 'You may live. You may not,' she whispered loudly.

'Right,' Hamish said, turning back around. 'Yes. I see what you mean,' he muttered, his gaze sweeping over some angrily written placards. He gawked at a woman wearing a "Fuck off Pollie" T-shirt, and a hostile man up the back, holding the hand of his male partner, glaring at him, no doubt wondering why the fuck he, straight Hamish, was chosen for their pin-up party and not him, a marginalised gay. Hamish guessed by the man's glare that he must have run for candidacy and was considered too marginal for what would get a significant Green vote. Too marginal to get past the traditional Liberal majority vote, in the stronghold Liberal area of Black Crag.

Hamish had read that gay or lesbian candidates in the political arena had to get past Labour strongholds as well, as both major parties were obliged to abide by the 100-plus year-old constitution of Australia, not known for its pro-gay stance, but for its long-term preservation of the Judeo-Christian state position. As Judeo-Christians were a heterosexist culture, gays, he'd read, were always going to face cultural exclusion. Hamish suspected some gays or lesbians were elected as tokenism, to appease a public that was growing increasingly intolerant of Judeo-Christian ideologies protected in law.

Hamish shook his reading out of his head and refocused on the crowd, waiting for him to speak.

He opened his mouth.

Nothing came out.

He saw Leanne frantically waving a bit of paper out to him, pointing at it. Hamish glanced down at the speech he'd written crumpled in his hand and put it on the podium, clumsily trying to smooth it out.

'Let's hear it for Hamish McColl,' yelled out Leanne, standing and clapping loudly.

Some people looked uneasily over at Leanne, some loudly murmured, and some laughed; but she didn't care. She kept clapping, stamping her foot loudly and whistling.

Some people got up and clapped as well. Some out of politeness. Some out of pity. Some out of a red flag opportunity, ready to lock horns with him.

Hamish leant in closer to the microphone.

'Hello,' he said, tapping at the microphone. It crackled loudly. *'Fuck!'* he swore.

'Not a good start,' Deanna said to Leanne loudly, shaking her head.

To Hamish's relief, he heard some *Hi's*; some *Hellos*; some *Fuck offs*; *piss offs*; and *Hurry the fuck up and speak,* in the crowd.

Hurry the fuck up and speak was Leanne.

Hamish remembered now. What Leanne had trained him to do.

Hamish looked slowly around the room, as taught by Leanne, catching the gaze of audience members. He gripped both edges of the podium and held his head centred, his gaze steady and direct.

'I don't want you all to think as me as just another politician,' Hamish began.

'Well you're not there yet, mate,' a man yelled out.

Smile at the shark, smile at the shark, smile at the shark.

Hamish managed to stretch his lips over his teeth.

The man sat slowly down.

Sugar the shark did work, Hamish thought, relieved, watching the man mutter to himself, examining a leaflet.

Hamish managed to widen his smile and began again. 'I don't want you all to think of me as just another politician. I want you to think of me as a Social Prophet.'

Hamish saw interest stir in the eyes of his audience. A few sat forward, their faces considering him.

'Prophets usually come in at a time when we have darkness in our society,' Hamish continued.

Silence fell over the crowd.

'The darkness in our society exists, because of a continuing cycle of social division which came from an ancient Western philosophy binary system. A system of opposites.' Hamish paused, looking carefully around at the crowd. 'It's a system which, today, determines what holds the greater cultural and social value. We have social opposites of non-gay/gay, non-indigenous/indigenous, sane/insane, rich/poor, nuclear family/single-parent family, non-disabled/disabled. We are *divided* from each other, by a system which determines what is of greater value and what is of lesser value.'

Leanne got up and clapped loudly. 'Yeah, scarecrow...I mean Social Prophet...you tell it as it is!'

Hamish tried not to smile. Waited until the murmurs of the crowd died down.

'You may be interested to know,' Hamish continued, taking a deep breath, 'that the first word of these binary opposites holds the greater value, the second the lesser value. That is the non-gay, the non-indigenous, the sane and the rich form the greater value to our society and the gay, the indigenous, the insane and the poor, the lesser value to our society.'

There was some loud clapping and whistling.

Hamish looked at the crowd, trying to sound firm, as taught to him by Leanne. 'What I want to do is become the new Social Prophet of Sydney. Help lead those on the lesser end of the social binary into the legally promised land where equal rights and equal opportunity and social inclusion exist. Because inclusion in law is one thing; in practice is another. Law, without social practice, is just token law.'

Some people stood and clapped loudly, whistling and stamping their feet. Hamish waited until the noise faded.

'So, we are in a social position of non-gay/gay, indigenous/non-indigenous, rich/poor, sane/insane, nuclear family/single-parent family, white/black,' Hamish continued. 'So I say this. Let's take ourselves out of opposing each other. Because as long as we are in opposition to each other, the greater value will always win as they are the ones with more social power. And those determined the lesser value will protest and riot, trying to get their unhappiness heard.'

More people in the room stood and clapped.

Hamish nervously smoothed over the crumpled bits of his paper, so he could clearly read the rest of his speech. 'So, I'm asking you on election day, to let me be your Social Prophet. And those of you who are religious, may remember reading that in Moses' time, ten plagues had to hit the land before the Pharaoh would consent to set the Israelite people free from a society that considered them of lesser value.' Hamish looked down a minute. 'The ninth plague was darkness,' he said quietly. 'And I say to you now, that our society is in a Moses type of ninth plague. We are in the dark because of an ancient system missing its social lightbulb.'

A hush fell over the crowd.

'So, help me lead you, not so much out of the wilderness, but out of the rigid equations of society, where the advantaged or those considered superior are given greater value and those considered inferior are marginalised and given lesser value. I'm asking you to vote me in, not just as a local councillor with a specific party platform, but as a Social Prophet, with the social knowledge, lesser value experience and determination to make a socially promised land happen. Right here. In our local government area.'

The entire room stood and clapped him, Leanne screaming and stamping her foot.

'Hamish, Hamish, Hamish, Hamish!' people screamed in unison.

'You know what was really good about that speech?' Leanne said to Hamish, stirring her black coffee.

'What?' Hamish asked, the peculiar feeling of triumph still pulsing through his veins.

'You even appealed to the conformists,' she said optimistically, 'because even the traditionalists of society have sons or daughters or wives or husbands or partners, who have a mental illness, who become gay, who maybe get a disability. But,' she said, lowering her spoon and looking at him warningly, 'if you want to stay politically appealing to the people, you must remember one very important thing.'

'What?' he asked contentedly, still basking in his new social approval.

'A lot of political candidates start off idealistic, with their strong social values and persuasive policy platforms. Then, the political Bermuda Triangle happens.'

'The what?' Hamish asked.

'The political Bermuda Triangle. Where the strong social values and persuasive political platform, which the political candidate started off with, suddenly and mysteriously disappear. Vanishes off the public horizon,' she drawled, snapping her fingers. 'It's a political pattern, Hamish, dating back a long time. She showed herself here in 1943, mate. The promise, the retraction, the promise, the retraction, the promise, the retraction,' she shook her head. 'How to flick a political rubber band, mate.'

'Who or what was in 1943?' Hamish asked interestedly.

'Curtin, mate. John Curtin. In World War I, he was *dead* set against conscription. He even became a jailbird briefly because he would not enlist. When he became Prime Minister in 1941, what did he do?'

'I don't know,' Hamish said. 'What?'

'He brought in conscription. After giving it the nose-up, after doing time, he then flicks the political rubber band and does the Bermuda, mate. Afterwards, he was politically ripped apart by some bulldogs in Labor, for doing it. And Curtin's not the only one. You've got the day the GST made it from ghost to flesh. It was going to be dead policy. But then, it mysteriously resurrected. Like Lazarus, mate, like Lazarus. Then there is the mystery of income tax cuts, suddenly repealed or butchered.'

'No political rubber band flicking,' Hamish repeated. 'I will remember.'

'Many a political head has come off that way,' Leanne warned, 'so don't you sell out on what you originally stood for. Because not only is it a betrayal of yourself, you have betrayed all those who had social and personal faith in you. They are looking to *you* to help change their life. Because they haven't got the social power to do it. And you, in your new political position do. So, remember that. Stick to the Social Prophet, leading your constituents to their legally promised land.'

'Now, Hamish, another important thing.'

'What?'

'Kevin Rudd's sorry speech was a big hit with the Australian public. Gave the Indigenous people some hope and most of the whites were impressed too, with a politician who didn't just speak the much-hated political rhetoric, but put a story in there, you know, blew up his words with a bit of heart pound. People listen to that, scarecrow. Congrats on your Moses seller of a Social Prophet, it had some throttle in it. So, good on you for that…' She leant back in her chair, grinning at him. 'Bring that social manna down, baby.'

Hamish nodded, 'Yeah, I remember Rudd's speech. And it's the stuff people want to hear, but—'

'But?' Leanne prompted.

'We've got to repair things in reality; not just repair on the symbolic level. I don't think just saying sorry is enough.'

'Well, Rudd did mention that in his sorry speech,' Leanne corrected him. 'He said: "Unless the great symbolism of reconciliation is accompanied by an even greater substance, it is little more than a clanging gong". '

'Maybe I should go Labor, you think?' Hamish asked uncertainly. He clutched his head, frustrated. Uncertainty had never existed in him before he went to the Looney Tunes hotel, and he hated the feel of it; of what it did to him. Caused a strange dipping in his mind.

'Hamish. No,' Leanne said firmly, 'you just study what works. And what works is telling a story. And I don't mean porkers. I mean something with a bit of *Days of Our Lives* in it, a few violins playing in the sentences. Rudd put in some flickering campfires, a bit of foot stomping, half-naked tribal elders and a grimly determined, yarn-spinning, 80-year-old Indigenous woman in his speech…and it worked, you know? The fucking speech got played over and over and over. Mind you, gays and lesbians are still waiting for *their* apology and sorry speech.'

'So are the mentally ill,' Hamish said.

'People with a mental illness,' Leanne corrected amicably.

'What? That makes mental illness sound like a handbag,' Hamish said irritably. 'People *with* something, like it's something they wear or carry around.'

'It's to distinguish the person from the mental illness,' Leanne explained. 'So they are not mistaken for one and the same.'

'Well no one told me all I had to do was throw away the handbag,' Hamish said. 'They just told me I *was* the handbag.'

'Which is exactly why the wording "People with a mental illness" was designed. So, you are not mistaken *for* the handbag.'

'I think it's wording that identifies "people with a mental illness" as a separate population, to the population just called people,' Hamish said.

'It could be population categorisation,' Leanne agreed mildly, 'but those sorts of categorisations are seen on forms everywhere.'

'I read an article where mentally ill people…'

'Hamish,' Leanne scolded, 'you have to use the correct language in politics. You'll be seen as either lazy, deriding or ignorant if you don't.'

'I read an article where mentally…I mean people with a mental illness,' he said through gritted teeth, 'are actually being called *consumers*.'

'That may be the effect of neo-liberalism, Hamish. Consumer is a market term,' Leanne said thoughtfully, crossing her arms across her chest.

'Right,' Hamish said, 'from Western Philosophy binary existence, that is non mentally ill/mentally ill, to a market pig, C/O neoliberalism and…*fuck* there go my thoughts.'

'It's your language starting to normalise, mate,' Leanne said soothingly. 'Your brain is putting on the brakes, as it doesn't recognise people with a mental illness as market pigs; because this comparison doesn't make sense to its new lithium logic.' She leant back in her chair. 'You need to speak more like you did in that speech, scarecrow. It was ingenious, mate.'

Hamish basked in her praise. 'I found a book in the hostel bookshelf, flipped through it and got drawn in by the writings in there. The rest of the speech came from the underpants I grew up in—Moses, the Promised Land, the plagues. And so on.'

'Scarecrow, Church undies? How to restrain your mind and your dick, mate.'

'Um…' Hamish said, 'my mind is already restrained by medication. The dick part I'm not even going to talk about, since the last time I talked about genitals, I ended up scheduled by mental health.'

She gave him an affectionate pat on the shoulder, and then wiped her hand on her pants. 'No offence, you stink of male.' She looked across at him. 'How about this for a fact, Hamish: some religions actually *do* have a philosophy of church undies for dick.'

'What?' Hamish asked, bewildered.

'Well, I read about a religion that recommends men bandage their dicks to their stomachs when dating a woman, so it doesn't spring out at the startled female on the first date.'

'I never heard of it…in Catholic practice…' Hamish said.

'I read about it in a Baptist newsletter,' Leanne said, 'of recommended dating practices for men.'

'What are you doing reading church newsletters?' Hamish asked, puzzled. 'That's not like you. I would have picked you as reading human rights books, where men are allowed to dick spring on the first date, not put it in a church lasso…*fuck*…my mind's gone mental again; not wanting to do social nit speak…*fuck*…'

'It will pass, mate, it will pass; once your mind stops returning to all those phrases considered abnormal. As for why I was reading a church newsletter, someone stuffed it into my haversack when I wasn't looking.'

'Probably someone from the church,' Hamish said.

Leanne scratched her head, 'Mate, they are forever trying to convince gays and lesbians of the proper heterosexist way to do things. Anyway, what were we talking about before our conversation about church-incarcerated dicks…was…that's right…interesting political speeches. If you can make a bit of soap work, you do that, scarecrow. Or should I call you Moses now? You keep giving that speech you made the other night to all the other political forums you have to go to before the council election. You just need a *little* more training in fielding questions; but you can handle crowd hostility pretty well. Now,' she said broodingly, drumming her fingers on the table, 'let's talk about our next step.'

The café door opened, and Hamish turned to see who was coming through the door. He turned back to Leanne, his face pained.

Leanne gave him a pitying look. 'You poor bastard,' she said.

Hamish watched, trying to control his anguish as they approached. Justine: his love, his sun, his altar. And *him*, Wall Street Man, in his stiff-black suit, with his smooth glossy black hair and confident eyes.

Justine slowed as she saw Hamish, her long white dress winging out like an angel as the breeze floated through the open café door.

'Hamish,' she said, her blue eyes looking at him steadily, 'I never would have recognised you.'

Hamish couldn't even manage a smile.

Justine turned to the man next to her, smiling up at him. 'This is Nick Carver, my fiancé.'

Hamish went white.

'Oh *fuck!*' Leanne said, covering one side of her face and looking away.

Hamish couldn't even speak. In agony, he turned away from her, refusing to look at her with her banker man; wearing his 18th-century corpse look.

Justine leant in close to Nick. 'Sometimes Hamish is like that,' she said quietly.

'Bloody bitch,' Leanne said, rising up out of her chair. 'Look how fucking patronising you were, just then. "Sometimes Hamish is like that",' she mimicked, 'like he's something you can only generally explain; as if you had to explain him at all, to your Wall Street prick. You don't even know how much he bloody loves you, do you?'

'I…think we better go,' Justine said, turning towards Nick.

'Yes. You do that,' Leanne jeered. 'And that bastard you're with may look cultured and well cut, but so did Ted Bundy, lollipop.'

'Who?' Justine asked, staring bewildered at Leanne.

'You know, Ted Bundy, the serial killer?'

'Fuck!' said Hamish, leaning his head in his hands and shaking. 'Fuck!'

'You *poor* bastard,' Leanne said. 'I would hug you, but that would be too much for me.'

'Come on, sweetheart,' Nick said soothingly to Justine, 'let's go.'

'That's it, lollipop,' Leanne said sarcastically. 'You go off with your cultured arsehole, there.'

‘Excuse me,’ the man said coldly, nodding stiffly at her and taking Justine’s hand and leaving.

Hamish heard Leanne’s voice, kind and concerned, ‘Hamish?’

Hamish couldn’t look up, nor could he speak. He kept rocking back and forth, his face in his hands, his voice strangled by a big knot of grief.

22

Hamish had lost track of how long he had been lying on his bed. Two days, maybe three.

He wasn't counting.

'Hamish.'

He heard Father Matthias's voice through the door, and turned over, facing the wall.

'I need to speak to the Social Prophet,' Father Matthias called out, 'not Hamish in angst.'

Hamish felt something stir in his consciousness: that new idea of what he wanted to be, but he couldn't seem to stop falling back into his old self again. His thoughts struggling with each other; objects in the room swelling out of their structural forms again.

He hadn't slept for two, three, four nights straight. He couldn't remember.

'What do you want?' Hamish asked dully.

'I need to speak to you about Justine,' Father Matthias said.

Pain struck hard at his soul, at the sound of her name.

He sat up, his face anguished. 'Is she OK?'

'She's not dead, Hamish. But she is upset.' There was a silence. 'Can you just open the door please?'

Hamish dragged himself to the door and opened it. The priest looked him up and down. 'You do look better with your hair crisp, short and sharp like that. Get rid of those trackie pants, however. Comfort does not hold you up.' He looked at the tracksuit pants, shaking his head. 'Mm-mmm-mm. No. They won't do. If you are going into politics, it must be crisp, snappy trousers.'

'I've seen a pollie in cargo pants,' Hamish mumbled.

'No. Really?' Father Matthias asked, pushing past him. 'He must have been having a trouser lazy day.'

'Or he hadn't done his washing,' Hamish said, yawning.

The priest looked around Hamish's hostel room, scrutinising everything with a disproving eye. 'The politicians I know don't do their own washing,' he commented crisply. 'They've got a wife to do that.'

'Bit 1950s isn't it?' Hamish asked, rubbing at his eyes.

'Some people are happy like that, Hamish. Know what their role is, are good at it, and they work together like smooth machinery.' He turned to Hamish and said, 'It's so dark in here, Hamish.' Father Matthias went to the curtains and threw it open. 'Let there be light,' he pronounced.

'Well, looks like you know your role too,' Hamish said weakly, slumping down on the chair by his small, brown wooden desk, as the sunlight streamed in. He turned and looked at the priest suspiciously. 'You're not here trying to get a confession out of me, are you?'

The priest narrowed his eyes, tilting his head to one side. 'Have you done anything, Hamish? Something I should know about?' he asked suspiciously.

'I haven't murdered anyone yet,' Hamish mumbled.

'No. Wouldn't look good on your political rap sheet,' the priest said drily, 'now, would it? Now,' he said firmly, patting the bed, 'sit next to me here and tell me all about it.'

Hamish staggered tiredly over to Father Matthias and slumped onto the bed, his head in his hands. 'Tell you about what?'

There was a silence.

Hamish looked up.

Father Matthias looked at him sternly.

'OK,' Hamish sighed, 'I had a mentally ill reaction to Justine announcing her engagement. She announced it right in front of me, with her plastic shark…plastic…thing…him; my words won't form when…*Fuck!*'

Father Matthias looked at him sharply. 'When they weigh in on the mental illness scale, Son. "Plastic shark"? Hamish,' he tutted, shaking his head. 'Your brain has sent out an alarm, saying your words don't make sense, you know. Your brain should associate sharks with things you learnt in school. Sharks have enormous teeth, smooth grey skin, gills, several fins, and swim in oceans. Those are the facts, Son.' Father Matthias tipped his head the other way. 'Hamish. When you call sharks *plastic*, your brain has registered that this is something you did not *learn*, but made up. So, it freaks out a bit. Anyway. Let's talk about why I'm here.'

Hamish looked down, unable to speak; his heart cracking, his mind too full of Justine, to even find a word.

'Hamish,' the priest called.

He raised his head finally, and looked at Father Matthias miserably.

The priest looked at him sternly. 'Your friend. She upset Justine very much.'

The words rushed out of his mouth, before he could stop them. 'Why isn't Justine talking to me about it?' Hamish demanded. 'Why you?'

'Justine felt it would be best coming from me,' the priest explained, putting a hand comfortingly on his shoulder. 'She said you went ill again after she told you her happy news. And then your friend, she abused her.'

'Leanne's just looking out for me. She knows how much I love Justine, and well...thinks Justine was cruel: standing in front of me, hand in hand, with her non-plastic shark telling me she was engaged.'

'Non-plastic...shark...no, Hamish, no. That's still a strange way to refer to a shark.'

'Justine's fiancé's name,' Hamish began, 'Father Matthias, his *name*. Nick Carver? Surely, that rings alarm bells for you,' Hamish said looking at Father Matthias significantly.

'Nick...Carver...in what way, is this name supposed to ring alarm bells for me, Hamish?'

Hamish looked at him. 'You know: Nick. The *Devil's* nickname.'

'No. No. Hamish. No. Let's not go that way. That he, Justine's fiancée...'

Hamish doubled over, as pain ripped apart his soul.

'Hamish?'

Hamish made a strangled noise. 'Her name, Father, her name. It sits in my soul like a wound.' He wrapped his arms around himself, rocking backward and forward.

The Priest looked at him gravely. 'Now let's not go comparing what's normal to what's abnormal, Son. The name, Justine, should not be compared to a wound. And as for the *significance* of names, Justine's fiancé Nick and *Old* Nick, the slang for the Devil, are not the same personage, Hamish.'

'Nick is not a Christian name, Father Matthias. His name should tell you he is heathen orientated; and prone to malicious behaviour.'

'I'm onto you, Hamish. Oh yes, I am,' Father Matthias said, raising his chin, his eyes rolling to the heavens. 'I think you have deliberately designed your argument to appeal to me. You did the same thing trying to explain your pagan dreadlocks to me, as a Samson hairstyle. So, let us look at the facts, Hamish. As per Francis Grose in his 1785 *A Classical Dictionary of the Vulgar Tongue* about the Devil's nickname, "Old Nick". Firstly, we will explore what contributed to the name "Old Nick". Grose says, in his dictionary, that the Devil was the angel given the job of making women.'

'What? Is that why the Church believe women are evil?' Hamish asked, 'Because some mothball scholar thinks the Devil designed them? That's—'

Father Matthias held up his hand. 'Let me continue. When the Devil made women, the Devil would nick the taller women with a small scratch, but the littler women had no such advantage; as they had shorter legs, and thus were within his vengeful and spiteful reach. He didn't just nick them, he slashed them. His tendency to nick women, tall or short, is how he became known as Nick, or *Old Nick*.'

Hamish looked at him worriedly. 'Well, can't you see Justine's in terrible danger then? She's not very tall, and…'

'Son,' Fr Matthias said, looking at him sternly, 'the Devil is not possessing Nick Carver because they share their name in slang. And Justine is in no danger just because she is engaged to a man called Nick. It is your association with the name that makes you *think* she's in danger. And if that association disease has come back to perch in your brain again, then that's why you are not thinking rightly.'

'Perhaps you should get Justine some high heels,' Hamish mumbled, 'to elevate her out of the Devil's reach.'

Father Matthias looked at him, exasperated. 'You have taken all of this too far, Hamish, and please keep in mind, it's best for you *not* to pronounce the Devil's name. My tongue has sanctity, so it won't affect me like it will affect you, should you pronounce the name. Perhaps,' he said staring at him suspiciously, '*this* is why you are becoming unwell again.'

'What?' Hamish asked irritably, 'You think I have become unwell, because my tongue is missing sanctity and I spoke an evil name? That my tongue is in holy poverty?'

'It is obvious the Devil is making you ill, Son. Because of the strange way you are speaking. That plastic shark? The belief that Nick Carver is related to the Devil by name and by nature? Justine needs high heels to avoid the Devil? You must get onto this at once, Hamish, and see your doctor. You don't want to end up in mental hospital for three months straight again. You see, with the Devil making you so ill, you have become your own enemy.'

'What happened to *Love thy enemy*?' Hamish mumbled.

The priest shook his head, 'See? You're not well at all, with that strange response to what I just said. *Love thy enemy* is contextual, Son, contextual. You should not love the enemy of sickness in your mind. Especially, if it is caused by the Devil. There's something wrong if you do.' The priest paused, looking at him grimly. 'You talked about binaries in your outstanding speech to the community. You've got to get out of your *own* mental binary of sane/insane, Son. You got to get above it. Otherwise, you will keep going like a metronome between sane and insane, back and forth, back and forth, back and forth. And it will take one little thing, like seeing Justine with another man, to send you back into that insane part of the mental binary you are in. You've got to get to the point, you can deal with things without slipping back into a past or unwell state.'

'You mean reach the transcendental point, above the sane/insane binary.' Hamish said miserably. 'So I'm not up and down, or backward and forward.'

'Yes, that,' Father Matthias said, his pulpit voice relenting, becoming kinder. 'You may be on medication to treat your condition neurologically, Hamish, but you need to know how to manage emotionally when you come across or encounter a Justine incident. It's triggered a very strange episode with you.'

'You want me to yoga my brain?' Hamish mumbled.

'See? There's another strange comment. All I meant was, emotionally manage it, Hamish. Emotionally manage it. You got to get the depression physically out of you, so it doesn't have a nice cosy room inside your head to live in. You won't get out of that Devil-produced state, staring at the wall in a dark room.'

The priest produced a pair of sneakers.

'What's that? The miracle of the sneakers?' Hamish muttered.

'I'm not Jesus, son,' Father Matthias said. 'That is something that should be obvious to you. But I did ask your father your sneaker size, and buy them for you. You have to run, Hamish. Get the depression out of your mind. I read all about it. Running produces serotonin, which is like an antihistamine to depression. You don't exercise, your mind it becomes one big anaphylactic condition. Nothing there to change it.' Father Matthias patted Hamish's knee and stood up. 'You're on the right track, you know, with your political aspirations and doing your degree to give you political and social credibility. But get the grenade out of your mind, Son. Because there will always be someone or something to pull the trigger on it. Best if the trigger's not there at all. Then it won't hurt you or others.' The priest handed the sneakers to Hamish and strode to the doorway, pausing. He turned, his hand on the handle. 'Get some counselling too, Hamish; talk about Justine, you know? She's part of the grenade in your mind called *things I can't and haven't dealt with*. You've *got* a chance of making it, *if* you get rid of plastic sharks, and name-implied Satan, and your unresolved feelings for Justine. Those are the sort of things that bring your mind down. Put it in civil war, make it fight with itself.' He grinned widely at Hamish. 'Come and see me sometime, huh? I don't want to just be catching up on your news by reading the paper and seeing you headlined as the new Social Prophet of our LGA, nor do I want to hear about you through Justine sobbing on my shoulder because she was called a heartless lollipop, asking me to do something about it.'

'Father, the woman who called her a lollipop is a lesbian. I think the word, lollipop, was her symbol for a heterosexual woman, you know; the stick sticking up into the round, sweet…'

The priest's voice cracked across the room like a whiplash, 'Hamish! No, no. *No* Devil-implying words. Go with what *is*. With what is *real.*' Father Matthias paused, looking down at Hamish's bare feet. 'Now get those on,' he said firmly, looking pointedly at the sneakers. 'You got to get that depression out of you.' The door closed behind Father Matthias like an exclamation mark.

Hamish, before he put the sneakers on, read that running was also about patterning; producing a rhythm and motion which was even, smooth, paced and repetitive. The same rhythm and motion as conformity, Hamish speculated. Maybe running would help him lose that innate defiance and intolerance he seemed to have of people locked into tight positions because of one-way thinking. He couldn't help being impatient with people who limited themselves that way; knotted themselves into one place or position. He hoped that running would inoculate him against that past mental speed and restlessness posing as his mind; a whirlwind of strange instincts, reactions and stimuli.

Now the whirlwind was spitting again, just as rain spits before it pours; tiny fractures in his mind, growing wider again.

Hamish, as he ran, thought about how he read that physical activity could alter thinking. Hamish ran faster, hoping to lose his Wizard of Oz mind, where everything existed as strange, symbolic and transformed; not as it actually was.

Hamish stopped running after fifteen minutes, realising with dismay how unfit he was. His ragged breathing sounded like someone with asthma, he thought dejectedly as he bent over, his hands on his knees, breathing hard, waiting to feel any difference in his mind. He felt a weak surge, like he had had a bit of a pot smoke, and then it went flat again. Maybe, he needed to do more of it, he thought, for the effect to last longer. He had to get his mind higher to reach the transcendental point, the escape route of out the mental binary he was in; sane one minute, suffering the next.

He straightened his body, his breathing returning to normal.

He hung his head.

He was tired of his mental seesaw.

Every time he thought of Justine, he practised putting her away again. Like the university counsellor had suggested. For as long as he could remember, Justine had eased his knife-flicked mind with her drifts of pink, white, softness and certainty.

'It's that certainty, I'm looking for…isn't it?' Hamish asked his counsellor, Paula Craven, running his hand agitatedly over his shorn head. 'The certainty I can see in Justine, so I keep trying to hold onto her; because she's the stable in my life, the granite, the something that doesn't shift and change like my mind or my life does. I'm having trouble giving up the restless ocean in me.'

Paula tapped her pen on her desk, looking at him pityingly.

'Can you not…make that noise?' Hamish asked tetchily. 'It makes me irritable, sets off, like, this OCD in me.'

'I thought Justine was your OCD,' Paula drawled, leaning back in her chair, spinning her pen around between her fingers.

'Yeah…I mean *yes,'* he corrected himself forcefully. Hamish considered Paula's laid-back curiosity, her small glasses with their red frames, her long brown plait hanging heavily down over one shoulder to her waist, her navy blue and white striped shift dress.

Explaining himself to Paula wouldn't be too hard. He found it hard to talk to immaculate people, in immaculate clothing, with immaculate speech.

They made him feel unclean.

'Yeah…yes…what?' Paula asked.

'I'm practising elocution,' Hamish explained, 'so I don't slang-scare people off when I'm speaking at political forums.'

'Right,' Paula said, looking at him considerately. 'Bob Hawke slanged it and people still worshipped him. But I take it what you mean is, you want to stop speaking like an ordinary citizen and start speaking in language more upper class, so you'll fit in that level. Is that right, Hamish? Fit in that level?'

'I've been told I will be taken more seriously as a politician if I stop slanging off in my social nit language. Use the caviar language.'

'Don't choke on it, will you,' Paula remarked and adjusted her glasses again, flipping the pages of his file. 'Now. Let's just deal with the need for certainty and the need for Justine; and see if they are one and the same need.'

Hamish leant forward, putting his face in his hands.

'Mate. You're going through a hard time, huh?' Paula said comfortingly.

Hamish raised his head, nodding, trying to get the flow of Justine's hair floating with feathers out of his mind. He could only remember the truth about her, not see it, since medication took his special eyes away.

Hamish wouldn't tell the counsellor that.

Not many understood. And those who he told related it to a crazed condition, the mental health DSM-IV manual, a pagan disease or a sick leprechaun living inside of him.

Hamish decided to stand by his decision, and not to say anything to Paula about his special eyes; especially as he could see the mental health 1800 number propped up near her phone.

The counsellor twirled her pen between her fingers, looking at him with that casualness that made him decide he would keep talking to her about his cracked heart, but not his cracked mind.

'Is there anything else, Hamish, aside from this girl's certainty that you love about her…and…' she checked her counselling notes, 'makes you want her so desperately?'

'Well. Yes. There is. She's not malicious, not a bitch you know. And she's straight. Doesn't fuck around…I mean, doesn't hide her mind from you, so you have no idea what she really thinks. She says what she thinks.'

'Honest then. That's good. At least you know where you are with her,' Paula remarked.

‘Well, that’s the painful part,’ Hamish said, his voice cracking. ‘I’m not anywhere with her. I’m not part of her insides or her outsides. I’m something in her periphery; just there discarded to one side,’ he said, looking at her painfully.

‘And inside of her is where you want to be, huh?’ Paula said, giving him a knowing, half wicked look.

Hamish got the joke. ‘Yeah, OK, I do. But I want to be in her heart and I’m not there. She’s got Jack the Ripper there instead.’

‘Oh, that sucks, doesn’t it? When they love the bastard, instead of the prince,’ she agreed.

‘I’m not exactly the prince. Neither am I the bastard,’ Hamish explained.

‘Well that’s the problem then,’ Paula drawled, twirling her pen again. Hamish tried hard not to look at the twirling pen; he was disturbed and irritated by it. ‘You are neither prince nor bastard. And I’ll tell you now. Women go for one or the other.’

‘Yeah, well, women have been trained on fairy tales, where it’s either Prince Charming or the Villain.’ Hamish agreed.

‘So, your girl’s looking at the Villain and not seeing where you are standing,’ the Counsellor said.

‘I’m standing right in front of her. Wanting to say *I love you*. But her face is turned towards the bastard who’s just going to rip her right up.’

‘And there’s no prince type around? To throw her on the back of his horse and gallop off with her, waving his sword and saying *Back I say*,’ she drawled.

‘Well if there is, I wouldn’t know. She doesn’t tell me anything,’ Hamish said.

‘Well, how would you defend her from this villain?’ Paula asked.

‘I don’t think I could do the horse thing; no, I don’t think I could do that. I would just reach out my hand to her, and see if she takes it.’

‘So that’s something-in-between,’ the counsellor said, ‘neither horse nor bloody knife.’

‘Yeah. I guess it is,’ Hamish said despondently.

‘And, where would you go after you reached out your hand to her and she clutched it?’

‘Home,’ he said simply.

‘So, home is free of bastards and of princes and is safe,’ Paula corroborated.

'Something like that,' Hamish said. He leant forward again, rubbing his eyes. 'But she doesn't want to take my hand; she's too busy holding hands with Edward Scissorhands.'

The counsellor spluttered in laughter and then managed to stop herself. 'Oh, that guy out of the movie you mean, that *Edward Scissorhands* movie, where he has scissors for hands.'

'I know his type, you know,' Hamish said, his voice uneven. 'It won't be long before he takes the rubber face off.'

'You mean she'll see him for what he is,' the counsellor said. 'As rubber faces belong somewhere in the world of fiction.'

Hamish decided to agree: 'Yeah, OK, they do.'

Sometimes his mind still skidded, but mostly it had been tarred with a new surface.

'So, you're hoping for the miracle, where *ta-da*, she sees that Jack the Ripper lives inside him, stroking her with his Edward Scissorhands,' Paula drawled.

Hamish rubbed his tired eyes and looked blearily at her. 'Justine's the sort of person who will stay with something, someone, even an idea or ideology, even if she reads criticisms of it or hears negative aspects of what she believes, she'll still stay with it.'

'So, she's a set sort of person,' Paula said, looking at him for confirmation, 'doesn't change.'

'It's why she has so much certainty,' Hamish said. 'Which is something I actually love about her. Me? I was always leaping from one idea to the next, or walking up the next mountain. Justine? She'd stay in one place, or one belief, or one idea,' he said, looking at Paula hopelessly.

'And probably has mountain phobia,' the counsellor added sarcastically.

Hamish considered this. 'Possibly,' he said, 'as it would lead her out of the place she's comfortable in.'

'So, is this why you decided to be a politician, get a new look, and become something which might change the way she thinks about you?' Paula suggested, twirling her pen.

Hamish looked resolutely away from the pen. 'And get the new mind that goes with the new persona,' he said, sighing. 'I have to get her to see me differently. There's a mental block there on her part, from when we were barely in our teens.' He looked down, his cheeks reddening. 'She heard something about me.'

Realisation crossed Paula's face, and she nodded to herself, as if something made sense. He glanced down and saw the word "Paranoia?" scribbled in lead pencil.

Hamish narrowed his eyes. 'This is a real incident I am discussing with you. Not something I made up.'

Paula put her pencil down. 'Yeah, OK. Go on.'

Hamish fought back any further comment, still trying to practise his new persona, free of the reactivity he used to have.

Hamish forced himself to go on and not walk out and slam the door. 'Justine never told me…actually she refused to tell me what it was. It put me in a position of anguish for years, wondering what it was and how it had put her off me.'

'Why don't you ask her again, Hamish?' Paula suggested. 'You are both a lot older now. She may tell you what she heard, specially, as you told me in our last session, if she's doing a Bachelor of Counselling. Studies like that would have brought her new ways of thinking; ways of thinking she didn't have before.'

Hamish looked at her hopefully. 'You think so?'

'Ask,' she said, 'or your mind will keep returning to it, because it's unresolved.'

'It will keep me in the insane position in my mental binary,' Hamish said bitterly.

The counsellor looked at him, as if he was a bit suspect. 'A what?'

'A priest I know. He told me I was in a mental binary.' He paused at her sceptical face and raised eyebrow; and once again fought his frustration that people didn't understand him.

Hamish remembered Father Matthias's words about managing his emotions, so he didn't have another crack-up. He waited until his mind was calm again, before he spoke. 'A mental binary. In civil war with myself,' he explained, trying to keep his voice level, 'sane one minute and insane the next.'

'That could be true, Hamish. That could be true. You've got to put the peace sign in your mind, not leave a ticking bomb there that's going to explode and send you mental. And do you know the best way to do that?'

He looked up at her, a bit lost, a bit hopeless. 'No?'

'Resolve the unresolved. Go clear it up with her.' She paused, pushing her glasses back up her nose. 'Be who you are, Hamish. Your mind won't fight itself then, if you are who you are.' She looked at him more seriously. 'There's no use being a pollie either, Hamish, if it's just to get into this girl's pants, and not genuinely part of who you are.'

Hamish resisted the cobra he could feel rearing up in his mind, and waited until it calmed.

He needed more lithium, he decided. If a cobra was starting to break through the new surface of his mind, he needed to be more deliberate, not just vomit the first thing out. Hamish practised considering things again. 'I want to change things in society. That's genuine. We have a constipated society, in a lot of ways. It needs a laxative, a clear out, too much conformist shit that won't shift.' Hamish stopped reminding himself not to use his social nit language anymore. He rubbed his forehead, squinting his eyes; there was just so much to mentally watch. And he wasn't used to being an observer of his own mind, he was used to being in it. *It's so hard*, Hamish thought despairingly.

'So, you are going into politics to give society a bum wipe,' Paula said, looking at him unconvinced, tapping her pen on the desk.

Hamish shifted in his chair, trying to stop the tide of irritability about to dump on the shore of his new resolutions. He looked pointedly at the pen Paula was tapping on the desk. 'Can you…stop doing that, please? People tapping their pens or incessantly clicking them on and off is one of my pet hates.'

Explaining himself was another pebble on his new shore. He never used to see why he had to explain anything. But he realised if he didn't explain himself, people would make assumptions. And avoid him. Or name him species type human-leprechaun.

Paula looked at him apologetically, and put her pen down. 'My pet hate is goldfish staring with big wide eyes through fish tank glass.'

'What?' he asked cautiously.

'They just irritate me,' she said, shrugging.

'Right,' he said, 'yes, of course.'

Paula leant back in her chair, looking at him wryly. 'So, you want to clear out the shit out of society,' she drawled. 'I hope you've got a lot of toilet paper.'

Hamish walked into the university café, looking around for Justine. She was usually here at 8 am, going through her textbooks and readings, with a cup of coffee. He pushed through the mingling students, looking for her.

He saw her sitting on the orange leather lounge in the corner. An orange lamp was glowing on a wooden stand by the lounge, easing the grey drizzle of rain on the windows. Hamish glanced at the small wooden table in front of her; magazines and newspapers spread carelessly over it. He watched as she put her coffee cup down on the table and straightened the magazines and papers up.

Things out of order have always bothered her, he thought, as he slowly came to a stop in front of her. He waited until she looked up.

'Hamish,' she said, her voice neither condemning nor welcoming. He looked down, shifting from one foot to the other, still embarrassed about the episode in the coffee shop, when she presented her fiancé who, despite his best efforts, still registered in his mind as Jack the Ripper. Hamish stopped shuffling his feet, reminding himself not to use his past body language, which, Leanne had told him, loudly announced he was feeling insecure.

Hamish straightened his body, standing completely still. Which he found hard as movement had always passed rapidly through his mind, making his body restless.

'Justine,' Hamish said, trying to keep his voice level and firm. 'I need to know something.'

Justine looked up from her textbook, her eyes steadily searching his as if she was looking for the presence of his so-called leprechaun.

'Do I pass?' he asked anxiously, then remembered he was not supposed to show any anxiety in his fight to be an A plus citizen.

Justine smiled, a hint of the affection she used to feel for him showing in her eyes. 'There's nothing strange in your eyes at the moment,' she said levelly. 'You pass.'

'Can I sit down?' he asked, encouraged she wasn't pulling out wooden crucifixes, trying to ward him off.

She placed her hand on the orange leather lounge and patted it. 'Sit down, Hamish. Please.'

Hamish sat down, stopping himself from automatically leaning forward, his head in his hands. Leanne had told him that sort of body language signalled to others that his mind had turned into the Titanic, about to sink itself.

Hamish turned to Justine instead, looking at her quietly, 'I'm seeing a counsellor, Justine.'

Her deep-blue eyes lit up. 'That's wonderful, Hamish.'

He ran a hand over his shorn head. 'Yeah…yes. I mean. It's very helpful.'

Justine closed the counselling textbook, looking at him with interest. 'And?' she asked.

'Well, Father Matthias, *and* the counsellor, both tell me it's important to resolve the unresolved. So, my mind doesn't piss all over itself,' Hamish stopped, reminding himself not to talk in social nit. 'Well I said that last part. About the piss. Father Matthias wouldn't use such unholy language. He's more into Moses linguistics.'

'What?' Justine asked, dismayed.

'Cut the last sentence.' Hamish sighed, rubbing his hand over his shorn head again. 'With all the antipsychotics drugging the strangeness in my mind, I really don't how that got through.'

Justine smiled a little. 'At least you're honest about it.'

Hamish looked at her pale face and blue eyes that held no questions in them, just answers. He worked up the courage to ask her what had been plaguing his mind for years.

Hamish opened his mouth, and in a panic closed it. Took a deep breath. Opened his mouth again. 'And I want you to be honest with me about something,' he said, managing to keep his voice steady, calm and firm.

Justine's eyes closed over a little, mentally pulling away from him, establishing distance. 'What is it you wanted to ask me, Hamish?'

'Do you remember when we were younger and I told you that I loved you?'

Her eyes lowered. 'Yes,' she said.

'And you said you'd heard something about me. Something you wouldn't tell me,' Hamish continued.

'Yes, Hamish,' she said definitely, her eyes lowering further, 'I remember.'

'What was it you heard, Justine?'

Justine was silent for a minute and then met his eyes, honestly and steadily. 'I heard you had sex with your sister.'

He looked at her in shock. 'Do you *really* think I would do that?'

'Hamish, I was only fourteen when I heard that. And it was a Church family I heard it from. You take the word of religious people as gospel at that age. Because you trust the value system they have; values like "Thou shalt not lie". So, naturally, I thought they were telling the truth.'

Hamish looked at her, white faced. 'Do you honestly believe, I would fuck…' he corrected himself, 'have sex with my sister?'

'Hamish. You had a mental illness. This was something that was well known in the parish due to your concerned parents asking anyone and everyone if they'd noticed any strange behaviour from you. To be honest, Hamish, it was well known in all the parish families that your entire family was mentally ill.' Justine was silent for a minute. 'The family who told me you slept with your sister said it was a mentally ill act you just couldn't help. Because you were untreated. I decided just to be friends with you after I heard the incest story, Hamish, because I knew you couldn't help your mental illness.'

Hamish struggled with his rage. 'Which parish family? *Which* family?'

'I can't tell you, Hamish. The family who told me, made me promise not to say it came from them.' She looked at him seriously. 'I always keep my promises, Hamish.'

'Well, you may tell them, next time you see them—'

She frowned. 'What?'

'That spreading stories around like that, without proof, can wreck a person's life. Even lead to suicide.'

'The family had an impeccable reputation, Hamish,' she said seriously.

'Socially credible doesn't mean truthful, Justine,' he answered, trying to suppress the rage still sputtering weakly in his mind, like a Bunsen burner set on low. He'd lost most of his heat with the God of psychiatry, who from his great mental height had prescribed him the stone tablets…*Thou shalt take thy lithium*…Hamish felt his mind started to thicken and slow again; his thoughts falling into the lithium crematorium, burning and dying.

Justine did not answer, just lowered her eyes to her textbook.

Hamish stood slowly, sadly looking down at her. Thinking about her straightforwardness, her concrete and unquestioned thoughts about him. He knew then, Justine was never going to see him any other way than a social nit who had, by the word of an inaccurate church family, fucked his sister.

Hamish made a decision as he realised eight years of longing to be in her steady, feathered presence, would turn into nine years; then ten years; then eleven years. Justine would marry her Nick Carver, in his starched suit; listen to his measured and careful words, all placed neatly in correct grammatical and sequential order; and she would be happy with someone who did things like that.

He would never, ever, be able to make her happy like that shark bastard.

He was just too damaged.

And too different.

‘Goodbye, Justine,’ he said, taking one last look at the creamy skin of her face and the beautiful blue certainty of her eyes as her face lifted to his.

‘Goodbye, Hamish,’ she said casually, her eyes already turning back to the textbook.

In anguish, he left.

23

'I'm so nervous. I'm so nervous,' Hamish said, stumbling over his words, panicking as he looked at the tightly packed town hall, where the Grand Debate of council candidates was about to take place.

'Don't be nervous, Hamish,' Leanne said comfortingly. 'Remember to speak from your beliefs if someone puts you on the spot, or you can't find the right word. You must answer the question from your own beliefs, not what you *think* you should say to sound politically impressive. Be the Social Prophet, the way out of social misery, no political arse speak. If you say fiscal policy, even one time, I will shoot you. Most people here won't know what fiscal means and how it relates to themselves and their families.'

'You do seem a little obsessed about destroying…that word…' Hamish said carefully.

'Well, yeah. I don't like it. It's English language with shark fins, mate. A word that opens its jaws right up and shows you its nasty teeth.'

'I had no idea the word fiscal was so feral,' Hamish said, alarmed.

'Don't even say it, mate; it's a predatory word designed to circle the ordinary citizen.'

'OK, I won't say it,' he promised.

'Now. Go get 'em, Moses,' she said, nodding towards the stage.

Hamish walked onto the stage, his legs wobbling with nerves. He glanced around the crowd, finding himself automatically searching for Justine.

Resolutely, he looked away.

Justine had become part of his past life now, something he was letting go of; part of losing his social victim self. *It is hard, so hard,* Hamish thought, his heart still struggling to let her go. She had been his rock, in all the chaos. Now, he was struggling out of the coal-glowing demons in his mind; those demons making and firing his thoughts, causing all that mind chaos.

Hamish sat down at the candidates table, his eyes falling on Father Matthias standing at the back of the room. The priest gave Hamish a quiet, solemn nod. The priest's presence brought back Sunday predictability; days of hot scones, jam and dripping cream, steaming black coffee and red underlined parables on faded Bible pages—a Sunday predictability which used to feel like a tight rope around his mind, yet felt strangely comforting now. He almost longed for the familiarity of Sunday predictability and church rituals which mapped his days as a child.

He felt now as if he was stumbling along, trying to get off the Wizard of Oz path. Trying to find his heart, his courage, and his real life.

A hush fell over the babbling crowd, as the community host cleared his throat. 'Welcome to our candidates here,' the host said loudly, 'and for those of you too far away to read the name tags in front of our candidates, we have from left to right…' He waved his hand expansively towards the candidates. 'On the left, representing the Labor Party, Mr Robert Belton.'

Hamish heard scattered applause, some hooting and some foot stamping.

'And next to Robert, we have Mrs Sue-Ellen Strong-off, representing the Independents.' Light applause spread through the room. 'And next to her we have, Mr Craig Pulverson representing the Liberal Party.'

Clapping rippled across the room, as Craig stood up briefly, and sat down.

'And next to our hometown rooster Craig, ruler of our LGA roost for the last three years, we have Mr Hamish McColl, representing The Greens Party.'

There was silence.

Just silence.

Fuck, Hamish thought, panicking, looking around the pitying and suspicious faces in the room.

'Hamish is new, so let us be generous with our praise and stingy with our criticism,' the community host said sombrely.

The crowd broke into applause. Leanne stood, stamping her foot and hooting his name. The community host waited until the applause died down and opened his mouth to speak.

'Hardly any women up there on the stage. *As* usual,' a woman called out from the crowd.

'Our selection process is based on merit and suitability,' Craig Pulverson explained to the woman.

'Yeah well, females haven't been suitable for a long time,' the woman said sarcastically. 'We are socially condemned to the Victorian ages of female docility and supporting thy husband.'

'Speak for yourself,' another woman yelled out. 'Some of us don't accept that.'

'Victorian era social rules still exist for women,' the other woman replied. 'Politics has repeatedly denied equal representation when it comes to the men–women ratio. There are a few token females but look how many women there are compared to men in Parliament? How many make it to PM? It's *always* a man. Women are always on the social crucifix in the suffering position.'

'With a sign above our gender cross that says, "Here lies the Socially Forbidden". Women have been up on that cross for centuries,' the woman debating with her returned.

'It was Eve that ate the apple,' a man called out loudly and confidently. 'Women are weaker. That's why we are in charge, not women.'

'Oh, fuck off to fable land,' Leanne yelled out.

'This…is not *really* a feminist debate,' the community host said hastily, 'although, we are happy to address any contemporary feminist issues. *If* you feel they are somehow a current issue in our LGA.'

'Well, of course, they bloody are,' Leanne called out. 'We need an LGA survey done on how many of God's roosters are in charge and how many women with CEO ability are forced into chicken form.'

'What?' asked a bewildered man, gripping the sides of his seat and leaning forward to look at her.

'Chicken form. Women who have to run around at the roosters' command, not able to challenge or question; because men hold the social power and make the rules in society, not women.'

'*White* men do,' objected an Indigenous man.

'Let's start with the speeches, shall we?' the community host said loudly and hurriedly. 'Afterwards, you are *all* free to ask questions. And just to make things clear, we have a chicken-free zone here tonight. Now. Robert. Would you like to start?'

Robert stood up and took the microphone. 'Yeah, look. We all know we need a new road coming into the town here. If it's not a 'roo that gets you, it's a pothole.'

Laughter cracked across the room.

Robert waited until the laughter faded and then continued. Hamish tried to concentrate on what Robert was saying but nerves kept snapping his mind. Hamish focused on Father Matthias's soothing presence at the back of the room, where he stood with quiet dignity, looking at him with his powerful, solemn eyes. Like the Noah of Town Hall, Hamish mused, and then pulled his mind back, reminding himself not to think in interesting phrases which could be considered delusional. He had to think in realist, concrete terms about people, as advised by his counsellor. Father Matthias was a priest, not the Noah of Town Hall. Yet, the sight of the priest made his mind stop lurching like a ship in tidal water. He supposed he should change his thought to Father Matthias: but it was nowhere near as interesting to his mind.

Hamish focused back on what Robert was saying. He was talking about new playground equipment for the local park for the kids. Hamish's mind struggled to find this interesting and he reminded himself that playground equipment was a community concern for people who had kids.

'…I mean that playground equipment's got to be seventy years old, right?' Robert asked, looking around the crowd, working it up.

'Forty-two years old, exactly,' corrected Sue-Ellen.

'The age estimate I just gave was appearance based,' Robert said generously.

'I hope you didn't pick your wife like that,' Leanne yelled out.

'OK, OK,' said the community host hastily through the laughter, 'Let's move on…shall we?'

The questions came hard and fast after that; *some hostile, some polite, some just way out there*, Hamish thought, trying to keep careful track of information, as he had been taught by his counsellor.

The questions were coming too fast for him to field properly and carefully sort through mentally.

'No, Mrs Petty,' Robert was saying, looking bewildered. 'Labor do not represent the Devil. We represent a fair go for the average Aussie; we are here to help the ordinary person. It's my understanding that the Devil is living in a different local government area, called Hell…'

More laughter broke out across the crowd.

'The Devil won't get many votes here, my word he won't,' an elderly man called out though the laughter.

Hamish knew Robert was serious competition. Robert's sense of humour was winning people over and he knew people were more likely to vote for someone who made them laugh. Hamish worried he was too solemn for them, not enough joker cards in him.

'Thank you, Robert,' the community host said encouragingly, clapping him as he left the podium and sat down. 'Let's move on. Would you all please welcome Mrs Sue-Ellen Strong-off, an Independent.'

Light applause scattered through the room, as Sue-Ellen walked over to the podium and adjusted the microphone. She took a small, elegant breath, ready to deliver her speech, which Hamish could see was typed on exactly one page. She laid it carefully and precisely on the podium stand.

'Look, Sue-Ellen,' a man called out, before she could begin, 'I don't believe there's much difference between you and the fucking Liberal party. Why the fuck should I vote for you when you're standing hand in hand with the fucking Libs?'

'Well, it's not like that at all, really,' said Sue-Ellen, fingering her pearl necklace. 'We do differ in several policy areas…'

Sue-Ellen's voice faded out as Hamish thought about how someone like Sue-Ellen would appeal more to the conservative and traditional people of Sydney, with her rationality and calm; but thought her formal language and appearance of wealth would put off the battlers, the strugglers, the bitter and the slangers. Political appearance was to many a political matter about what you understood and what you didn't. He looked uncomfortably at the suit he had been forced by Leanne and Deanna to wear for this occasion. He didn't think it would attract too much hostility; it was just plain black, with a deep-blue shirt, not too threatening, to either conservative people or the battlers. *But Sue?* he thought warily, *She looks like the Australian Mint has dressed her*, and he could tell it wasn't going down well with the crowd. The questions came hard and fast at her as the downside of town reacted to her polished language, her upper-class accent and clipped responses.

'What the fuck would you know about what it's like to search the back of your lounge or under the car seat for the extra ten cents you need to buy the loaf of bread to feed your family?' a man sarcastically asked. 'What the fuck would you know about it, you rich bitch, you poor excuse for suffering…'

'Call security,' the community host yelled to a man standing at the side of the stage. Two security guards found the sarcastic man and hurriedly took him out of the building.

'I think I'll leave it at that,' Sue-Ellen said, visibly upset, sitting down.

'Are you OK, love?' Robert asked, leaning forward, looking at her.

Sue-Ellen nodded, blinking back tears in her eyes. 'I still cry like everyone else,' she said, 'even if I don't search my lounge, or car, for the extra ten cents.'

Robert gave her a sympathetic look and patted her hand. She clutched at it, trying to stop her bottom lip from wobbling.

'Next, we have reigning Liberal councillor, Mr Craig Pulverson. Please stand and make him welcome.'

Chairs slid back. People stood, clapping solidly. Craig looked politely on, his smile correctly pitched, waiting for the applause to fade. He adjusted the microphone, and touched his tightly knotted tie.

'I would like to talk about some of the achievements I have accomplished during my time as your hardworking councillor.' Craig's face grew serious and intent. 'I have helped build a stronger town and a stronger local economy, generating more employment opportunities for the youth of this town.'

Scattered applause sounded across the room.

Hamish remembered some things about Craig that Leanne had briefed him on. People liked his reliability and his efficiency; but the feedback was he lacked magnetism and social appeal. He talked conservatively, addressed many people, in fact so many, he was nicknamed Microphone Man by some sarcastic members of the community.

Hamish forced himself to pay attention to what was happening around him. A hard thing to master, as he had been used to his thought-winds moving his mind across the top of mountains.

'One of my major, major accomplishments,' Craig continued, looking up from his speech, his face earnest, 'was to successfully obtain extra funding for special works in the area to help feed and house struggling and homeless families who, like in many other local government areas, were experiencing accommodation crises.'

Some of the crowd stood and clapped him. Things like that mattered. A lot, Hamish conceded. He had been unhappy in the Catholic box he lived in with his family, but at least he didn't have rain pissing on his face, a piece of wet cardboard to sleep on, and mouldy bread from the public rubbish bins as his dinner.

Hamish brooded more on the polite and lightly compassionate Craig; a social relief compared to some of the strange who roamed the city. Yes. Craig was reliable but without social or mental disorder, and while politically addressing the suffering position, did not understand it.

'Let's all work together to make our place in Sydney a safer and stronger community.' Craig finished talking, tidied his papers, and left the podium.

'Questions please,' called out the community host.

'What's your plan for the next round, champ?' asked an elderly man, his voice thin and wavering.

'Well, sir,' Craig began. Hamish reminded himself to concentrate on what he was saying, but nerves kept wrenching his stomach apart as the clock slowly ticked towards his appointed time. It seemed to Hamish that time slowed when you were waiting for something or someone you either feared or wanted.

Hamish took another suffering look at the clock.

He closed his eyes as the audience finished clapping Craig. *Not yet, not yet, not yet...* His eyes struggled open, knowing any second he was going to be asked up to that stage. His eyes frantically sought Father Matthias. The priest nodded quietly and seriously at him, slowly mouthing a quote by Francis Webb he'd said to him years ago: *"Down with the mind a moment, and let Eden be fullness without the prompted unnatural hunger, without the doomed shapely ersatz thought; see faith..."*

Hamish got up unsteadily, feeling some relief at the reassurance from Father Matthias, who he both trusted and respected. He tried to let go of the strange thoughts strangling his political Eden; that political vision he had to help people like himself and Leanne. The marginalised. The scorned. Those turned away from collectives, because they were different or because of those wary of individuality; the lone piece of clothing hanging in the wardrobe.

'Would you all please give a big welcome, to new political boy on the block, Mr Hamish McColl.'

Applause filled the room, a few loud whistles piercing through.

The Priest's words rang loudly in his head. *Be fullness...*Hamish closed his human eyes and opened his Social Prophet eyes.

He took a deep breath. 'I'd like to start tonight with some words from the poet Robert Gray,' Hamish began, his voice shaking a little. 'I want you to think about those words as I have. Words which tell a story about the price of becoming a social model, part of the beautiful people of society and ignoring what's suffering around us dressed in something not so beautiful. The homeless. The poor. The lonely. The suffering. The discarded. The rejected.'

Silence fell across the room.

Hamish looked down briefly, took another shaking breath, and read the lines: '*So we take the dark roads in beautiful clothing, greeting each other; sorry for the void that cannot see what we have become.*' Hamish looked up, relieved at the hushed audience, and took yet another shaking breath. 'I think, as a society, a lot of us cannot see what we have become. We're in a system of order where we think historically and traditionally about things, which is why those who are marginalised, such as gays, non-whites, the single parents, those with a mental illness or a disability, are regarded as the *disorder* in society, not the *order*, and are thus classed as the lesser value. This is why those with the greater value, those in the beautiful clothing, who are white, married, heterosexual, religious, able-bodied, and mentally sane cannot see what they have become at the cost of others less beautiful; because of a void in them, a historical blindness to the actual reality, where suffering is everywhere.'

Hamish paused, looking with his Social Prophet eyes around the room.

No hostile faces. Just quietness.

Hamish looked down at his speech, relieved. 'As a potential Greens councillor for local council and as a Social Prophet, ready to talk to the burning bush of constituent wisdom, I propose we bring in some new social commandments:

1. Thou shalt not discriminate against thy neighbour because of sexuality, race, class or disability or belief. Having said that, shoot the paedophiles, who do not have a right to their beliefs.
2. Racial appearance shalt not have the social meaning of lesser.
3. Single parents shalt be given community and social support and respect; so they do not feel so alone and isolated or experience social stigma.
4. Thou shalt recognise the rights of different sexualities outside the traditional heterosexist model, and recognise that different sexualities have the same social and legal rights as heterosexuals.

5. Thou shalt not ignore the dolphins, whales and seagulls choking on plastic dumped in the ocean.
6. Thou shalt not ignore the capacities and strengths of those with a disability.
7. Thou shalt not treat those with a mental illness as social lepers or objects of pity.
8. Thou shalt not walk straight past the homeless.
9. Thou shalt not ignore someone in suffering around you.
10. Thou shalt recognise the rights of the indigenous persons of our country, not just symbolically, but in practice.'

Hamish looked bravely around at the silent, sad and contemplative crowd. He noticed some faces were dismissive, but decided they were the beautiful people on the dark road.

He looked at those quietly listening, *...see faith...*

'All of you,' Hamish continued, 'no matter what your social status in life, know someone or something that fits into one of those commandments. And I'm hoping that not only will you help them, but ask them to talk to me, as your new Greens councillor; so we can address these issues plaguing our town, causing darkness on our roads. Thank you.'

People stood one by one, clapping Hamish loudly. Some people started stamping their feet and yelling.

'Hamish, Hamish, Hamish, Hamish, Hamish!' they yelled.

His supporters ran up on stage, lifting him up on their shoulders. The crowd roared with approval, as they carried Hamish up the aisle.

'Hamish, Hamish, Hamish, Hamish, Hamish!' they screamed, as they carried him out the door.

24

Hamish sat up in bed, startled by a knock on his hostel room door. A series of names ran through his head about who it could be, from Father Matthias to Leanne, before he thought to open the door.

He stood looking at her in shock.

Justine. His beautiful Justine.

With a big bruise under her right eye, tears running down her face.

'Justine,' he managed to say, shaken by the bruise on her face. He reached out, took her hand and gently pulled her inside.

She stood inside his room, clutching his hand, shaking. 'I…I…' she broke off.

He looked at her eyes, and for the first time in all the years he had known her, saw breaking points, little fractures of pain. Hamish led her to the bed and sat gently down beside her, holding her hand, waiting for her to speak.

'Hamish,' she said, her voice breaking.

He waited silently.

'I thought he was everything I wanted,' she said shakily, her body trembling. 'He seemed so together, so logical, so warm and such a gentleman. But he wasn't really.' She let go of his hand, putting her face in her hands, her body shuddering. 'Nick was hiding something ugly inside, something really ugly. Hamish…he…he…' She laid her head on his shoulder, crying.

Hamish put his arms around her and held her tightly, as her tears fell on his shoulder. He kissed the top of her hair, and just let her cry.

Hamish sat in his chair with a blanket around him, watching Justine sleep. He'd given her his single, little bed to sleep in and she didn't mind; she was just happy to have a safe place to stay. He looked at the ugly bruise, mottling her beautiful white skin, and thought how untouched she'd been by any ugliness until now. *Well*, he corrected himself, *maybe I*, Hamish, *used to be the ugliness in her life; but that was in my social nit days*.

He still loved Justine, he admitted to himself. She was a flow in his blood, a natural movement in his heart he couldn't change; no matter how she saw him. Hamish stayed in the chair with the blanket wrapped tightly around him, watching her as the hours passed. Keeping an ear out for the bastard.

Justine stirred around 3 am, sitting up and rubbing her eyes. He stood up, hesitating for a minute, wondering if he should let her go back to sleep. Then again, *she might need comfort*, he thought, as he saw her deep blue eyes, still in shock, looking around. Maybe she was still in a half-asleep panic, looking for the bastard, he thought.

Hamish sat down beside her, tentatively touching the bruise on her cheek.

She lifted her hand, to touching his.

25

Justine clutched his hand all the way to the local police station, leaning in close to his body, looking anxiously around.

'Do you want me to call your parents, Justine,' he asked, 'and let them know what happened?'

'I can't go to my parents, Hamish, I can't. It is a family expectation I marry Nick. He's been especially chosen by them.'

'What?' he asked, staring at Justine in disbelief. 'Why would your parents expect you to go back to the bastard even after he gave you a bruiser like that?'

'They would ask what I did to deserve it, Hamish,' Justine said unevenly.

'Fuck!' he exclaimed, 'Your parents are even worse than mine.' He gave her hair a gentle stroke, as they approached the police station. Hamish was still trying to get used to the new unsteadiness in her eyes, the trembling of her voice; after years of knowing her in an unchanging calmness and unchanging certainty, a new view of her, like looking out the window and seeing a new choppy grey sea, suddenly there. Instead of a neatly trimmed green lawn, white feathers drifting across it, and flowers, in a light flush of pink; Justine standing there on the green lawn, her pink dress drifting lightly in the wind; her soft pink mouth, slowly smiling at him, her blue eyes looking calmly and certainly at him.

It was strange how *he,* the wild and socially unforgivable Hamish, had become the new certainty in her life, after she, Justine, had been *his* certainty for so many years.

Hamish slowed to a stop with Justine, outside the police station.

'Are you ready?' Hamish asked, lifting her hand, and holding it tightly against his chest.

'No,' she said, her hand tightening around his. 'I've never…had anything like this happen…and my mind doesn't know what to do, Hamish. That's just as scary to me, as his fist in my face.'

'Your mind doesn't know what to do because it's never walked over rough ground before,' he said.

She looked at him, her eyes catching with regret. 'I wish I hadn't judged you so much, Hamish,' she said. 'I…I just hadn't been through what you have so I didn't really understand where you were coming from.' She lifted his hand to her face. 'I'm really sorry I believed that Church family now.'

'Well, I can't say that's alright, because it's not,' Hamish said honestly. 'But you were only thirteen when you heard that, before you were aware that socially tall people do not always tell the truth. For whatever reason…' he broke off, grinning wryly. 'Oh no, there I go again, mouthing off in my social nit language.'

Justine smiled slowly, in that way he used to love, and he looked at her in relief. She wasn't fully smashed by what the bastard had done. Maybe because she'd got out of the relationship before he could do a complete knockout of her.

'Come on,' Hamish said unevenly, 'let's go.'

The doors to the police station slid open and he walked in with her, his hand tightening reassuringly around hers. On the pin board at the top of the stairs were some pinned-up fliers of community groups and phone numbers. He pointed one out to Justine.

'Look,' he said, pointing out the domestic violence flier, offering court assistance to victims of domestic violence.

'I don't want to have to look at him in court, Hamish,' she said, her voice trembling again.

He drew her in his arms and gave her a hug. 'Maybe you can speak to an officer in there about that,' he murmured into her ear. 'They might come to some other arrangement for you, where you don't have to look at the bastard.'

Hamish heard the police radio crackling in the background, with information about a perpetrator, and turned to see an irritated-looking constable walking towards the counter reception.

A cop who'd had a bad day, he assumed, and reminded himself not to assume; but to look at concrete reality, so his thoughts didn't skate off in ten different directions.

'For fuck's sake,' the constable called out, to another cop up the back of the room, as the radio crackled with more talk. 'Can you get that prick locked up? This is the third time he's done this.'

The cop turned to Justine and Hamish.

'Yes. Can I help you?' he asked brusquely.

Hamish pointed wordlessly at the bruise under Justine's eye.

The cop's eyes narrowed suspiciously at him.

'It wasn't me!' Hamish protested.

'No,' said a female cop, walking over to the counter reception, 'not Sydney's new Social Prophet. I was there that night at your town hall talk, Hamish, when you proposed to replace Moses' ten commandments with something a little more socially relevant. And you should think about adding a few more, Hamish. Like hangings for crims who touch kids and belt women up.' She looked at Justine, her face pitying. 'Come through. Tell us all about the bastard.' She nodded over at Hamish. 'Bring Moses with you. No burning bushes here, mate. Arson is a crime.'

Justine broke into a smile.

'Good to see,' she said, 'the bastard hasn't completely done a domestic TNT job on you. Some women I've seen? Two years later, they're still not smiling. Come on, darlin', I've got a bastard report to write up.'

The female cop opened the door and let them through.

'Ready, Hamish?' Leanne asked, scrutinising him.

He drew in a deep breath, 'Ready.'

'Come on then, scarecrow. This is either your last supper or the start of many political feasts you will be VIP invited to.'

'Voter crucifixion, or voter-paid feasts,' Hamish said. 'Australia really is a country of extremes. They'll either leave me rotting in the desert or give me a camel to travel over it.'

'Well some feasts you have to pay out a few cents for,' Leanne answered casually, 'but others are on the house.' She looked at him warningly. 'You must give your skinny, lentils life up and go the doughnut, mate.'

'Hurry up,' Deanna called out through the door, 'the polling is about to start.'

'Where's Lollipop?' Leanne asked, looking around, as she walked through the door.

Hamish looked around. 'Over there,' he said, his face lighting up as he saw Justine sitting at one of the round tables draped with a dark green cloth. 'Sitting with Deanna.'

'Good,' Leanne said firmly. 'Deanna will give her some hard, practical advice, on what to do about domestically violent bastards.'

'The domestic violence refuge the police took her to are sorting her out. There's an AVO out on the bastard as well. She'll be safe,' Hamish said.

'Plenty of us to shoot him, fucking animal,' Leanne said. 'If he tries to come after her again.'

'Do you think you can shoot the rest of the other bastards, bitches and animals around,' Hamish muttered, 'as there are some of us still suffering at their hands? And while we are on this subject, I know you and Catholics don't see eye to eye, but you and Father Matthias over there, both go into bat for those suffering under bastards, or bitches, or animals. You have more in common than you think.' He paused at seeing her sceptical face. 'Go talk to him. He won't try and ward you off with the Bible. He's not that sort of person.'

'As long as he doesn't talk to me in anti-homosexual parables, I can put up with him. Now, where is he?' she asked, looking around.

Hamish pointed at the priest. 'Over there. By the window, arguing with a party official.'

Leanne looked at the priest and back at Hamish. 'All is forgiven. He's black, belongs to the marginalised and he argues with officials. What the fuck is he doing in a social control system?'

'Well, there's a new word for the Catholic faith,' Hamish said, scratching his cheek.

'All collectives are social control systems, Hamish, all of them. Religion, family, law, mental health—'

'And politics?' Hamish asked worriedly.

'Well, that's the biggest collective arse of all,' Leanne said, looking at him with surprise. She stopped suddenly, her eyes narrowing at a teenager skulking near Hamish's poster on the wall. 'No!' she yelled. 'No! Don't take that poster down. Leave that there, skank.'

Hamish looked pityingly at the frightened teenager shrinking back against the wall, his fingers edging around the poster.

'What? Do you think he's fucking lost already?' Leanne demanded, striding over to the teenager looking at her, terrified, as she came closer. His fingers gripped the poster so tightly, it almost ripped.

'I just wanted his picture,' the teenager said, his voice cracking with fear.

'Do you have gay longings for Hamish?' Hamish heard her ask the teenager. 'Because if you do, come out of the closet now and save yourself years of suffering trying to be a man, as per social code.'

'*Fuck,*' Hamish said, 'Leane...*Fuck*...I mean...Oh, my goodness...No. That's even worse than slang, I sound like a fainting girl...what am I supposed to say instead?'

'Talking...to yourself... Son?' Father Matthias asked, his face grave.

'Reasoning things out, Father Matthias, reasoning things out,' Hamish explained.

Father Matthias tapped his forehead. 'Best done up here, Son.'

'That's what got me into trouble in the first place,' Hamish explained. 'Trying to reason out things alone, in my head. She helped sort me out.'

'Who?'

He hesitated, 'You won't like this, because of your Catholicism, but my lesbian friend Leanne.' He looked gratefully over at Leanne, standing with her hands on her hips, tearing strips off the teenager.

'Leanne taught me about how to wrap a bullet in normality, so people accept the message and respect the messenger. Leanne's the one who got me to run for Council.'

'Son. I don't care what she is, if she pulled you out of the social mud hole you were in. And that's our job for all of us in society, Hamish, to stop each other sinking. That's all that matters.' He looked interestedly over at Leanne. 'I'd like to have a word with her, later on.'

Hamish hesitated, 'You maybe...well...shouldn't use the word of God,' Hamish advised solemnly, 'when having a word with her.' He paused, looking over at Leanne. 'Leanne's wary you may fling a thunder and lightning anti-homosexual parable at her,' Hamish explained hastily.

'No, no, no,' the Priest laughed.

'You've also got a dick,' Hamish added, 'which scores highly on the wariness scale with her too.'

'Hamish. None of that talk is welcome with me,' Father Matthias said sternly.

'I'm still on my socially appropriate L Plates, Father,' Hamish said.

'Hmmm,' Father Matthias said, looking at him suspiciously. 'I think you may need more lithium, Son, that strange language of unrelated objects and concepts is starting to come back.'

'I'm just saying, be careful. Leanne's suffered a lot. She's in the thin side of society.'

'No. Anything suffering is on the fat side of society, not the thin. So many of us.' Father Matthias said wearily, 'You have no idea how much time I spend getting people out of corners in back alleys, or answering calls for help.' He looked over at Leanne, who was firmly sticking the poster back on the wall. 'I'll go introduce myself, huh?'

'Good luck,' Hamish muttered, 'I can't guarantee the outcome, if you piss her off.'

The priest whipped his head around, staring at him sternly.

'I mean…if she becomes angry,' he said. '*Fuck!*' he swore as the priest strode off. 'I can't stand all this funeral language. Nothing alive in it,' he said to himself, watching the priest approach Leanne. She put her hands on her hips, regarding him warily.

'Are you one of those fundamentalist Catholics with a bullet for gays?' Leanne asked the priest bluntly.

'No!' Father Matthias protested. 'No! I'm not like that. I wanted to thank you for the good care you took of Hamish. You see…'

The priest's voice faded as Hamish looked around for Justine. She caught his eyes, smiling a little. It still tore him up, to see that sadness in her eyes; those fractures of pain, which had never existed until now. He watched her rise from her table; her long, light, pink dress, swirling softly around her brown sandals. Her blonde, bobbed hair shone under the overhead lights; her creamy white skin lightly flushed pink in the heat of the room. The bruise on her cheek had faded to an ugly yellow and grey colour. Tears pricked his eyes at the sight of his beautiful Justine, his sun, his altar, bruised by bastard balls. His fists tightened at the thought of her crumpling to the ground, defenceless against him.

'How's the vote count going?' Justine asked, standing behind him and putting her arms around him. He felt her soft cheek against his back, and a warmth ran through his body, suffusing him with calm and peace.

Happiness flooded him.

She loved him at last.

26

Hamish looked up at the television, his friends and supporters crowded around him. 'Closest contender is Labor smiles man, Robert,' Leanne said intently, staring at the vote count for Ward 4, 'but I knew he would be. People like having their ribs tickled; instead of having to reach for the paracetamol at all the political rhetoric.'

'I'm about 33 votes ahead now,' Hamish said, looking at the tally. 'And the Labor smiles man just got another five…'

'And you just got another seven,' Justine said, excited, her hand tightening on his arm.

Hamish sat on the edge of the table, Leanne clutching one arm tightly, and Justine clutching the other arm as the votes came in.

'I don't usually do this, Hamish, clutch a man, but you are excepted on urgent political grounds,' Leanne told him, her eyes intent on the voting count.

'I just want him to win,' Justine said, her blue eyes lighting with determination, as the tally continued.

'Of course, you do, Lollipop,' Leanne said comfortingly.

Hamish knew that Justine was more tolerable to Leanne now, as his church princess had been through an experience of the marginalised. The experience of being marked out from the ordinary or cherished citizen, as per the Constitution, had landed right on Justine's cheek.

Leanne gave Justine another comforting look and turned her head to look at the television.

Hamish heard Father Matthias come up behind him, and felt his strong hands on his shoulders. He felt that reassuring sense of Sunday predictability again; and he smiled wistfully, remembering the days of challenging and being challenged; before the meds stoned his mind. Hamish didn't argue anymore, he just went and found the right book, for the right answer, helplessly sad about his lost nit self, yet more at home in Social Prophet citizenship.

‘Are you giving “The Blessing of the Political”, Rap man?’ Leanne asked sardonically, looking at the priest’s hands on Hamish’s shoulders.

‘I’m not sure there are many blessings reserved for the Political,’ Father Matthias said, his voice dry.

‘Humour. I like it,’ Leanne said categorically.

‘Just because I’m Catholic doesn’t mean humour is excluded from the title,’ Father Matthias said mildly.

‘Catholics are a personality type,’ Leanne said firmly. ‘Individuality in lockdown, Rap man.’

‘OK,’ Father Matthias said, ‘you like the self, I like the collective.’

‘There would be no Sunday Mass if you just liked the self, Rap man. It would be just you and the empty church, with the collective moved to a new collective.’

‘Every day, I pray that doesn’t happen,’ Father Matthias said, his eyes raising to the ceiling.

‘Good luck getting any answer,’ Leanne answered caustically.

‘Look, Hamish, look!’ Justine said, jumping up and down.

Hamish looked at the television. Father Matthias and Leanne dropped their prickly conversation and looked as well.

‘Hamish McColl has won Ward 4, by 922 votes,’ said the political commentator, ‘and we can safely say he has it, even after postal votes are counted; given the rankings of the other political candidates and the population count in Ward 4.’

‘You won! You won!’ Leanne screamed, clutching his arm. She let go of his arm and ran around the room whooping, her hand clapping her mouth like a caricature of a Native American Indian.

Father Matthias looked at him, his eyes brimming with tears. ‘Well done, Son, well done.’

Hamish fell against Father Matthias’s chest, sobbing. ‘Fuck you, Dad… Screw you, Mum… Bye-bye, vicious sister…’

‘Er…Hamish?’ the priest said. ‘You have to leave all of that behind, OK?’

A crowd pushed in around Hamish. They tore him out of the priest’s comforting, Sunday arms and lifted him up, running around the room with him.

‘Hamish, Hamish, Hamish!’ they screamed in unison.

27

Hamish took a deep breath, straightening the new, silk, deep-blue tie Justine had bought him as a congratulations present. He caught sight of himself in his crisp white shirt, dark brown hair parted neatly to the side, and his pressed black suit. For a second, just for a second, he caught sight of his past self in the mirror: his long, knotted, dark-brown dreadlocks, eyes red with insomnia, his psychedelic shirt and jeans hanging off his hips.

The image faded.

And he was in the mirror, as he was now.

Hamish took a deep breath, opened his Social Prophet eyes and pushed open the doors of the council chamber.

The council members and new mayor rose from their seats, clapping.

The doors shut behind him.

The End